Welcome to

A Rocky Malone Adventure

by

Rollie Johnson

the Peppertree Press
Sarasota, Florida

Graphic design by Rebecca Barbier.
Illustrations by Rollie Johnson.

For information regarding permission,
call 941-922-2662 or contact us at our website:
www.peppertreepublishing.com or write to:
the Peppertree Press, LLC.
Attention: Publisher
1269 First Street, Suite 7
Sarasota, Florida 34236

ISBN: 978-1-61493-425-7

Library of Congress Number: 2016901321

Printed February 2016

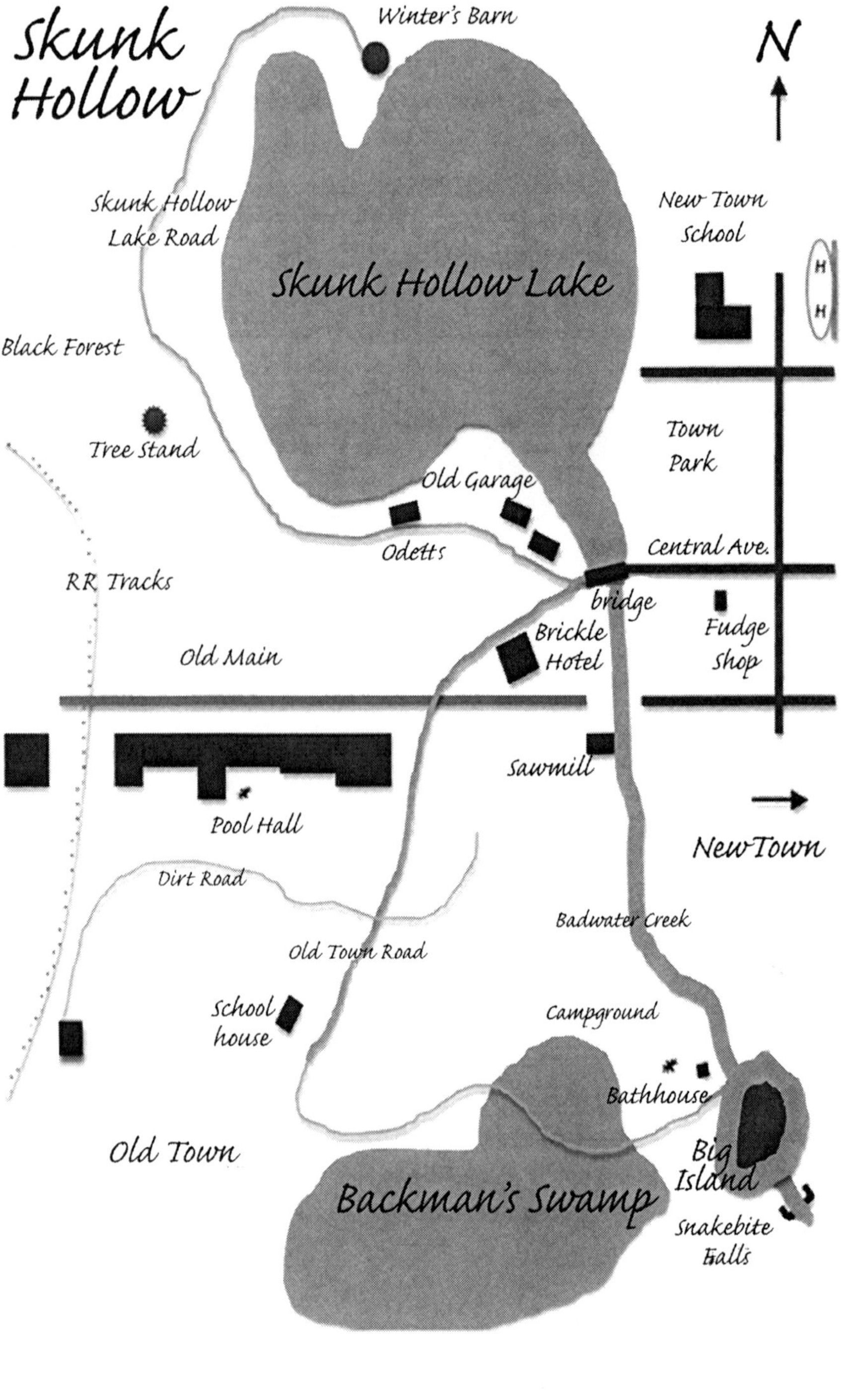

Skunk Hollow
Winter's Barn
N
Skunk Hollow Lake Road
Skunk Hollow Lake
New Town School
H
H
Black Forest
Tree Stand
Town Park
Old Garage
Odetts
Central Ave.
RR Tracks
bridge
Brickle Hotel
Fudge Shop
Old Main
Sawmill
Pool Hall
NewTown
Dirt Road
Badwater Creek
Old Town Road
School house
Campground
Bathhouse
Old Town
Big Island
Backman's Swamp
Snakebite Falls

Prologue

Lost again. Beauregard Puce was always lost, but this time he figured he was in real trouble. He'd been asked to deliver two saddlebags of gold to some G. Custer who was on his way to Fort Lincoln, but somehow Beauregard had gotten lost and ended up in Dakota Territory with no clue which way to go or even where to hide. Things didn't quite work out like Beauregard planned. Two years ago he had joined the army for fun and adventure out West, but ended up as a desk clerk at Fort Snelling in Minnesota. When the army asked for a volunteer to catch up with General Custer, Beauregard jumped at the chance for an adventure and promotion. Captain Puce, Hero of the Great Plains. Let the adventure begin!

He figured the 7th Cavalry could only be a day ahead of him, so of course he'd easily catch them in a day or so. He'd ridden a horse a few times and he knew it would be easy to follow the tracks of the entire 7th Cavalry. He also knew what horse tracks looked like. Beauregard had packed enough food for three days figuring that would be plenty. He'd just hunt for food if he ran out. How hard could that be? The army had given him a rifle. All he had to do was learn how to load and shoot it.

Days had turned into weeks and Beauregard had managed to survive, but was beginning to realize he was in way over his head. Some shady men had heard him bragging about his adventure back at the fort and he was pretty sure they were following him. He spotted a campfire behind him just about every night. He'd also seen some Indians jumping around a bonfire. Fearing for his life, Beauregard decided to bury the bags of gold, let his packhorse loose, and ride pony express-style as fast as he could west to Fort Lincoln. He dug a deep hole under a small oak tree near a creek he had just stumbled across. Even though he wasn't good with maps, he thought it best to draw one and send it to someone just in case something happened to Custer.

His sister Julian in St. Louis was the obvious choice. She'd love to read about his adventures and she'd know what to do with the map. Good thing he brought a pencil and his diary. A desk clerk is always prepared. He had just three unanswered questions. Who was following him, how could he get his diary to his sister, and why does this creek smell so bad?

Oh yeah, one more question: which way was west?

Chapter One

So what's the big deal? I wasn't sailing solo across the Pacific or climbing the mighty Kilimanjaro, I was just moving across two states to a small town in South Dakota. I didn't really want to move, but I knew I didn't have much of a choice. My father, Harold "Buzz" Malone, had sold our house in Chicago and bought a run-down old gas station in a town called Skunk Hollow about 600 miles away. I tried to convince my father and mother that we were better off staying put, but Dad wanted to make a fresh start. He'd been talking about a fresh start for years and nothing ever happened. I had always thought it was just a lot of hot air but when the *SOLD* sign went up in the front yard, I knew I was a goner. We were going to move, and soon.

Buzz (everybody called my dad Buzz) had seen an ad in a local paper about two weeks ago. It read something like this: *"Are you tired of the same old grind? Be your own boss in beautiful Skunk Hollow. Promising business for sale. Price includes a three-bedroom fixer-upper on the property. Call Slim Stanley at SKunk Hollow1-3325. That's SK1-3325. Time's a wasting. Let's make a deal."* My dad called that same day and closed "the deal" a week later.

My best friends in Chicago had always been my dog, my snake, my mother when she didn't have me cleaning my room or helping with dishes, and Ernie. Ernie's dad had just been transferred to a job in Denver so my summer was already slowing down to a crawl. Ernie and I really didn't have much in common, but he loved snakes so he was always hanging around keeping me company and playing with Gerty, my pet snake. Even though we had different interests, I always knew I could count on Ernie in a pinch. I guess that's what makes a good friend. I will miss him and his goofy Roy Rogers outfits even if he wasn't into solving mysteries like me.

Mom and Dad named me Rocky the day I was born. Dad told me that Mom had a pretty tough time that day. It wasn't too easy on me either. I had heard that the first words Dad said to Mom when I took my first breath were "Boy Irene, that sure was a rocky start."

The name stuck; from then on I was *Rocky*. I was so glad that my dad didn't blurt out something like "Boy Irene, what a little weenie," or "Boy Irene, his head looks just like a potato." I could have been named Little Weenie or Potato Head Malone. Dad could do that without a second thought. The Big Guy Upstairs must have been watching over me that day. Rocky works just fine, thank you.

Mom told me that Dad was a boxer before the war. He was always listed on the boxing card as Harold '*Buzzsaw*' Malone. Mom started calling him Buzz after they got married. She thought Buzzsaw was too violent. Dad didn't mind. He even got a haircut to match his shorter nickname. All the cool kids at school had crew cuts. Dad had a buzz. It wasn't quite the same. I wish he had stuck with Buzzsaw. I could picture Dad's arms flying as he mowed down opponents in the ring.

I often heard people in our community say "Irene's just an old-fashioned farm girl." I always figured it was because Mom was always doing chores for other people in town and cooking big meals for everyone. Somebody told me farm girls did that. Maybe it was Ernie. Mom always had a smile on her face and sang the silliest tunes. She even smiled when my dad told her about Skunk Hollow. As she cooked up a celebration dinner in the kitchen the night of Dad's announcement, she was singing a tune I had heard on the radio, " I'm counting on you, dear . . ." I don't think Dad picked up on it but I did, and Elvis would be proud. I thought my mother was a gem.

Ned would probably like the change as well. He spent most of his dog life tied to the clothesline in the back yard. The neighbors all called him a mangy mutt but I knew that Ned was the smartest dog around. Of course, no one had ever seen my dog eat only the chips out of a chocolate chip cookie or climb a stepladder. Ned always let me know that someone was coming even before they got to the sidewalk in front of our house. He never barked at anyone, at least not that I can remember. As soon as he knew someone was coming into the yard, Ned would position himself between the visitor and me. It had to be a little disconcerting to be face-to-face with a ninety pound shepherd/lab mix, teeth and gums exposed, when all the salesman wanted to do was sell some spices or an accordion.

Ned was a fantastic friend but he didn't carry on a conversation very well. People always seemed to understand him though. Only fools and friends tried to pet him. Fools never tried again. Yeah, maybe Ned would like the change in scenery. There were just too many fools and too few friends in Chicago. Dad didn't think Skunk Hollow had a leash law or a dogcatcher. That would be a great change from Chicago. With my help, Ned could get into all kinds of mischief in South Dakota, and I'd be right there with him as we worked on some brand new mysteries.

My 5-foot corn snake Gerty wouldn't care where she lived as long as she could curl up in a corner and occasionally snack on a mouse or two. Although she never told me, I think Gerty really liked riding in my bike basket when I pedaled around the city. I had to admit, my bike was always safe, no matter where I parked it. Corn snakes are pretty harmless, but most people shy away thinking snakes were slimy or they might bite. Gerty would never bite anyone but that was our little secret.

With Gerty and Ned guarding my space, I was always protected from the bad guys. This new town of Skunk Hollow might have some great biking trails that Gerty would love, if she really thought about stuff like that. She'd have to find a new Ernie to dote over her though. And of course, she'd protect me from all the bad guys. I had heard there were lots of them out West. That's what Ernie told me anyway.

I got to visit Skunk Hollow with my dad the very next weekend when he drove there to close the deal with Slim Stanley. Mom said she trusted Buzz to make the right decision so she stayed back and worked on getting the house in order. I think she was just finding a way not to ride in our pickup late at night. I had no trouble sleeping in the truck, so I was game.

Dad really loved *Bette Lou*. (Yeah, he named his truck.) He'd spend hours tuning and polishing her every weekend. Dad told me on several occasions, "Rocky, if you take care of your ride, it'll take care of you." I wonder if that applies to bikes? My bike needed some major work. The trip went by fast and the old Chevy truck ran like a top.

We arrived in Skunk Hollow just as the sun was coming up over the hills to the east of the town. We hung a left off of Highway 15 onto a road called Central Avenue. I was immediately and totally impressed. Skunk Hollow looked like one of those towns right out of a fancy magazine–super-wide sidewalks, beautiful shops, manicured lawns, and a fudge shop right next to a park. Things were looking up. This move might actually be okay. Maybe they needed a fudge sampler. I could apply.

We had the address of the old gas station so we made our way west to an old covered bridge. The bridge looked like it needed repair, but maybe it had some *historic* value. I had heard that you couldn't change old buildings that were historic. Maybe that rule applied to bridges as well.

As *Bette Lou* (our truck) entered the bridge everything went dark. Dad turned on the lights as we crept over the old, creaky expanse. A cold shiver raced down my spine as we inched along over warped and cracked wooden beams. Finally, we popped out on the other side of the bridge and we were on safe ground again. Talk about creepy!

What spread out before us on this side of the bridge wasn't *historic* at all. It wasn't picture-perfect like the part of town we had just driven through. It was an abrupt trip to the dark side. Dad and I had just entered a ghost town complete with unpaved roads, weather-worn buildings, and tumbleweeds. As my friend Ernie would have screamed if he were here, "Rocky, this is disgusting. Mount up. We need to leave . . . pronto."

"Dad, I think we must have turned the wrong way. Let's go back to the fudge shop." When I'm creeped out, a piece of fudge always helps.

I swallowed hard and a giant lump crash-landed in the pit of my stomach. Can kids my age swallow their own Adam's apple? I was glad that the sun was out but somehow it still felt darker in this part of town. I wouldn't want to be here at night. No way! What was my father thinking? I know what I'm thinking. I'm going to be sick.

Dad must have felt my inner pain. He grabbed my knee with his big, steady hand and commented, "Keep an open mind son. It's always darkest before the rainbow." What the heck did that mean?

We drove south a few blocks and took in an even more dark and dingy street. Years of neglect and weather had taken its toll on all of the buildings and sidewalks. I couldn't imagine calling this place home. Our appointment with Slim Stanley wasn't until 10 a.m. so Dad decided to see if we could catch some breakfast in this "quaint little burg." Who's he kidding? Who wants to munch on tumble-weeds, and what's that smell?

"A restaurant here? Dad, there aren't even people here. Maybe only zombies and they'll be having us for breakfast. Let's go back across the bridge. I saw a real restaurant close to the fudge shop."

Just as I finished wailing, Dad spotted an old, rusted-out Studebaker just down the street. It was easy to spot since it was the only car around. It was parked right in front of a crusty, old building with a very worn, but readable "Winter's Pool Hall" sign. We figured the owner of that nasty, old car must be inside the pool hall since no other living thing was moving on the street, unless you counted a mangy black cat that suddenly appeared in front of us as we parked the pickup. Not a good omen!

Dad insisted that bartenders always had a "treasure-trove" of information and quite possibly this local could give us some good insight as well as good food. He loved eating at what he called "greasy spoons."

We stepped out of the truck, avoided the cat, and made our way through the double swinging doors into the pool hall. If I hadn't been in ghost town shock, I might have imagined myself as a gunslinger in the Old West stopping by for a cool one after a tough shootout. Ernie would have been in cowboy heaven. He'd probably say something like "Let's belly up to the bar."

Actually, I wanted to hide out in the truck until Dad got this silly idea out of his system. We could begin our journey home right now as far as I was concerned. I took another look around and made a quick decision to stay with my dad. No telling what could get to me if I hid in the truck.

There was only one person in the pool hall, the local bartender, Willie the Wanderer. He seemed friendly enough once you got over his wild hair, missing teeth, and wandering eye. When I was little, I had some funny glasses with springs connected to eyeballs. That was what Willie's eye was doing, bouncing around without the springs. I wondered if it was a glass eye that he could pop out. I saw a guy at a circus do that once. Gross!

The bartender said he was called Willie the Wanderer because years ago he was a hobo wandering the countryside looking for work. Hobos gave each other nicknames and would use the name as kind of an official title. I guess his name had nothing to do with his wandering eye.

That's what he told us, and who was I to argue with a rather scary guy about a nickname or a wandering glass eye. I made the decision to not say anything and take him at his word. Sometimes saying nothing is my best detective move. He could be a vampire for all I knew, friendly by day and a one-eyed bloodsucker by night.

I decided to make a pledge to myself not to hang around the pool hall at night if we did end up moving into this "quaint little burg." I whispered "Please Dad. Let's think about this. Chicago's not so bad."

After Willie and Dad warmed up to each other, Willie talked non-stop about Skunk Hollow. Since we were his only customers, we sat at the bar and Willie gave us his undivided attention. We didn't get any breakfast though. The pool hall had sodas, beer, candy, and Cracker Jacks – my kind of food. I wondered if they served meals at night. I bet that it had lots of blood in it. Dad said we'd eat later, but he did give me some change for a root beer and Cracker Jacks to keep me occupied.

I was up for something cold to drink and since I still had a rock in my stomach, I wasn't really up for a big meal right then. Carmel corn and peanuts would be perfect. Sometimes I barf when I drink soda pop too fast or I'm stressed. I was already stressed to the max, so I took my time sipping the root beer. Barfing is never a good impression, even if it was just Willie, possible local vampire, watching my every move with one eye.

As I listened, I sipped my root beer and fiddled with a deck of very worn and stained cards. I thought about sitting in this bar in the Old West and wondered if Wild Bill Hickok ever used these cards? Ernie taught me all about Aces and Eights, the Deadman's Hand. I decided to put the cards away.

Here's what came out of Willie's mouth. "Skunk Hollow gots named by some ol' drunken army guy named Beauregard Puce who probaly got losted on his way to some battle. Some say he got real thirsty, drank some water from the creek, den spit it out 'cause it taste sooooo bad. So's he named it Badwater Creek. Couple days later, some old-timers comes up the creek looking for this Puce guy. They doesn't fine him so they sets up a camp hopin' he'd stumble back south. They'd done 'nough trackin' and searchin' for this guy. It was time for Puce to find his self and them."

Willie the Wanderer talked slow and funny, and we both found it very hard to look him in the eyes when he was talking. I chose to look at his mouth to see if he had any large, sharp fangs. If we concentrated real hard we could follow most of what Willie was saying.

Later I asked Dad if everyone around here talked like Willie the Wonderer. Dad said Willie just had a colorful country drawl. When I asked what country, Dad laughed. I thought it was a good question.

Continuing his story, Willie went on to say that days, weeks, and months went by. The old-timers tents changed to claim shanties with wooden floors, shanties became houses, and all of a sudden a town sprung up. The water from the creek still smelled and Beauregard Puce was never seen again.

The only good thing that ever came out of that ol' creek was catfish, and "they's only good when they's fried right." Willie's brain had a tendency to wander, just like his right eye.

I thought that the missing army guy had to be another mystery just waiting to be solved. Maybe something bad happened to Beauregard and just maybe he hid some treasure somewhere in Skunk Hollow. Someone had told me Custer found gold in Dakota Territory; maybe this Captain Beauregard Puce found some too. Captains don't normally just disappear either. Army officers usually died fighting Indians or died in some army hospital in Washington D.C. That's what Ernie said once, and Ernie never lied. I'd need to do some research, under-cover of course.

The whole history of Skunk Hollow made absolutely no sense to me, but here it was, a small town planted right in the middle of nowhere, too far from anything worthwhile. Who would want to come to a town named after a smelly animal next to a creek with bad water? Buzz and Irene Malone did. Go figure!

We couldn't make sense out of everything Willie the Wanderer threw our way, but we did learn that although the town wasn't very big it was slowly expanding east toward the highway. It sat on the southeast corner of Skunk Hollow Lake. Badwater Creek ran almost north to south and divided Skunk Hollow into two communities, Old Town and New Town. New Town had sprung up in the last ten years and was now almost six times larger than Old Town. Based on the last census, Skunk Hollow had reached a whopping 274 people, 59 in Old Town if you counted the goatman and Miss Odetts' brother, Lenny. He would get lost in the swamp some times for days, but always managed to show up after everyone gave up the search.

I used to have a cat that did the same thing at least twice a year. Just when you had given up all hope and were excited about getting a new cat, Tiger would stroll in looking for a handout. I wondered if Miss Odetts ever thought about getting a new brother. Could she do that? I'd have to ask her.

That old, single-lane covered bridge that strung across the mouth of Badwater Creek connected the two communities just south of the lake. Although cars rarely met on the bridge, it was always a challenge to bike or walk across because the bridge was so narrow. It was also impossible to see a car entering from the opposite side. Buses and eighteen-wheelers were too wide and heavy to cross the bridge. A small car and a bike could pass each other, but meeting a big Cadillac meant you and your bike were going to be crushed or creek-bound. Only the very foolish or desperate would ever attempt to cross that old bridge on foot.

On school days, the New Town school bus would pull up in front of the bridge blocking all traffic. Old Town kids were required to walk together across the bridge to get on the bus. New Town kids got picked up at their houses. That seemed a little unfair to me.

Willie the Wanderer didn't know too much about the people in New Town. He didn't get over there very often. He said he liked sports and occasionally traveled to the high school to watch Old Town's sports hero, Eddie Brickle, score some points in some basketball games, but that was about it. Everyone figured that Eddie would probably become a pro in some sport after college. Even the New Town crowd cheered for Eddie.

Old and New Towns were completely different and divided. I really wondered if the townsfolk wanted it that way. It sure looked like a tough trip just getting across that bridge. I was really beginning to worry about Dad closing the deal with this Slim Stanley character and our family living on the wrong side of Badwater Creek. Maybe we could find a nice house near the fudge shop.

Slim Stanley met us at the door of the old garage. Mr. Stanley was a big pudgy man with jet-black hair, combed back Elvis-style. He wore a very loud, plaid sport coat, wrinkled tan pants, and shiny black cowboy boots. His string tie was bright red, almost the color of his cheeks. There was nothing slim or cool about Slim. If he was trying to look like Elvis Presley or Johnny Cash, he failed big time. The only cool part of Mr. Stanley's outfit was his big silver and gold belt buckle shaped like a horseshoe. I thought the buckle would look better on a big stallion than on a big stomach.

Slim grabbed and shook our hands as if we were long, lost friends or he was about to close the deal of the century. I was sure we'd never met, and we were a long way from any deal. I endured his sweaty handshake and then quickly wiped my palms on my jeans as soon as he released me from his gross, humongous paws. I had been officially slimed by Slim!

Slim Stanley would have to do some serious convincing to get me excited about this place. It had nothing that I needed and even less that I wanted. Mom always said, "Needs and wants are two different things. You might really want something, but you really don't need it to survive." What I needed was some fresh air. What I wanted was to put some distance between Mr. Slim Stanley and me. Looked like I was going to get neither one today.

The garage had two big barn doors off to the left and a small office door on the right side of the building. Other than the 12'x12' office, the garage had no interior walls. All the windows were built to let light in, but nothing else. It had to be a furnace in there with the summer heat.

The bay on the far left had deep pit dug into the middle of the floor. I had no clue why it was there but the pit reminded me of a giant grave for a bloodsucking vampire. Maybe there was a vampire buried in a casket right in the middle of this garage just waiting for a nice, juicy kid like me.

I didn't see myself as any kind of vampire slayer and I sure didn't want to be hanging out in that garage at night looking for a new friend with sharp teeth. I was a super crimefighter, solving mysteries and fighting bad guys on bright, sunny days. I didn't do well with wooden stakes and garlic. I wasn't afraid of the dark, just the creepy-crawly things that roamed around in the dark.

The house and garage sat on a piece of land just to the right of the covered bridge coming into Old Town. Both buildings faced a gravel road with the house closest to the bridge, closer to the road, and about 75 feet from the lake. The house and garage were identical in size and shape. They were both big, ugly wooden buildings with no curb appeal. The so-called house must have been some kind of store at one time.

No one that I knew would build a house to look that bad. Slim was just making the two buildings a packaged deal to hook us in. Lake property, what a steal!

Dad was super excited when we found a huge pile of metal parts and rusted out engines next to the left side of the garage. He said it was worth its weight in gold– maybe fool's gold.

Dad had a completely different explanation for the pit. "Rocky, no one is trapping or burying vampires in there. When this was a gas station, cars would park over the pit and mechanics would climb down for an oil change or work on the motor with no need to crawl under the car."

Really? I was glad my father was going to work on small engines. That big hole was way beyond creepy. No sane person would want to enter *the pit;* only car mechanics, monster slayers, and mindless teenagers would enter on a dare. I now had two buildings to avoid at night. This road trip really wasn't going well at all. Please Dad, let's end this nightmare. Chicago's still a good place to live, even without friends.

The house was equally big and just as ugly. Looking at the building from the street, two large store windows were on the left and a smaller front door was located on the right. Instead of glass block windows around the sides and in back, someone had actually put in regular house windows. The inside wasn't much to look at either. Even though the walls needed new plaster, there were at least walls. The front of the house had a huge dining/living room on the left and what I think was a galley kitchen on the right. All the appliances were missing. The back of the house had a center hallway, two fairly large rooms on the left, a bathroom and another room on the right.

There were no fixtures, lights, or furniture anywhere in the house – a few broken radiators, an old bathtub, and a rusted-out water heater that took up space and would need to be trashed. Out the back, a door opened onto a big, ugly, concrete slab. Dad called it a patio. I thought the slab was more likely a slimy nesting area for every kind of bug ever hatched in South Dakota.

"Perfect on those hot, summer days when you want a cold lemonade, some fresh air, and beautiful sunshine. Look Rocky. You can even see the lake." The lake was visible through the weeds so I guess that was a plus. Let's see, on my tally, one plus and fourteen minuses. I vote no on this move!

Dad was excited that we would be living right on the lake. He probably thought this was going to be our dream beach house. The so-called house was way beyond a "fixer-upper" and the lake was, well, gross. And what was that smell? Buzz really missed this time. Mom wasn't going to be happy if Dad took the plunge. We couldn't live in that dump without some major repairs, like maybe blowing it up and starting over.

Dad had other ideas. He thought we could rent hotel rooms for a couple of weeks until the renovation work was completed. Was he dreaming? It would be months. My idea was much better. I bet we could buy some dynamite someplace around here. Maybe Willie had some.

After our tour we followed Slim across the bridge into New Town. His real estate office was right next to the Bank on Central Avenue. He was also the bank president and the town's biggest land baron. Slim walked us from our truck to the office and herded us into his "Signing Room". The small talk began with Slim assuring us there were "plenty of fish to be caught in Skunk Hollow Lake if you had the right bait. If the fish weren't biting, you could always go catfishin' in Badwater Creek."

I wasn't sure why he was talking about fish. Willie the Wanderer had talked about catfish too. Was there a connection between Willie and Mr. Stanley? I vowed to get to the bottom of this fishy mystery. Hopefully, that would take my mind off vampires and pits to the underworld.

Slim Stanley told us the people of New Town once petitioned to get the Skunk Hollow name changed, but the governor said the name had "historical significance" and he wouldn't allow it. That was too bad. I thought a good name might have been *Nowhere.* That's where we were, right in the middle of nowhere.

I figured that the people in New Town wanted a better image to attract new businesses and tourists. Visualizing someone spitting into the creek was probably not a big draw. I'd have to see if there was a bronze statue of Beauregard Puce spitting into Badwater Creek. That would be cool if they actually hooked up water to it and some creek spit came out of his mouth. I was pretty good with tools and was sure I could probably rig up something. Might be a good project to keep me out of trouble.

"Mr. Stanley, are there any buildings that have *historical value* in Skunk Hollow?" I wanted to make sure that we could blow up the old gas station and the house without hearing from the governor. Kaboom! No more buildings and no more vampires! That would be a fresh start.

Slim answered "Only the old round barn on the north side of our beautiful lake. It belonged to one of the first families to settle here, the Winter family. Still a few Winters in Old Town."

Dad scratched his head and then asked, "Does that mean once we sign, we can do anything we want to the property inside and out?"

"It's all yours, hook, line, and sinker. Do whatever you want. No charge for the engine parts on the west side of the garage either. If you do any renovating, I can get you a real nice improvement loan to help move things along."

Engine parts? Was he kidding? That was a junk pile. Slim was working all the angles to squeeze Dad out of even more money. A realtor, closer, banker, and land baron all wrapped together in one big, pudgy, Elvis-want-to-be package. Something really did smell fishy, and I would get to the bottom of it.

After all, wasn't I the infamous Inspector Rocky Malone, Super Crimefighter and Mystery Solver? Of course, my title was a well-kept secret. The best crimefighters never revealed their true identity. I'd have to solve this case in secret, and from all appearances, all by myself. Well, Ned could help a little, but Gerty would be pretty useless. Maybe Ernie could drive up for a visit.

And then the Chicago chapter in my life came to a close. The bait had been cast, Buzz grabbed it, and Slim Stanley reeled us in. My dad signed on the dotted line and we became the proud owners of a big pile of old concrete, rotted wood, and rusty engine parts. Dad said we made out like bandits, but I was pretty sure by this time that Slim Stanley was the bandit and we just got robbed. This wasn't exactly the "fresh start" I was looking for, but Dad was happy, so that was worth something, I guess. I promised Dad I would do my best to make it work from my end. I promised myself I'd uncover Stanley's scam.

After we signed the loan papers, Dad and I decided to explore our new community. New Town had a new school, new park, lots of new homes, and a snazzy downtown with all kinds of shops and a couple of restaurants. I planned on spending lots of time at the fudge shop whenever I could get across the bridge. It would have to be on bright, sunny days and I'd need some fast wheels. I'd need a bigger allowance after we moved.

Old Town had a lot of "former" businesses. There was the former theater, the former school, the former feed store and elevator, and the former gas station. Main Street had several empty buildings crying for occupancy and a coat of paint. Maybe some buildings were occupied, but by what? I bet Alfred Hitchock would love this place.

Sidewalks, curbs, and gutters had years of neglect. The most prevalent flower was the dandelion; it had taken over most of the grassy areas along the gravel roadways. At least they added some life and color to this dreary town. The only real businesses were a small hotel, a mercantile, a sawmill, a secondhand store, and Winter's Pool Hall. If my dad could make a go of it, that would bring the total number of Old Town businesses to a whopping six. Dad made an attempt at being optimistic. "Room to grow Son, room to grow."

Yeah, just like all the dandelions. I heard that people make tea out of that weed. I prefer a big mug of frosty root beer. I bet root beer was made from really good stuff, not weeds.

We made a quick stop at the Brickle Hotel in Old Town. I had seen enough old buildings today so I stayed in the truck. Buzz was only gone a few minutes and then we were on the road again. "Good news, Rocky," Buzz said as we retraced our drive back over the bridge. "The hotel has plenty of room so we'll have a roof over our heads while we work on our new house and garage."

I hoped the hotel had inside walls, lights, a bathroom, and no blood-sucking vampire pits. I wasn't optimistic, but anything would be better than Malone's Small Engine Repair Shop and the Pit of Doom.

The day was finally winding down and after a quick stop at the fudge shop we pointed our pickup east toward Chicago. Dad was in need of some sleep so we stopped for a few hours at a truck stop in a town called Montevideo, someplace in Minnesota. We were back on the road again just before midnight.

I had the feeling that Dad was excited to tell Mom all about Skunk Hollow and his great plans. His idea was to turn that old gas station into a family gold mine and his services, of course, would be in high demand throughout the county. The beach house was an added bonus and would be the envy of everyone in town. Get real Dad!

"Irene," Buzz exclaimed as he burst through the kitchen door the next morning, "with a little TLC our beach house and my new business will be our lifetime dream come true. It's a glorious day for the Malones." Irene just smiled.

I was still in shock and felt like throwing up for the second time this weekend. Maybe some ice cream would help. "Does anyone want a hot fudge sundae? I'm hungry," I moaned parking myself at the kitchen table.

"Rocky, it's Sunday morning. Have some cereal and milk." Rats! Back to reality again! I wasn't going to get any ice cream and I knew all we had was bran flakes and toast. I should have bought more fudge at the New Town Fudge Shop.

Once I had food in my stomach, I calmed down a little and began to think about a few of the positive things about moving. I figured it really wouldn't be that hard to leave East Side School or my friends. I wasn't fond of the school anyway, and my friend Ernie had moved to Colorado. Anyway, most of the other kids in my class thought I was a little weird and standoffish. Somehow, I never really connected with the neighborhood kids. Maybe Gerty and Ned scared them off, or maybe they all had their own friends. My mother told me many times that not knowing me was their loss. I always felt better after talking to Mom.

As exciting as everyone thought it was, sometimes growing up in the nineteen fifties was a real drag. It also didn't help that I was an only child. I hoped that I could make some friends in Skunk Hollow who maybe liked what I liked. Mom would get busy like she always did, sewing, cooking, and helping people. Dad would put all of his time and energy into getting his new business going. I knew I would have to pretty much fend for myself in this new old town, at least until school started in September. I was glad I had Gerty and Ned to keep me company. That part wouldn't change.

I had always been able to handle things on my own in Chicago, but this move was a new wrinkle in my life. Of course there would be some new mysteries to work on. Just maybe I could find some friends in New Town to help me track down a bad guy or two. I'd probably have to wait for school to start to meet new kids. It looked like Old Town was short on live kids, and I sure wasn't interested in making connections with any of the local zombies or vampires. I really wanted to keep my skin on and my blood in.

Chapter Two

Buzz and Irene decided that an estate auction would be best if they really were going to make a fresh start. I was pretty worried that they'd try to sell everything, including my tools, gadgets, and toys. Mom assured me that we would have plenty of space in the truck, but that we should only take what we needed and what we really wanted. Plenty of space? Who are they kidding? We had a pickup, not a moving van.

My parents said anything that went on the sale that was in my bedroom or that I built would be "money in the bank" for me. I could use the money I earned from the auction to buy fudge and wooden stakes in Skunk Hollow.

All those green backs sounded awfully good to me. I could use a new pair of jeans without knee patches. Maybe I'd sell my old bike at the auction for a little extra cash. I was ready for an upgrade in the bike department anyway. Bring on the auctioneer.

Dad needed to finish out the week at the hardware store so much of the work getting things ready for the auction fell to Mom and me. We did have some help from Mrs. Beeson down the street but she spent most of the time digging through Mom's clothes. Absolutely nothing would ever fit her since she was at least 100 pounds and six dress sizes bigger than my mother. One day she managed to pull on what I was told was a woman's girdle. I think I'll be having nightmares the rest of my life.

Cowboy Bill's auction crew came in a few days early to help organize boxes and displays. Our family had to put red tags on everything not to be sold. My mother had a tough time sorting out some of her china, but most of the furniture and appliances would never make the trip. Mom was hoping to clear closets as well, but Cowboy Bill said people around East Chicago didn't buy many clothes at auctions unless they belonged to someone famous. I was really hoping to unload my old clothes. Maybe I could convince some kid they belonged to Elvis when he was a little boy.

I had what I thought were outstanding collectables in my room – an old wire birdcage, a marble collection, some paint by numbers books. I was sure they would be real treasures in the right hands. Maybe Mrs. Beeson's daughter might be interested in a few of my things. She was always looking for something different and unique at garage sales. I needed to tell her about my treasures before the sale.

Dad had several chainsaws, mowers, and trimmers to sell. He kept a few of the better ones back to peddle in his new store. Of course his pride and joy, his toolboxes would make the trip to South Dakota. "You can't even tighten a toilet seat without the proper tools. And then where are you?" I bet you'd still be in the bathroom.

Cowboy Bill parked two flatbed trailers in our driveway. His crew placed all the boxes and small items on the trailers in an order that Bill thought would spark the most interest. Furniture and appliances were put in rows in the front yard. People could come by two hours before the start to view auction items, get their auction number, and find a convenient spot close to the auctioneer. I got a number just in case something came up that I really needed. I wonder if you can bid on your own stuff?

Cowboy Bill asked me to keep Gerty in the house. Even though Gerty was harmless, he didn't want to scare anyone away. He agreed that Ned could roam around as long as I promised he wouldn't bark or bite anyone. Ned would be fine with the crowd; he'd have fun just people watching.

The day before the auction and two days before we left Chicago for good, Golden Hardware put on a big barbeque to thank Dad for all his years of service. Mrs. Golden had finally convinced Mr. Golden that he could stand to spend a little money celebrating one of the store's best employees. The BBQ was held in the parking lot by the hardware store. Never missing the chance to make a buck, Ralph Golden kept the store open during the party and even considered charging guests for the BBQ. We were all surprised that Golden didn't ask Dad to run the store during the BBQ.

To recognize all of Dad's years of service, Mr. Golden gave a long and boring speech about the hardware business mentioning Dad's contribution in the last sentence at the end of his speech. What I took away from it was "Blah, blah, blah, blah . . . and we wish to recognize a good guy, Harold Malone, for his (How many?) years of service. I forget. Thanks Buzz. Now let's get that barbeque going. Our store's still open. Don't forget to check out our new inventory."

I was hoping Dad would be honored with a new truck, a big check, or at least a gold watch. Dad got a big handshake, a card, and a gift certificate to Golden's Hardware for $10 off any purchase of a seasonal or discontinued item valued at more than $20. What an amazing send-off!

Our whole family was just thrilled with Mr. Golden's generosity. Now we could get that pink toilet seat or the giant set of big plastic reindeer to remind us of all those wonderful years at Golden's Hardware. This gift was right up there with all the great raises Dad was promised but never given.

The thank you card was equally bad. *"Dear Buzz – Thanks a million. We won't forget you. Ralph Golden -1957."* I was pretty sure Buzz would be forgotten before we left the city, and that was only days away.

Mom smiled and said "What a Chump!" under her breath as Mr. Golden finished his speech. Mrs. Golden must have heard my mom because she turned red with embarrassment and wouldn't look at Mom the rest of the BBQ. Dad was right about needing a fresh start. This hardware career was a bust. Dad knew his skills would be in high demand out West although he'd probably branch out to boat and motorcycle motors once he got the business going. He was a natural when it came to small engines.

Auction Day arrived and I hopped out of bed even before Mom had breakfast on the kitchen table. Today was a cereal and toast day, just like most days. Once in a while we had bacon and eggs, but all the pots and pans were packed for the move or out on the trailer to be sold at the auction. Mom greeted me with a smile and some OJ as I slid into my chair.

"When does the auction start Mom? Are we going to bid on our own stuff? Can I be the auctioneer? Do we get to keep all the money? What if stuff doesn't sell? Is there any jelly? Where's Dad? Are we selling the stove and fridge? Can I sell lemonade? Ned can guard the cash if you want. Can I ride my bike around and find customers? Is Cowboy Bill a real cowboy? Does he wear a gun? I think I'm done eating. Thanks Mom."

"Your welcome Rocky" Mom replied. "Now go help your dad in the yard. He's making sure everything looks nice."

Mom must have known that I didn't expect any answers to my questions. I scrambled out of my chair and bolted through the front door, tripped down the steps and launched myself face-first into our local busybody, Mrs. Beeson. (She must have come early to pick through the good stuff.) Did I mention she was a rather plump lady? With no time to react, my entire eighty-five pound rocket was instantly enveloped in a mass of human flesh. Her massive breasts surrounded my eyes, ears, and mouth. No sound or breath came from my mouth, only the telltale "pthupt" as I saw my life flash before me. (Not really, but I'll always remember that sound.)

"Oh Rocky!" she groaned. "I'm going to miss you too. You are such a wonderful young man. I could just hug you to death." From my point of view and my sudden loss of breathable air, that was a distinct possibility.

"Thanks Mrs. Beeson," I stammered. Missing her would not be a big loss. Cowboy Bill arrived just then all dressed up in his cowboy attire. From boots, fringed vest, to ten-gallon hat, he almost looked the part. No six-shooter, but he did have a super wide belt with a silver buckle that was as big as my head. I think he needed it to hide his rather large stomach. His assistant was dressed in the same attire, but she looked much better. Kinda like Annie Oakley from Ernie's "Wild West" magazine.

I wasn't a huge cowboy fan, but Ernie gave me one copy before he left for Colorado. He thought that the magazine would remind me of him. I don't think so. Even in his Roy Rogers outfit Ernie didn't look like a cowboy; he looked more like a kid in a Halloween costume. Cowboy Bill's assistant sure looked like a cowgirl though. I bet she was from Texas.

Eight o'clock came around fast and at least seventy people showed up to put bids on our stuff. Cowboy Bill rolled up onto the first trailer and yelled out "Welcome ladies and gentlemen, boys, and girls. Bidding will begin in five minutes, so park yourself and pull out your green. We've got some amazing items here today. If you don't have a bid number yet, please register at the back table. Don't get caught with your hands in your pockets."

Ned and I found a good spot on top of a hay bale close to the wagon. Cowboy Bill's crew had put bales of hay around the trailer so people could sit or stand and have a good view of the proceedings. I had my spot and I was ready to have the big money roll on in. I could tell Ned was excited too. He jumped up on the bale with me, licked my face, and sat down facing the auctioneer. Ned knew something was up and he wasn't going to miss the action.

CB (Cowboy Bill) grabbed the first box next to him, held it up for all to see and barked, "Our first prize is a fabulous sterling silver tea set with all the accoutrements. Let's start the bidding at five dollars." CB began his rapid chant. "Do I hear five? Now five. Now five. Yup! Now six. Do I hear six? Yup! Now seven. Lookin' at seven. Yup! Can I get eight? Now at eight. Anyone eight? Seven fifty now. Yup! Back to eight. I'm at eight. Seven fifty once. Seven fifty twice. Sold to number 34 for seven fifty. Bring your number to the back table to collect and pay. Next up . . ." Every time CB said "Yup!"

he acknowledged the bidder with a quick look and headshake and continued on with his chant.

Ned and I tried to keep up with his looks and nods, but finally settled for identifying the last bid. CB was shaking and talking way too fast for me. The auction was off to a great start and I was super excited. I was with Mom when she bought that tea set at a garage sale for fifty cents. I wasn't sure what accoutrement meant, but I could tell it was going to be a great day. The cash was already rolling in. I bet my bike would sell for big bucks.

I hadn't been to many auctions so I was surprised when something didn't get a bid. That didn't slow CB down at all. He just put that item together with the next item and people had to take both if they bid on the second. CB called it "bundling." That's what he meant when he said "Everything goes." Slim Stanley had "bundled" the garage and house in Old Town to make the sale too. Dad bought both to get what he wanted, a new business and a fresh start.

Finally, my bike was up for bids. I can't say the bidding was fierce, but I did end up with three dollars. It wouldn't buy a new bike, but maybe I could find a good used one in Skunk Hollow and paint it my favorite colors, red and yellow. I could maybe name my new bike *Big Red* or *Flame.* Ernie would think that was really cool. I'd send him a picture if I ever got his Colorado address.

By the end of the day, everything was gone, and I mean everything. Nothing was left in the garage or yard. Our house was also practically empty. Mom and Dad had decided to sell all the furniture, beds and appliances. Even the old paint cans in the basement made it to the trailer. We kept our clothes, blankets, and a few treasures. Mom kept her cooking utensils and sewing machine. Dad kept his best tools and a few motors he said would help him get started. I kept Gerty's cage, Ned's bed, and of course my crime-fighter magazines. I would need them to help me solve the mystery of Beauregard Puce and the Skunk Hollow treasure.

Outside, CB's crew picked up their tables, threw the bales up on the trailers, attached the trailers to their trucks, and headed out. CB's assistant counted up the cash, took 15% off the top and handed Dad a check for $649.33. Everyone was happy, including me. That was more money than I had ever seen. I hoped my cut would give me some good green.

Then it hit me. All the beds were gone. Where were we sleeping tonight? Maybe we'd sleep in one of those big hotels downtown. Wrong again! I had to sleep on the floor. At least I had a few blankets to lie on. Ned was lucky; he got to keep his bed.

Dad bought a small trailer from CB that he hooked up to our pickup. He thought it would help in the move and he could use it to haul mowers in his new business. Everything that we now owned could easily fit in the trailer and the truck. What a relief. I had visions of them giving away Gerty or Ned because there just wasn't enough space in the truck for everything.

Chapter Three

It was official. We finally arrived in Skunk Hollow and increased Old Town's population by three. Our first stop was our future home to unload all of our belongings. Dad decided that it should all fit in one of the "back bedrooms" in our new house. He picked the room that was closest to the back door and would take the least amount of repair. We didn't have much left so everything fit in the 15x15 room. Dad called it the master bedroom with a view. It did have a view – a junk pile by the garage. When everything was finally unloaded, Dad installed a lock on the bedroom door to make sure all was safe during the upcoming renovation.

After unpacking the truck and trailer we made our way to the Brickle Hotel. We were all tired and hungry, and I definitely needed sleep. Mrs. Brickle met us in the lobby and welcomed us to Old Town with some cold lemonade and some big blueberry muffins. What a great treat! I almost swallowed my first muffin whole. Mom asked me to eat the next one slower. "Good food should be enjoyed, not devoured." I enjoyed devouring food, but made a decision to listen to my mother and show Mrs. Brickle that even boys my age can sometimes have good manners. I suppose that means I should hold my burps in as well. Being a kid can sure be tough, especially when you're hungry.

The Brickle Hotel was a three story building right on Old Town Road. It had to be the biggest building around. The first floor had a small lobby, a dining room, a kitchen, and the manager's living quarters. That's where the Brickles lived. The second and third floors were all hotel rooms, six on each floor with a shared bathroom. I wasn't too sure how old the hotel was, but at least it didn't look haunted.

"I just saw the house Buzz bought this morning." said Irene. "I think it will take several months to get it in shape. Do you mind having guests for an extended time?"

"No problem." said Mrs. Brickle. "In fact, I was thinking that you could use the third floor for your temporary home. We have three rooms up there that we never rent out. They're clean and tidy, but we just don't get that many customers. The other three rooms are just storage – tables, chairs, dressers, and a couch or two."

Before anyone could respond, I blurted out "That would be super. I could have my own room, mom and dad could have theirs, and we could make the third into a kitchen." I was always watching out for my stomach.

Mrs. Brickle laughed and said "I'm afraid there is no stove or fridge up there, but you're welcome to use the ones in the back of the dining room on this floor. After my husband passed on, we gave up running a restaurant here, but everything still works."

Mom had a few ideas of her own. "I think I could use that third room as a living room and sewing room. I might be able to start a little sewing business of my own. Would we be able to switch out the bed in that room for a small table and one of the couches?"

"Of course. Take whatever you need to make it comfy," said Mrs. Brickle. "It will be wonderful having that floor occupied again."

Mom was an amazing seamstress. She could take my torn old blue jeans and turn them into jackets, caps, shorts, and even dresses to sell. I was always outgrowing and tearing holes in my jeans, so we always had an endless supply of denim. Mrs. Brickle thought a sewing room was a great idea and offered to ask Mrs. Gittemeire at the thrift store if she would consider selling some of Mom's denim creations. As usual, Mom was all smiles.

With a little food in our stomachs, we were ready to move upstairs. I ran out to get Ned and Gerty to show them our new room. Ned jumped out of the back end of the pickup and I wrapped Gerty around my neck. I could tell both were eager to get some water and take a much-needed nap. This had been a long trip for all of us. As I charged through the front door, I ran right into another person. That made two in less than a week. At least this time I didn't get smothered in large breasts, just a small collision.

"Well hello to you too." said this girl, now only inches from my face. "I love your necklace. May I try it on?"

And there she was, someone my age in Skunk Hollow. I had just collided with Mrs. Brickle's daughter Cindy, a freckle-faced redhead in a bright yellow T-shirt and blue jeans. She was about my height and weight, and "cute as a button." (I heard my dad say that.) I'd never seen a cute button, but for a girl, this Cindy had a look that made me sweat.

"I'm Cindy Brickle by the way, but you can call me Cinnamon. Everyone does."

I stumbled over my reply. "Okay a . . . Cinnamon, and ssssure. This is my snake Gerty and my dog Ned."

Ned could tell she was friendly. He licked Cinnamon's face as soon as she bent down to greet him. I carefully placed Gerty around Cinnamon's neck and she ran off to show her mom. As she darted away with my snake wrapped around her neck she turned her head and yelled, "By the way, what's your name?"

Tongue-tied again. " Errrrrocky." I blurted out. I was so smooth.

"Okay Errrrrocky. Funny name. See you in a bit."

And that was my first encounter with a girl that would soon

become a life-long friend. Me? Friends with a girl? Who would have believed it? Not me in a million-quadrillion years. Truth be told, I was more than a little shy around girls; *scared to death* would be really how I felt most of the time.

Ned and I continued on our journey to the third floor. After two long flights of stairs we finally arrived at my room. Ned and I both crashed on the bed; sleep was our number one priority. I'd unpack my clothes later. Right now I needed some shuteye. That's what Dad called sleep.

I had been in dreamland for about two hours when a light knock woke me up from my beauty sleep and brought me back to the real world.

"Room service!" said a muffled voice from behind the door. I pulled myself out of bed and stumbled across the room. After a couple of tries, I twisted the old glass doorknob just right and the door opened with a creak. There was Cinnamon again with Gerty still wrapped around her neck.

"Thought I'd return your snake, Errrrrocky. Dinner's at six. I think we need to do something about your hair. Here she is," Cinnamon said as she handed Gerty to me. "See you later."

I was once again speechless. I took Gerty and closed my door as Cinnamon darted down the hall and down the steps. "What's wrong with my hair?" I thought out loud. I located a mirror on the closet door and then I knew. What a disaster! My hair was spiked in all different directions; porcupines look better. I guess I needed to cut down on the Brylcreem. I always thought if "*a little dab'll do ya*" a little more would be even better.

How to impress a girl in three easy steps; have a head-on collision, put my foot in my mouth, and have a bad hair day. I really am one smooth guy. I wonder what dinner was going to be like? Maybe I could just stuff food in my mouth all night and then I wouldn't have to talk to this "cute as a button" girl.

I had to do something about my hair. A bath was out, but maybe

I could put my head in the sink and soak out some of the grease. I thought this was a good plan until I put my head under the faucet in the third floor bathroom. I forgot that Mrs. Brickle had said the third floor rooms hadn't been used in a while. Now my usually blond hair was spiked, greasy, and slightly rust colored. I really hoped I could wear my baseball cap at dinner.

Dinner was served buffet-style in the hotel dining room. Breakfast and dinner were served to all registered guests and the Brickles. Today, we were the only guests at the hotel. Mrs. Brickle cooked up a great pot roast with carrots and potatoes, some huge biscuits, and apple pie for dessert. I couldn't wait to dig in.

Of course, my mother made me take off my cap and after a few laughs from everyone, we all sat down together at a big, round table. Cinnamon picked a chair right next to me. Mrs. Brickle introduced everybody and then asked us all to bow our heads in prayer. I silently prayed that I didn't spill anything on Cinnamon and that I could pack plenty of food in my mouth so I didn't have to talk.

Cinnamon's brother Eddie was at the table as well. He didn't say much, but from everyone's comments we found out Eddie really was a superstar high school athlete. He played just about every sport at the school, and helped his teams win lots of games. I didn't know many athletes but I was impressed. Eddie asked me to come and watch a football practice next week and he'd introduce me to his teammates. I had potatoes in my mouth but I made sure I shook my head vigorously, so he knew I was excited to go.

Mrs. Brickle and my mother continued talking about all the stuff women talk about. Dad tried to interject a few comments here and there but eventually just settled back and listened. I thought this was a good plan.

"So your name is really Rocky?" asked Cinnamon between bites.

With my mouth full again, I just shook my head. This no talking idea was pretty tough when someone sitting right next to you asked you a direct question. Just when I thought it might be time to slow down and try a few words, Dad asked me another question.

"Rocky, did you put Gerty in her cage?"

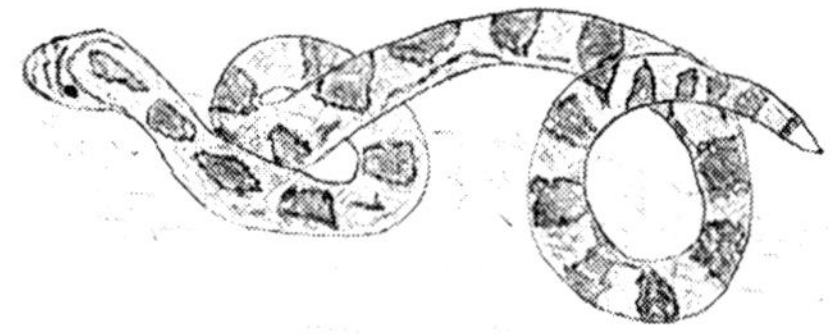

Oh great! I left the cage in the truck. "I left her on the bed," I said sheepishly. "She'll be all right." I could only hope. Gerty could move pretty fast when she was hungry, and she hadn't had a mouse in quite a while. She could be anywhere in the hotel by now. Even though no other guests had checked in, I sure didn't want Gerty to end up in someone's room late at night. I knew that would be big trouble. I had to finish up, excuse myself, and find her quick. But a big piece of apple pie was calling my name. Gerty would just have to wait. After my second piece of pie, I asked to be excused and took off for my room.

"I'll go with you," said Cinnamon as we pushed away from the table.

"Cindy, you need to help clean up," said Mrs. Brickle.

"Buzz and I will do the clean up tonight," my mother said. "After such a great meal, it's the least we can do. Run along kids." My mother knew Gerty was loose and I would need any help I could get in tracking her down in a new environment. We bolted out of the room and took the stairs two at a time. We were on a mission.

As we entered my room, I crossed my fingers and wished for the best. Rats! Gerty wasn't on the bed or anywhere else in sight. This was not a good sign.

"Here Gerty, here Gerty." said Cinnamon.

"Cinnamon, Gerty can probably hear you, but she doesn't come when you call. Only Ned does that. We'll have to find her or coax her out with some food." Finally, I got out a couple of complete sentences. I hoped Cinnamon didn't think I thought she was clueless about snakes.

"I figured that, but thought it was worth a try anyway," she said as she looked under the bed. "She's not here."

"Hey Cinnamon. One of the things I like to do is solve mysteries. I think we could treat this like a mystery and follow some steps I learned to help find Gerty. "

"Sounds like a good plan. How do we start?"

"Well, I follow the seven easy steps to solving a mystery that are outlined in my Crimefighter magazine. *Step #1 is Survey the scene.* Is anything unusual or different?" I pulled out some paper and a pencil from my suitcase and jotted down: #1. Nothing unusual in my room.

"Do you think that there was a crime here?" asked Cinnamon. I could hear the strain in her voice.

"I don't think so, but we can't rule out anything until we have all the facts." Now I was in my element. "Our second step is to *Record and examine all the facts.* What do we know for sure? Did we see anyone go up or come down the stairs during dinner? Are there other ways to get into my room? Did Gerty leave any clues? Are there back stairs? Do doors lock from the inside? Can anyone climb through a window on the third floor?"

"Next we try to *Establish possible motives.*"

"She was hungry, she wanted to explore, she got scared, or someone took her. Oh no Rocky! Do you think someone took Gerty?"

Trying to look official, I jotted down Cinnamon's ideas behind #3. Cinnamon must really like snakes. I never knew many girls in Chicago but the ones I did know would scream and run away when Gerty was around. Gerty got me out of a few girl jams.

I handed Cinnamon my pencil and she drew a quick map of the third floor. Cinnamon could draw great maps, just what every good investigator needs when solving tough cases. She handed the pencil back and I tucked it behind my ear. It stuck like glue; at least my greasy hair was good for something.

We moved on from my room into what my magazine calls "the perimeter" checking and noting every detail as we went. That was the start of Step *#4: Expand the search. Observe and Listen. Be methodical as you search.* We looked for dark places, warm places, holes, and possible feeding areas. We checked windows, doors, and locks as we went.

Step #5: Eliminate the obvious. We could rule out someone taking Gerty. No one had come up the stairs during dinner. The second and third floors were unoccupied tonight, and everyone in the hotel, other than the two of us, was still in the dining room. Even though we hadn't found Gerty yet, Cinnamon was visibly relieved.

After talking about snakes in general, we also eliminated Gerty being scared. Snakes aren't afraid of much. That left two possibilities – she's hungry or she's exploring new surroundings.

#6: After searching, collecting, and recording all data, identify the most probable solutions. "Have you seen any mice up here?" I asked as we continued down the hallway looking for clues.

"I saw a mouse in the storage room at the end of the hall a few weeks ago." Cinnamon said. "Mom was going to set some traps or get a cat, but we haven't done anything yet."

We both looked at each other and then made a beeline for the storage room. It was just two doors down from my room – a very short trip for a hungry snake. We opened the door and sure enough, there was Gerty lying on an old rug. She was definitely a little fatter than she was an hour ago.

Case solved! We could close the book on this mystery. That was #7. We were both excited and relieved. Cinnamon gave me a big hug and almost kissed Gerty. I knew we both would have sweet dreams tonight; mine wouldn't be about finding Gerty.

This wasn't a big mystery, but it gave me a chance to get to know Cinnamon and prove to her that I wasn't just a clueless Errrrrocky, fumbling for words. I also figured that if I could get Cinnamon to like solving mysteries, she might help me work on the big ones that had been nagging at me since we signed our agreement with Slim Stanley.

My big, unanswered questions were: What was Slim Stanley up to? What ever happened to Beauregard Puce? Was there really a treasure hidden in Skunk Hollow? Was there more in Badwater Creek than just catfish? And, what was that smell?

We had two weeks before school started. Plenty of time to solve at least one big-time mystery if I got some help from Cinnamon. I was pretty sure we wouldn't be tracking down any vampires – maybe a few crooks and plenty of gold. But, under Step # 3: *Examine all the facts* the official rule was *take nothing for granted.* I couldn't rule out bloodsuckers just yet. That would be a tough assignment since I didn't plan on going out at night.

After letting our families know about Gerty and the mouse, it was time for me to fix up my room and head for bed. Cinnamon offered to help, but I let her know in a nice way that I wanted to unpack myself. Actually, I didn't want her to see my red pajamas or my stacks of worn and holy underwear. I'd put those away myself, thank you. I thanked Mrs. Brickle again, wished everyone good-night and headed up the stairs to my room.

"Good night Rocky. Tonight was fun," said Cinnamon as I took to the stairs. "See you in the morning. Hope your hair looks better."

Oh great! I forgot about my Rocky, spiked, greasy hair. I bet she thought I was a zombie-look-alike. Maybe it was time for a bath. I'd run the water in the morning before breakfast. I was way too tired to take a bath tonight. I'd just wear my baseball cap so I didn't get the pillow dirty.

I was thankful mom wasn't tucking me in anymore. She'd make me take a bath tonight. Mothers are like that. Dads don't really care. Dad would probably say something like "Bath today, bath tomorrow. Whatever works."

Chapter Four

After a good night's sleep and a scrub down in the tub the next morning, I was ready to face the day. My hair was clean and I made myself as presentable as possible. I dressed myself in clean blue jeans with identical knee patches, my favorite brown belt with the double star buckle, a green T-shirt with no holes, and my black high-top tennis shoes. It was the best I could do with what I had to work with. I ran a comb through my hair, brushed my teeth, called Ned, and headed downstairs. My parents had already eaten and were off to explore their new purchase. I bet my mother had a few choice words for Dad when she finally saw the inside of their new beach house. I was happy I didn't get up early to make that trip.

Breakfast at the hotel was great. Mrs. Brickle had fried up dozens of pancakes with lots of maple syrup. I love pancakes. I bet I ate at least six. After filling all the gaps in my stomach, I was ready to explore Old Town with Cinnamon as my guide. Then I remembered – no bike. I had sold it at the auction back in Chicago. This could be a major setback. I didn't think Cinnamon would be up for us riding double.

"I think you could borrow Eddie's bike," Cinnamon mumbled between mouthfuls of pancakes. "He hasn't ridden it in years. You could ask him. He'll be here in a few minutes. He's still in his bedroom admiring his muscles in front of his mirror."

I never looked at myself in a mirror unless I needed to comb my hair. There was nothing I needed to see. Dad always said "Rocky, don't break the camera." In my case, I was sure that comment also applied to mirrors.

Eddie was soon parked at the table dishing up a huge stack of pancakes. I was thoroughly impressed with the number and gawked at his plate until Cinnamon poked me. "Hey Rocky, don't you want to ask Eddie something?"

"Oh yeah. Eddie, I sold my bike back in Chicago and was wondering if I could borrow yours today while Cinnamon shows me the town. I'd be happy to rent it, I have three dollars from our auction."

"I'll sell you that bike for three bills," said Eddie. "I haven't ridden that thing in years. The tires need air, but otherwise it's in pretty good shape. Anyway, I need some gas money for my wheels."

Eddie had inherited his dad's car, a '49 Chevy coupe. The car was definitely hot. I never knew when to call something hot or cool, so I just used both whenever. Eddie was cool; his car was hot. Some day I hoped someone other than Ernie would think I was cool.

"Sold!" I said without hesitation. I had a feeling Eddie's bike was probably pretty hot, just like Eddie's car.

Cinnamon laughed. "Don't you think you should look at the bike first, Rocky. It could be a lemon."

"A yellow bike? I could go for that. Nothing wrong with yellow." A little red paint here and there and I would have some great looking wheels.

"No Rocky," laughed Cinnamon. "A lemon means something isn't worth buying. You don't want a lemon. Come on. Let's go look."

"It's out back," said Eddie. "Cinnamon will get you the pump. Take it for test ride and if you like it, it's yours for three bucks."

"I know I'll like it," I said excitedly. We're going to take in the sights today and I need some good wheels to keep up with Cinnamon." I really wasn't up for riding double with a girl just yet.

Things were working out pretty well so far today; a full stomach, a new friend, and wheels. I couldn't wait to see my new ride. I was ready to rock regardless of the color of the bike!

And there it was – a 26 inch red and chrome *Schwinn Phantom Cruiser* complete with tank and back rack. I couldn't believe my luck.

Pinch me; I think I'm in heaven. I was going to be chasing down bad guys and making daring escapes on some very cool, hot wheels. I grabbed the pump from Cinnamon and after a few pumps and some drops of oil from the Brickle toolbox I was ready to roll.

Even though I could have been on the move right then, Cinnamon convinced me to go back into the hotel to pack a lunch and get some change for a stop later at the fudge shop. She tucked our supplies into her front bike basket, and off we went, me astride my new set wheels and Cinnamon on a bike she had appropriately named *Black Beauty*.

Of course, I had to name my ride; *Phantom* seemed to fit since the name was already stenciled on the tank. The world's best mystery solver and crimefighter had wheels that could help me fade in and out as fast as I needed in almost any situation.

We said goodbye to Mrs. Brickle, told Ned to guard the hotel, tumbled out the door, and mounted our bikes, eager to start our quest. This was going to be a great day exploring Old Town. We headed north toward Skunk Hollow Road and the old Winter barn. "Might as well start with Old Town's only tourist attraction," Cinnamon said.

"Let's lay down some tracks!" I said as we pedaled north on the gravel road that led past our new estate. I wasn't sure if "laying down some tracks" was the right line to use, but Cinnamon seemed impressed with my comment. First time for everything! I'd have to drop some other cool, one-liners on her like "Off to the races," or my favorite "Let's rock and roll."

The new Malone estate was right at the corner of Old Town Road and Skunk Hollow Road. I told Cinnamon we could stop on the way back if she wanted to take a look. As we traveled around the lake, I took in the sites and tried to commit them to memory. It wasn't too hard since there were very few check points, buildings, or turn-offs along the way. We passed Miss Odetts' house early on and she gave us a big wave from her vegetable garden.

After that we passed lots of big oak and elm trees with overhanging branches that seemed to threaten the existence of the road any time the road took a slight turn. We pedaled along the west side of the lake. I only saw the lake through the trees one time on our entire trip to the barn. It looked pretty big and uninviting. Cinnamon said the Winter barn was about three miles out, but as fast as we were pedaling *Phantom* and *Black Beauty*, we were there in short order.

The historic round barn stood on a small peninsula surrounded by acres of plush green grass, several chokecherry bushes, and tons of crab apple trees. The barn was weathered and unpainted, but had somehow defied nature for decades – no rotted boards, broken windows, or holes in the roof. It looked like a picture on a postcard that you'd send to a friend with a quote, "Look what I found on my vacation."

Cinnamon didn't know if the site ever had more than just the barn. If there ever was a farmhouse on the peninsula, it was long gone. The Winters must have lived somewhere; we'd have to explore. I was sure we could find an old foundation and maybe even some hidden treasures.

I couldn't quite figure out why the grass around the barn was so short. "If this building was abandoned years ago, weeds should have made the barn almost invisible from the road." Before Cinnamon could even respond, six goats came around the barn on a trot. That was a short-lived mystery. My old science teacher would have called this an "Aha" moment.

These goats were pretty funny as they raced to greet us. They bumped, brayed, and bit each other as they jockeyed for the lead on their way to greet us. As they approached we got off our bikes and then the licking began. The goats were worse than a bunch of hungry kittens. They licked everything – face, hands, and my bike tires. Good thing I liked goats.

I had my eyes on the goats and didn't notice a huge man following about twenty yards behind the herd. "Whoa kids!" boomed a voice as loud as thunder. I was sure he was yelling a warning, so I did what any normal skinny kid would do. I hopped back on my bike as fast as humanly possible. I was scared, and I was going to get the "heck out of Dodge."

"Don't run off Little Ones; just keeping my goats at bay," grumbled man-mountain. He had to be calling us "Little Ones." I guess we were. Compared to this giant, most humans would be considered little. He was way taller than my dad and twice as wide. With a full beard, thick dark hair, and limbs as big as tree trunks, this giant was quite imposing. I decided to keep my distance and keep my grip on *Phantom*. Even if I was little, I was fast and I was ready to put *Phantom* to the test. I hoped Cinnamon and *Black Beauty* were ready to blast out of here as well.

"Hey Mr. Jingles. How's life?" Cinnamon said with confidence.

"Life is good Little One," replied man-mountain with a much kinder, softer voice. "What brings you out here?"

"Just showing my new friend the town. Rocky, this is Mr. Jingles. These are his goats and he lives in the barn. He's Old Town's one and only goatman. He's famous around these parts. Maybe you've heard of him."

Mr. Jingles put out his massive hand and we shook. "Welcome

to my home Rocky." Sometimes you can read a lot about a person just by shaking hands. Mr. Jingles could have crushed my hand, yet I sensed as soon as we shook that this was a gentle man who was honest, sincere, and loved life.

I immediately felt at ease even though this was the first time I had ever met a real, live, giant goatman. What a difference from Slim Stanley and his creepy, sweaty grip.

"Can you stay a while and have a little chokecherry juice and goat cheese? I made fresh batches of both this morning."

The goatman seemed eager to have visitors and of course, I was hungry. I'm always hungry.

"Sure Mr. Jingles." I said. "I've never had goat cheese or chokecherry juice. Hope they don't make me sick." Why do I say stupid things? I hope I didn't offend man-mountain. He seemed friendly enough, but I was pretty sure upsetting him wasn't a good plan.

Mr. Jingles just laughed. What a relief. "You'll be fine. You might get a few freckles out of it though. Cinnamon here has been drinking my juice and eating my cheese for years and look what happened to her."

I looked over at Cinnamon as she twisted her face and crossed her eyes. I laughed right along with Mr. Jingles. Although I'd just met him, I liked this gentle giant. If he was Cinnamon's friend maybe someday he would like to be my friend as well. I made a promise to myself to not say any more stupid things around him. Fat chance on that one!

We had a great time talking about the barn, the goats, and riding the rails. I learned that Mr. Jingles had moved from town to town by train during the Depression and had finally settled in Skunk Hollow.

It seems Old Man Winter told Mr. Jingles he could stay in the barn as long as he kept the barn tidy and the grass around it trimmed. A local farmer gave Mr. Jingles a pair of goats and in a few years he had a whole herd to take care of the grass. Mr. Jingles said he was "a man of simple means" and was able to live off the land and the goats. Occasionally he sold cheese and milk to the locals but mainly hunted, fished, and farmed. It seemed like a great life.

"Where do you get your bib overalls?" This was just one of the many goofy questions I asked as we munched on cheese and juice. I didn't think Mr. Jingles had a sewing machine and I'd never seen clothing that large in any store. I was pretty curious about where he did his laundry as well. I didn't see any electric wires coming into the barn.

"I order my bibs and shirts out of a Sears and Roebuck catalog that Mr. Potts keeps at the post office. He's a good man. You should get to know him. His son Charlie is a regular visitor here."

It sounded like Mr. Jingles had lots of visitors, mostly kids. "Do you walk to town? Where do the goats stay when you're in town?" I asked.

"Most of the time they just want to stay here; they love the grass. On really nice days we all go for a walk. It's pretty fun to see the New Town folk's reactions. They pretty much steer clear of me, especially when I have my goats. Come to think of it, they steer clear of me most of the time unless they know I have cheese or milk to sell. Got some pretty uppity people over there. I much prefer Cinnamon's visits." He winked at Cinnamon who immediately twisted her face again.

We talked for almost an hour. Once we decided to continue our tour, I promised Mr. Jingles I'd be back to see him soon and I'd bring him some of my mom's chocolate chip cookies for a treat. He seemed pleased and invited us both back for a wildlife picnic next week. I wasn't sure what the menu would be, but if it was anything like chokecherry juice and goat cheese, I would be there.

As I mounted *Phantom* I had to ask one more question. "Mr. Jingles, do you know anything about Beauregard Puce and the lost treasure?"

"I know enough. I think I can help you out with your mystery. We'll talk next week."

How did he know I was into mystery solving? I guess I need to work on being more discrete. Could be trouble if people knew I was searching for clues.

"All righty then. Let's burn some rubber." I thought that was another good one liner until I glanced over and saw Cinnamon roll her eyes. Okay, maybe I was pushing it just a bit with my one-liners, but it got us moving again. I could hear Mr. Jingles laughing as we pedaled away.

We made our next stop about a mile south of the barn. There was a small, barely visible path leading back into the woods. "What's back here?" Inquiring minds wanted to know. There wasn't much of a trail to follow.

Cinnamon guided me to a huge deer stand up in an old oak tree. "What do you think Rocky? It's big enough for four or five adults and all their gear," said Cinnamon. "And it has a roof to keep you dry in the rain. No walls though; just a rail to keep you from falling."

We located the long ladder hidden in the bushes and pretty soon were up in the stand looking out over the woods to the west and Skunk Hollow Road to the east. The stand was so well hidden you really couldn't see it from the road but from the stand you could see at least a mile in any direction. You could even see a bit of the lake through the treetops. With a good lookout, it would be hard to sneak up on anyone in the stand. Ned could be our lookout when he came along on our next trip.

"Is it okay to be up here?" I asked. "We're not trespassing are we?"

"It's okay. My father built this stand years ago. Since he died, I'm the only one who ever comes here. I miss him so much." Cinnamon quickly turned her back to me, but I didn't miss the tears she was trying to hide.

I felt bad for Cinnamon. I didn't know what to say make it better for her. "This is an amazing place. Thank you for bringing me here."

She gave me a quick hug again, the second in just two days, and then barked in her best tough-girl voice as she headed down the ladder "Come on Malone. Let's rock and roll."

Hey, that's my line, I thought to myself. I was saving my special line for a big mystery finale. "Okay then," I blurted out following her down the ladder. Maybe I need a new favorite line. I hadn't used "Let's motor!" or the Lone Ranger's line, "Hi-yo Silver! Away." Maybe I could yell " Hi-yo *Phantom*! Away." Nothing I could think of was quite as cool as "Let's rock and roll." Rats!

"Our next stop should be for lunch," said Cinnamon. "I know this place right on the lake. It has an old picnic table and I'm sure no one will mind if we use it."

I was ready for a picnic. I'm always hungry and if given the chance could probably scarf down one of our sandwiches as we pedaled down the road. We passed Miss. Odetts' house and got another wave from the garden. From the road, her garden looked amazing. All those vegetables made me even more hungry, if that's possible.

"Not too far now, Rocky." Cinnamon could really cruise on *Black Beauty*. I wouldn't have been able to keep up on my old bike, but *Phantom* was up to the task. Where were we heading? We passed the new Malone garage and house, and then veered left. The old bridge was straight ahead. I bet we were picnicking in New Town. Maybe we could stop for fudge.

Cinnamon put on the brakes right at the bridge. "We'll have to leave our bikes here," she said. They'll be safe behind the fence." She parked her bike, and before I could even jump off mine, she disappeared down an overgrown path next to the bridge.

"Bring the sandwiches and cookies from my basket," said a voice down and off to the left.

"Okay," my voice crackled. I hate when that happens. It sure sounds goofy, especially whenever I tried to sing, which was mostly never. I slid down the path and landed in a heap. I picked myself up, brushed myself off, and pretended I meant to slide. I thought it was a great performance.

"Nice entrance!" remarked another voice, and it wasn't Cinnamon's.

"Rocky, these are my friends Tommy Two Feathers and his sister." Cinnamon said. "Their families have lived around here forever. Would you two like to join us for lunch? We have plenty of sandwiches."

"My name's Sarah, but you can call me Little Mouse. Everybody does. Thank you for inviting us," she squeaked. The name fit her to a T.

We all sat down at the old picnic table no more than a stone's throw from my new back yard. How cool was that? I could walk from my back door to the lake and plant myself right under the covered bridge. What a great place to hang out. It was a little scary when cars drove over though. That bridge was old and creaky. I wouldn't want to be down here when the bridge collapsed and I was sure that would happen very soon.

I broke out the peanut butter and jelly sandwiches and we all dug in. Cinnamon had packed enough sandwiches and cookies to feed an army. I wondered if she knew Tommy and Little Mouse would be here.

"What are you doing here under the bridge?" I asked eying the bridgework to make sure nothing was going to collapse on my head.

"I come here all the time to skip rocks," Tommy said. "Want to see me hit the other side of the lake?"

I didn't know Tommy, but figured that he was boasting since the far bank was at least one hundred yards. "I'll bet. Do your rocks have wings?"

"No, he has a sling," chirped Little Mouse, "and he's pretty good with it." She was obviously a fan of her big brother.

Tommy took his sling out of his back pocket and dropped it

on the table. I wasn't impressed. It was just two long leather laces attached to a small flat piece of buckskin. "One hundred yards with this thing. No way."

"Time for a demonstration," Tommy said as he got up from the table. He tied one of the laces around his right wrist, and then held both laces in his right hand. He placed a small rock in the rawhide pouch. After a couple of full-circle swings above his head, Tommy released his grip on the untied lace and the rock was airborne. A small splash about five feet from the shoreline told me Tommy was a little short.

"Had to show you a splash first," Tommy stated as if that was his plan. "The rocks are hard to see when they hit the bank." Look close for this next one." Tommy released the next rock effortlessly and it exploded into the base of a huge oak on the opposite bank.

"Cool!" After seeing two throws, I was hooked. I knew I had to learn how to use a sling. What a great way to waste an afternoon. "Tommy, can you teach me how to use one of those? I've only thrown baseballs."

Tommy smiled and agreed to meet the next day for some serious lessons. I was hoping that we could sling rocks without an audience. I was pretty sure I would bean anyone close. I wasn't too hot at throwing baseballs either, but no one had to know that right now.

We sat down again at the table and Tommy shared some of his family history. Tommy and Little Mouse were full-blooded Lakota. Their ancestors had lived and hunted around Skunk Hollow Lake for generations. As white settlers moved west through the Plains, most of the Lakota fled north to Canada. Chief Henry Two Feathers made every attempt to stay and live with his wife and children on Badwater Creek, but a raging fire took the lives of his entire family with one exception. Tommy's father, Daniel Two Feathers, had pulled himself to safety as his home, family, and possessions were reduced to ashes. Daniel was sure someone had started the fire, but his suspicions fell on deaf ears. No one seemed to listen or care about one little Indian boy.

All seemed lost until Old Man Winter took Daniel in, protected his claim to his family land, and kept his spirit alive.

Old Man Winter convinced Daniel to finish school. It was tough for him but Tommy's dad was determined to keep his promise to his ancestors. He would survive and bring honor to his family and his heritage.

With Mr. Winter's help, Daniel was able to build and operate a small sawmill on his land. Two Feathers Sawmill was located at the east end of Old Main right on Badwater Creek. Logs could be floated down the creek from the forests surrounding the lake. It was also a straight shot west on Old Main to the train station. Unfortunately, the train rarely stopped in Old Town since the elevator and feed store had closed. Semi-trailers were used to transport goods these days. That was a problem for Old Town businesses. Trucks couldn't cross the Skunk Hollow bridge.

Daniel worked very hard and the sawmill produced high quality lumber that was sought after by many contractors and cabinetmakers. Lately however, many of the local contractors were getting low-grade lumber from a big lumber mill up north. Daniel was eager to find more buyers interested in quality lumber, but it wasn't going so well for the Two Feathers family. The push to build "fast and cheap" housing came right out of the mouth of New Town's finest, Slim Stanley.

"My father won't do business with Slim Stanley; says he's a liar and a cheat. Father can't stand to be in the same room with that blowhard. He also believes Mr. Stanley had something to do with my grandparents' death. I … I think I said too much."

Even though Tommy stopped talking, the conversation didn't end there. Little Mouse chimed in, "I hate him. I call him *Slime* Stanley."

I had the feeling that Little Mouse wasn't afraid to voice her opinion, especially about Mr. Stanley. After a good laugh, we all agreed that Slim was Slime and we needed to keep an eye on him.

After a great PB&J lunch, we said our goodbyes to Tommy and Little Mouse and continued our bike tour of Old Town.

"Our next stop is the Grand Theater. It's been closed for a long time but I know how to get in. Sometimes I jump up on the stage and pretend I'm a star. Some people say ghosts of famous actors still perform there at night. Maybe we can come back some night and see for ourselves. Rocky, are you afraid of the dark?

"Not at all," I lied through my teeth. "Bring on those ghosts and ghouls." Oh great! Just when things were going well I'm probably going to do something stupid like scream in fear, wet my pants, or cry like a baby. I didn't even want to see the theater in broad daylight. No way was I going there in the middle of the night. If Cinnamon ever wanted to visit the theater at night, I knew I'd be busy with something else.

We parked our bikes behind the theater and wiggled through a gap in a boarded-up door. Nobody seemed to care that anyone or anything could crawl into this building. As we moved through the building I could see why people said this place was haunted. Every step brought a deep, sad groan from the well-worn wooden floor. The musty air hinted of years of neglect and decay. Stage props and sets were left broken and scattered. Red velvet curtains would never again rise to the rafters announcing the start of another grand performance. The Grand Theater was no longer grand.

"What happened here?" I asked with a voice barely above a whisper.

"When the town's population started to decline there weren't enough people coming to performances. The money just ran out so the theater had to close. The Stanley Bank now owns the building."

Slime was once again in the picture. What's up with this guy?

Just as we were about to step onto the stage, a light came on in the balcony. "Who's there?" boomed a deep, threatening voice.

I was going to reply, but Cinnamon had placed a hand over my mouth and whispered softly, "Stay quiet, Rocky. I don't think he saw us. We'll just have to hide until he's gone or he loses interest."

Hide in here? I'd rather run and take my chances. *Phantom* was right out back and no one would catch me on my new wheels, unless of course he could turn into a bat. Then I was toast. I guess I'd have to trust her. And the day was going so well.

With Cinnamon in the lead, we slowly crawled almost to the center of the stage. It was a good thing the place was filled with boxes and props. It would be difficult to spot us, even with some light. Luckily, it was as dark as a tomb on the stage. I couldn't believe I was glad I was in the dark.

There was a small trap door in the middle of the stage. Luck was with us again as the door was open. We moved down the old steps as slowly as we possibly could to avoid making any sound. I grabbed Cinnamon's hand just in case she might be scared or need my support.

If the stage was dark, this hole was pitch black. I hoped Cinnamon knew what she was doing. I sure didn't. We held hands all the way down the steps into what felt like a small room. I couldn't see or feel any doors or windows. We sat down on the last step and waited in the dark for about twenty minutes. The only sounds we heard were our breathing and my pounding heart. My imagination was going wild. I was sure something evil was listening for us and would devour us as soon as we made any attempt to move. What a nightmare in the middle of the afternoon.

Finally Cinnamon whispered, "I think he's gone Rocky. Let's go find our bikes. Be as quiet as you can, just in case."

No-brainer for me. I couldn't stop my heart from pounding though. Right now it was as loud as a base drum. I probably wouldn't calm down until we were back in the hotel.

As we got back on our bikes Cinnamon blurted out, "Boy, that was fun, Rocky! We're pretty good at hiding. Bet that was Mr. Stanley. Let's go back tonight with flashlights to see what he was looking for in the balcony."

"Not a chance. I'm busy tonight." It wasn't true, but I was sure I could come up with something a lot less scary. Maybe we could sit around and listen to the Lone Ranger on the radio. I didn't even like westerns, but I guess I could learn.

"Okay Rocky." Cinnamon sounded disappointed. "Let's ride over to Torgeson's Mercantile. Maybe Sam will be in the back room working on something."

"Who's this Sam guy?"

"Oh, just a friend," said Cinnamon. I bet you two will hit it off right away. Sam's kind of a bookworm."

I'm really not a bookworm, more a crimefighter magazine junkie. Maybe Sam reads book mysteries like Sherlock Holmes. That would be a great connection.

We pedaled across the street to Torgeson's, hopped off our bikes, and headed inside. "Hello Mr. T," Cinnamon said as she passed the counter. "Is Sam in the back?"

"As always, Cinnamon. How are you and whose your friend?" asked Mr. Torgeson.

"This is Rocky. He just moved here from out east. Big city somewhere." Cinnamon didn't know about Chicago? She had to know about Chicago. It was on every U.S. map and much bigger than Skunk Hollow. I'd have to fill her in later.

"Hello Mr. T. Glad to meet you." I really was happy to meet someone who didn't scare me or lurch around in the dark looking for my blood. Mr. T seemed like a regular guy. I continued walking to the back of the store thinking Cinnamon was right behind me. She wasn't.

I poked my head into the back room and saw a girl with long blond hair sitting in an overstuffed chair reading a very big book. "Hi, I'm Rocky. I'm looking for Sam. Cinnamon said he's back here. Have you seen him today?"

The girl jumped out of her chair, straightened her gingham dress, adjusted her thick glasses, and quickly positioned herself just inches from my face before I could even think about planning a retreat.

"Yes, I know where Sam is. Sam's right here."

I did my best to look around her, but as thin as she was, she was right in my face blocking my view of the room. "Sorry, but I don't see him. You're kinda blocking my view."

"I'm Sam, you gumball, Samantha Torgeson. You can take your foot out of your mouth any time now."

Cinnamon finally arrived. Eying my predicament she joked "Hey red. My favorite color, even if it's on your face. I see you've met Sam. Did I miss something?"

"Yes . . . no. I just met Sam, I mean Samantha. I . . . err was just a little flushed because it's kinda warm back here." It sounded like a good excuse for my red face, but from the laugh I got from both girls, I knew neither bought it.

The good new was I found out that Sam and I did have something in common. We both loved mysteries. She loved reading books more than magazines. We both loved to solve the case before the story ended. Sometimes I read the last pages in my magazines first. I guess that was cheating, but if I already figured out who did the crime, why waste my time getting to the end. Just *eliminate the obvious.* I was pretty sure Sam read her books from front to back.

Sam wanted to talk about the book she was just reading. Something called *Hound of*

the Baskervilles. I thought it would be fun to talk about some dogs. Maybe they were just like Ned. Cinnamon had to drag me out of the room just when it started to get interesting. She told me we had a lot more to see in Old Town.

On our way out, Cinnamon invited Sam to have lunch with us tomorrow. That sounded great, even though I didn't know I was having lunch with Cinnamon. Although I hadn't thought that far ahead, I was thinking about dinner tonight back at the hotel.

Our next stop on the tour was the old schoolhouse. After nearly getting slimed by Slim, the Vampire at the theater, I was hoping we weren't walking into another run-down building with pits or black holes in the floor. Please make this next stop bright and cheerful. My stomach couldn't take much more excitement today and I sure didn't want to lose it. Maybe I could just hang out outside.

We made our way south on Old Town Road and came upon the old schoolhouse about a mile south of Old Main. Unlike the other buildings in town, the school looked great. The exterior had been recently painted, all windows and doors were clean and in working order. The grass and bushes were neatly trimmed, and the playground had equipment that looked like it was ready for kids. Maybe we could take a spin on the merry-go-round. I could maybe use that as an excuse for my stomach going topsy-turvy.

"Come on Rocky. This is a really neat place. I love coming

out here."

We jumped off our bikes and walked up the steps to the schoolhouse door. The door was unlocked so we stepped inside. The desks were all cleaned, polished, and lined up. Chalkboards were washed and maps were rolled up tight. "This is amazing. Do they use this for classes?" I had heard that everyone now went to the New Town School.

"Not really. Miss Odetts' brother, Lenny Odetts, takes care of the building. No one pays him to do it, but he thinks it's his job. He went to elementary school here and really loves the place. His challenges didn't allow him to go beyond the sixth grade, but he came to school everyday anyway. He's a great friend, even if he is much older than me."

"Lenny's been taking care of this school for over thirty years," Cinnamon remarked. "Sometimes some of us come here and Lenny pretends he's a teacher. We have so much fun, and Lenny just loves pretending."

I had heard about Miss Odetts' brother and how some of the New Town punks made fun of him. I hadn't met Lenny yet, but I was sure that I'd like him. Maybe I could introduce Ned to those punks the next time Lenny got picked on. He'd be more than willing to teach them a lesson.

We did a little more exploring and then decided to get back for dinner. I was hungry again. My stomach was growling loud enough that Cinnamon thought I was making animal sounds on the way back to the hotel. Bring on the meat and potatoes my stomach roared.

After another amazing dinner Cinnamon and I talked over our plans for solving the big mysteries. We needed the help of quite a few people if were ever going to get to the bottom of some of these questions. We'd have to keep our investigations "under wraps" so it was important to find people we could trust to keep their ears open but their mouths shut. We also agreed that each person on our team had to have a skill that would help us in our search. We'd need a special meeting place – a place that was easy to get to but only our team knew about.

I suggested the table under the bridge, but Cinnamon had a much better idea. "We can use my father's stand. Everyone can get there in a few minutes by bike and we can hide everything in the woods. My father would be thrilled that it was being used for something really important like solving mysteries."

What a super meeting place. Our next step was to choose our team of investigators. Tommy was at the top of my list. He was brave, cunning, and good with a sling. He knew the woods, river, and swamp better than anyone, except for his father. Tommy's dad had taught him all of the Lakota ways. He was a loner but I was pretty sure he'd agree to help.

Of course we'd have to include Little Mouse. She was always tagging along with Tommy. I was pretty sure Tommy was responsible for Little Mouse when they weren't at school. Cinnamon said that her family called Little Mouse a "finder". She paid attention to the smallest details and could even find a "needle in a haystack." That's what Mr. Jingles said. She could help uncover even the tiniest clues. We'd count her in.

"What's my talent?" Cinnamon asked with a sigh. "I'm not going to be much help."

"You're kidding, right?" I could not imagine how she thought she had no talent. "Your drawings are amazing, you know everybody, you're super smart, and you're cool under pressure. Without you, I'm not doing this."

Another hug. I'm finally learning how to be smooth around girls. Most of the time I just stumble along and get embarrassed.

"Who else do you know that could help us? I don't know many people in Old Town."

"I can think of two other kids that would be great, Charlie Potts and Sammy Torgeson. You met Sam. She can really help with research. You haven't met Charlie but he knows a lot of people in Old and New Towns. He can help us get any supplies that we might need. If you agree, I'll see if they both can meet us at the bridge tomorrow."

"Sounds like a plan," I said as we packed up our notes. "I'm meeting Tommy tomorrow morning. Should we meet under the bridge at noon?"

"I'll be there with a surprise lunch for everybody," said Cinnamon.

I was hungry again just thinking about a surprise lunch. Of course, I'd probably eat anything Cinnamon gave me, except maybe crab apples. They were just too bitter.

Chapter Five

Ned and I met Tommy bright and early the next morning. He was waiting for me under the bridge near the old picnic table. I knew something was up as soon as I slid down the hill because he greeted me with an ear-to-ear grin. Ned wagged his tail, walked over to Tommy, and prepared for an old-fashioned ear rub. He got one right away and Ned was in heaven.

"This is Ned. He's decided you're one of the good guys."

"In Lakota we call our friends *kola*. Those we call kola have special places in our hearts," said Tommy. " Ned is *le mita kola,* my friend." After a good ear rub, Ned decided to crawl under the picnic table to get out of the sun and take a morning nap. Sleeping was one of Ned's favorite pastimes.

"Got something for you," he said reaching in his back pocket. "I made it last night."

Tommy pulled a brand new sling out of his back pocket. It was complete with leather straps and buckskin pouch with my initials tooled into the side.

"Wow, this is really cool. Now if I only knew how to use it." I could probably learn to throw rocks easily enough, but accuracy was going to be a real challenge. I was hoping Tommy was a patient teacher. Based on past experience, this was going to take some time.

"That's my job," said Tommy. "I know you'll get the hang of it. I'll bet you'll be scaring crows out of trees in just a few hours."

Tommy was a great teacher. He taught me the ties, the grip, how to swing my arm correctly, when to release, and even what to look for

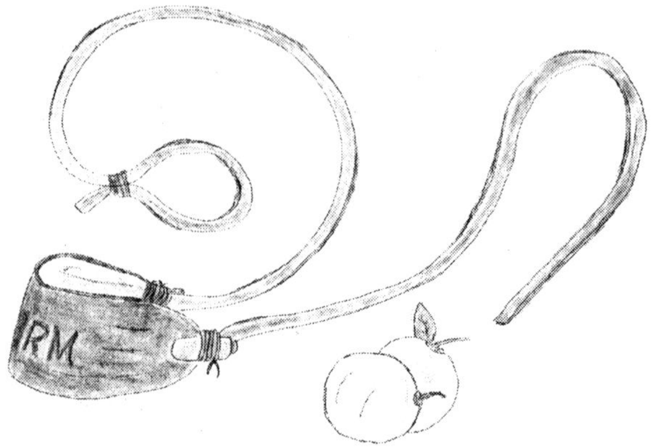

in a throwing rock. "My favorite ammo is a small crab apple. They're the right size, Mother Earth approves, and the squirrels and geese love them. Mr. Jingles gives me all I want. I got a bag from him this morning."

Cinnamon had told me that Tommy was very quiet in school and that he really didn't have many friends. He kept to himself most of the time and, other than Little Mouse, always shied away from just about everyone. He was making up for it today. I was happy about that.

It had surprised Cinnamon when Tommy had talked about his family and had offered to meet me. It was sure going to surprise her even more when I showed her my new skill, thanks to Tommy the Teacher. I don't know why it happened, but in just a few hours we had developed a strong friendship.

After an hour or so, I had mastered the sling enough that I could actually hit the far bank. I did hit the big oak tree above the bank once in a while, but I attributed it to blind luck. Tommy was very patient, commenting and making suggestions on each throw. He even told me the way I stood made a difference in the flight. I found that hard to believe, but went along with his suggestions.

Tommy could hit just about any target within 200 feet. He could be a great partner if some bad guys or vampires were after us. Getting beaned by a crab apple would give any creep something to think about. In between throws, I asked him if he wanted to help me work on some big mysteries.

"Ohan Rocky," said Tommy. "That's yes in Lakota."

We stopped slinging crab apples when we heard some bikes rattle across the bridge. "A-oh," said Tommy almost under his breath, but loud enough that I could hear trouble in his voice. (I found out later that a-oh actually meant trouble.)

Three boys had crossed the bridge and emerged on the downward trail. They looked to be a few years older than Tommy and me. "Well lookie here! Little Indian Boy found um new friend," said the first punk sporting a mop of greasy black hair.

The other two laughed with snorts that would have made any pig run for cover.

It wasn't possible. A younger, skinnier Slim Stanley? Boy, was this town in trouble. It was too late to run up the hill to my bike. Besides, I didn't think I should leave Tommy there all by himself. I did the only thing I could think of on such short notice. I thought I'd try to kill 'em with kindness.

"Hello. I'm Rocky Malone. I just moved here from Chicago. I was hoping to meet some people from New Town, and here you are."

I put out my right hand to shake and moved a step towards the apparent leader of this threesome. That was probably my first mistake.

"Hear that George," said the skinny greaseball to the right. "He wants to be our friend."

"I don't shake the hand of any Old Town creep. Don't care if you did just arrive from some big city. You're not wanted here." George unloaded a wad of spit just where my hand would have been if I had kept it extended. Luckily, I recoiled rapid fire. I learned that skill watching Gerty.

"Since you already know my name, let me introduce you to my two friends. The big guy here is Freddie. He likes to smash things. My other friend is Clyde. He likes to pick up the pieces after Freddie's done." All three snorted out their pig-in-pain laugh this time. This conversation wasn't going well at all.

While all this was going on Tommy just sat there as calm as could be, not even looking their way. Was he getting ready to run? Did he know something I didn't, because I was sweating bullets? These three were definitely not interested in becoming friends, and I wasn't up for any bruises on my body.

I didn't really care if they made fun of Chicago. That city was not my favorite city and no skin off my back.

Then it hit me. I hadn't introduced all my friends. "Oh sorry," I said in my most charming voice. "I forgot to introduce you to our friend Ned. Oh, Ned. Come out and say hello." All this time, Ned had been keeping a watchful eye on the three toughs from under the table. They hadn't seen him yet, but Tommy had; that smile was on Tommy's face again.

Ned lazily crawled out from under the table, shook his head a few times for effect, looked over at the three party-crashers, bared his fangs, and slowly walked toward them. With his ears back, head down, and a growl in his throat, Ned was communicating. George got the message.

"Okay, were outta here," squeaked George as they backtracked up the hill. I heard a distant voice yell out as three bikes tore across the bridge to safety, "Just wait 'til school starts, you worms. You won't have that mangy mutt around to protect you."

"Worms?" Tommy and I both laughed, scratched Ned's ears, and sat down to wait for lunch. To pass the time, I wiggled around in my best worm imitation. Tommy thought it was hilarious. Ned had seen enough and decided to park under the table again. I guess he wasn't impressed with my act. He sure had earned a good lunch though.

"Hey, where's Little Mouse," I asked. "Doesn't she hang out with you every day?" Sometimes I was just a little slow on the draw.

"Oh, we stopped by the hotel this morning," said Tommy. "Sarah stayed to help Cinnamon make our surprise lunch."

Now I was really hungry. What kind of lunch took that much preparation? Not PB&J sandwiches.

It was finally noon and my new friends were arriving for the picnic. First down the hill was Samantha. She parked her cute pink bike right next to *Phantom* and gingerly walked down the hill. "Hello Tommy. Hello Rocky. Remember me? I'm that guy Sam you met yesterday." She wasn't going to let me off the hook yet.

Today Sam was wearing a flowery dress with some lace around the collar, white socks, and black patent shoes. She was also wearing a little white hat adorned with a pink ribbon. "Are you going to church after our picnic?" I asked. I thought it was a good question.

Sam's eyes met mine and I knew I was in trouble again. Her piercing eyes were as cold as ice, even though they were bright green. "Don't you like my dress?"

Oh boy! How do I get out of this mess? Someone help me please!

"Your dress is just as beautiful as Mother Earth's flowers after a gentle morning rain. Hello Sam," said Tommy.

Calm again! I owed Tommy a big thank you after that close encounter. Why couldn't she just wear blue jeans? I didn't think that I would suggest a new wardrobe just yet.

Charlie Potts made a grand entrance, almost as good as mine the first time I slid down the bank. His was more of a roll and tuck than a slide, but the effect was the same, a complete lack of body control. He got up, dusted himself of, and proclaimed, "I meant to do that."

We all clapped our approval. Charlie bowed, stuck his hand out, and said, "Thanks so very much. I'm Charlie Potts. Most everyone calls me Cryin' Charlie. I have allergies and it always looks like I'm crying." With that, he took out a big red bandana, wiped his eyes, and blew his nose. I was sure that any moose in the area would recognize the sound.

I reminded myself to never ask to use his bandana. "I'm Rocky Malone. Pleased to meet you. Should I call you Cryin' Charlie or Chuck?"

Charlie grinned and said, " I'm okay with Cryin' Charlie as long as you don't tease me about my runny nose and constant tears. Not much I can do about it anyway. I never did like the name Chuck. George Stanley calls me Upchuck or Chuckles and I really hate those nicknames."

"It's a deal," I said. I was hoping he could control his moose honk even just a little bit. Nice guy but that honk was a little annoying.

"Hey, are you ready for some lunch?" Cinnamon yelled from the top of the bank. I need some help getting everything down. Tommy, you're the most sure-footed. No offense Rocky and Charlie."

"None taken. Can't wait to see what you two cooked up," I said as Tommy glided effortlessly up the hill. That guy moves like a cat.

We weren't disappointed. Cinnamon and Little Mouse had cooked up tons of fried chicken, biscuits with honey, and homemade lemonade. Mrs. Brickle had sent along a checkered tablecloth, plates, cups, and a ton of napkins. This was a feast for kings and queens. I vowed to take my time eating so I could actually taste the food. Mom would have been impressed.

The six of us had a great time eating, talking, and laughing. We made sure Ned got some food too. He was the hero of the day. After we told our story Little Mouse named our local toughs "Gorgeous George and the Slimeballs." Sounded like some kind of band, but the name fit, even though I thought calling George Stanley gorgeous was a bit of a stretch. Little Mouse said that was the point. She had a sharp mind and sharper tongue. Maybe she could come up with a name for our crime fighting team.

Everyone was excited about my plans to solve some of the local mysteries. They all wanted to get started right away. I thought it best to let Cinnamon explain how we would get organized and where. She was good at that stuff, and they'd all listen to her.

We decided to meet tomorrow afternoon at the tree stand. Cinnamon told us to come separately and park our bikes in the trees so we wouldn't draw attention. Tommy and Sarah didn't have bikes, but everyone knew they'd be there long before the rest of us, and no one would see them on the road. I made Tommy promise to show me some of his trails.

"Anyone up for a swim this afternoon?" asked Cinnamon. "I was going to show Rocky Big Island Trail, the campgrounds, and the dam. It's a hot day and the water will feel good after baking in the sun. We could all get our suits and meet there about three o'clock."

"Great idea Cinnamon," I said. I wasn't much of a swimmer, but I loved the water. I just hope I could find my suit. I also couldn't wait to see Sam's suit. I was sure it would be all pink and lacy. I also bet she brought along a flowery swim cap and thick goggles. I'd really have to work on keeping my comments about her attire to myself though. I was in enough trouble with her already and we'd only just met a day ago.

Tommy thought a dip was a great idea since he and Little Mouse were planning on hunting for frogs out in Backman's Swamp anyway. "It's just a short hop away from the dam." Tommy glanced over at me to see if I'd take the bait and hop around like a frog. We looked at each other and I could see the grin coming.

My worm impersonation earlier that morning had been a big hit, but I decided to pass. I wasn't quite ready to make a fool out of myself in front of three girls. I was sure that time would come soon enough. Why push it.

I was amazed at how Tommy and Sarah got around. Cinnamon told me Big Island was about three miles away. That's a lot of walking. Sam and Charlie both had bikes and were excited to be included.

We finished eating and all chipped in on the clean up. "That's the best chicken and biscuits I ever had. Thanks so much." I really meant it. Everyone else agreed.

"You're welcome," said Cinnamon. It was my mom's fried chicken recipe and a Two Feather's recipe for the biscuits. We can't take any credit for the honey. That came from Miss Odetts."

Little Mouse grinned from ear to ear. "My mamma said the secret to great tasting biscuits is a hungry man. Guess you were really hungry." She was right of course, but I'm always hungry. The food was amazing.

We packed everything back into Cinnamon's basket. I hung the cooler over my handlebars, and off we went to get our swim gear. I hoped the water by Big Island was clean and tasteless. I couldn't help thinking what Willie the Wanderer had told me about Beauregard Puce and the creek water he tried to drink. Gross!

Chapter Six

We stopped back at the hotel just long enough to put our picnic gear away and change into our suits. I found the faded blue suit I used in swim classes back at Eastside Elementary. I was sure Cinnamon's suit would be either red or yellow. No-brainer there. Mrs. Brickle gave us a couple of old towels and told us to be careful. Cinnamon and her brother had been swimming there for years, but I was the new, untested kid on the block. She wanted to make sure I was safe. "Come to think of it," she said, "you need to run up to your new place and let your parents know where you're headed."

I agreed, even though my parents let me go to the community pool any time I wanted. I suppose not having a lifeguard around could be a challenge. It delayed our departure a few minutes, but we had almost two hours before we met up at the dam.

The trip out to the dam was uneventful. We passed the schoolhouse and in ten minutes were pedaling down Big Island Trail, an old, single-lane, dirt road. It made the gravel roads in Old Town look like super highways. I bet a few cars broke axles on this giant pothole.

Ned decided to see how much mud he could get on his coat along the way. By the time we reached the lake he was covered head to toe. Ned really needed a bath.

The trail went right through the northeast corner of Backman's Swamp. We could hear a ton of big old frogs croaking in the summer heat. Tommy said he found lots of frogs out here. I forgot to ask him what he did with them.

We arrived at the bathhouse about two thirty. Of course Tommy and Sarah were already there. (I was still having trouble calling Sarah Little Mouse.) Tommy was wearing blue jean cut-offs for his suit and Sarah had what looked like a buckskin suit. Pretty cute outfit. They'd already tested the water and said it was *minne-waste*, good water.

"How'd you get here so fast?" I asked. They must have come on a dead-run from the bridge.

"I'll let you in on an old Indian secret. It's called a *motor scooter.* My dad gave it to me a few years ago. I have a lot of trouble with the engine, but I got it running today. I think it goes about 40 on the open road. Not really sure though, the speedometer's broken. No brakes, bald tires, and it needs a tune-up. I'm not really good with motors."

"Hey, that's my dad's business. I bet he can get your scooter purring like a kitten. I'm sure he'd love to look at it. He loves small engine work." I knew Buzz would eat this up. If the engine was already running, a quick tune-up wouldn't take long at all.

Charlie and Samantha arrived a few minutes later. They had run into each other in front of Torgeson's and decided to bike out together. Sam had a long T-shirt on so I couldn't see her suit, but I was ready to work on holding in my biggest laugh of the day. Charlie was really the perfect picture of what not to wear at the local swimming hole. I wasn't sure where I'd ever seen such an ugly suit– mostly white with green, red, and black stripes. Oh yeah! Now I remembered. My Dad's old boxer shorts! Mom made Dad throw them out before we moved. She said they were gross.

Sam was finally ready to swim. I prepared myself for the big no-laugh. What a disappointment! She had an emerald green suit with a green ponytail ribbon to match. No thick goggles, no flowery cap, and no pink suit with laces. She looked great.

"What are you staring at, Gumball?" she said. "Don't you like my suit either?"

I was in minor shock and had to refocus. "No really, it's ummm, great," I blubbered. Tommy was too far away to help on this one. I really needed to find a way to let Sam know I liked her, but right now

I wasn't connecting. Hopefully, I could get her talking about mysteries again.

Except for Ned, we all finally made it into the water and I had to admit, it was the best swimming hole I'd ever been in. Well, it was the only one I'd ever been in, but it was still tops in my book. After baking his muddy body in the sun for a while, Ned eventually joined the fun. I was happy about that because he couldn't come up to my room tonight caked in mud. Swimming saved me from having to hose him off back at the hotel.

Tommy tied a big rope over a tree branch; with a good swing we could soar out into deep water. We set up all kinds of contests off the rope swing. Cryin' Charlie won the biggest splash, Sam won most twists, and I won best landing. Everyone was impressed with my belly flop. I pretended it didn't hurt even though my stomach turned beet red.

After almost two hours of swinging, swimming, and laughing, we were all exhausted and decided to head home. We reminded each other to meet at the tree stand after lunch tomorrow and bring anything we thought might be useful, but wouldn't be missed. I'd bring my clipboards, paper, pencils, and my toolbox. Might need a hammer for some quick repairs.

On the way back Cinnamon and I stopped by the old schoolhouse. "Something's not right here Rocky," said Cinnamon as she got off her bike. We parked *Black Beauty* and *Phantom* and took a closer look. While we were swimming, someone had been in the school. Doors and windows were left open, the desks were shoved out of place, and a note had been written on the blackboard–"See you later alligator." Lenny Odetts would never write that. The schoolhouse was his pride and joy.

We put everything back as best we could, but this didn't feel right. We couldn't jump to conclusions, but our minds were racing. We made a beeline to Miss Odetts to check on Lenny.

"We need to fly, Rocky," exclaimed Cinnamon as she pumped *Black Beauty's* pedals. I was glad *Phantom* was up for the task. Ned thought it was a race and led the charge all the way to the Odetts' house.

Ned was surprised when we passed the hotel, but he didn't complain. He just stopped long enough for a quick drink from his bowl and then rejoined us in a matter of seconds. As we rode up to her house, we saw Miss Odetts pacing back and forth on the porch. "Oh my, oh my! What can I do? Lenny's missing."

We jumped off our bikes and raced to Miss Odetts' side. "Children, have you seen my Lenny?" The strain in her voice was way beyond normal, almost a desperate sob.

"We haven't seen him, but we're here to help," said Cinnamon. "What happened?"

It took a few minutes, but we finally got Miss Odetts calmed down enough to tell us what she knew. She told us that Lenny would often disappear for days, but he always told her what he was doing and always took some extra clothes and food. This time, he just vanished. No extra clothes, no food, no word. "Lenny wouldn't leave like that," she said. "Something's wrong, and I have no idea where to look. Can you help me?"

"Of course we will," said Cinnamon. "Rocky's pretty good at finding people. I'm sure we can find Lenny."

I wasn't so sure I was good at finding people, but I wasn't going to let Miss Odetts or Cinnamon down. I'd uncover every clue and track down every lead. If Lenny was in Skunk Hollow, we'd find him.

"We'll check with everyone in Old Town right away to see if anyone has seen him. It might take a few hours, but we'll come back tonight," I said trying to sound reassuring.

"You stay here, make yourself some dinner, and try to stay calm. Lenny could just be out for a walk."

"Lenny's been gone since yesterday. His bed hasn't been slept in and he didn't take anything with him. Something must have happened."

She really cared about her brother. We both gave Miss Odetts a hug and took off for the hotel. It was almost dinnertime and we had lots of people to see. Maybe we could get our parents to help in the search. There was still plenty of daylight left and I was hoping we could find Lenny before dark. I promised myself I'd do whatever it took, even if it meant a night search – just not in the theater. We could do a search right after dinner.

"Cinnamon, if we don't find Lenny tonight, do you think we can get our team together right away tomorrow morning?" I knew that the first days in any investigation were crucial. That's what I read in my crimefighter magazines.

"Great idea," said Cinnamon. "Let's ask them tonight when we're searching Old Town."

"Wash up kids. Dinner's on the table," said Mrs. Brickle. "We're having shepherd's pie."

I wasn't a fan of green beans, but what kid is? Mrs. Brickle seemed to have a way with making everything super tasty. If we had time, I was sure this would be another great meal, but we were on a mission.

"Mom, Lenny's really missing and Miss Odetts is in a panic. Can we eat fast, tell you what we know, and get everyone out to try to find him?" Cinnamon said in rapid fire. " We promised her we'd help if we could."

"We'll all do what we can, but we do need to eat," said my mother. "You can fill us in at the table."

"Let all bow our heads in prayer for a moment," said Mrs. Brickle. I prayed for Lenny's safe return.

After a quick meal and a short explanation about what we knew, we divided up Old Town and our search began. On my suggestion, we went in pairs. Dad and Eddie took the pickup and headed out toward the old barn and Mr. Jingles. My mother and Mrs. Brickle would go to all the homes in Old Town. Cinnamon and I took Old Main. I had a feeling I'd end up in that old theater again – just not so soon. We all agreed to take any help that was offered and to report back to the hotel at nine p.m. with any news or leads.

"Mom, can you ask Charlie Potts, Sam Torgeson, and the Two Feathers kids to meet us on Old Main whenever they can? They can help us there." Mom had no idea who these people were or where they lived, but Mrs. B. said she'd make sure they got the message.

We all stacked our dishes in the kitchen and made our way out to find Lenny. Other than the pool hall, all of Old Town's stores were closed for the day. Although it would be better to search them, I decided that Lenny would have been noticed in a store. We could cross the stores off our lists. We decided to take on the theater right away. That was my idea. Might as well get it over with during daylight hours. I absolutely didn't want to go into that building after dark.

We entered the theater the same way we did before, but this time carried flashlights and made as much noise as we could. Ned thought it was great fun and actually barked once. That was new. If Lenny or anyone else was here, they would hear us. I was okay with finding Lenny on stage. I wasn't interested in running into anyone else, especially some nightwalker.

We searched everywhere in that old building and didn't find any trace of Lenny. We did discover a pile of old books up in the balcony office. I was pretty sure it was an office at one time; it had a desk, files, and a working lamp. An old ledger was opened on the desk. It was pretty obvious that someone had recently been looking through the old books searching for something. We decided to do a more thorough investigation after we found Lenny.

"Hey, are you guys in here?" It was Tommy and Little Mouse.

"Yeah, we're up in the balcony. Watch your step. There's junk all over." I couldn't believe I was telling Tommy to watch his step. If anyone was going to trip over something, it was going to be me. Tommy was Mr. Surefoot.

I just a few seconds, they both were in the office with us. I never even heard them take a step. "How do you do that?" I asked.

"Do what?" said Tommy.

"Move without a sound," I said.

"I thought I was being noisy. I'm much quieter in the woods."

I bet Tommy and Little Mouse could sneak up on anyone. Could be a good skill to learn. I was pretty sure it would take him a lot longer to teach me how to walk without a sound than teaching me how to use a sling. Coordination and keeping quiet weren't my strong suits. We filled them in on what we knew as we made our way out of the theater and back on to Old Main.

"Sarah and I went frogging in the swamp after our swim this afternoon. Lenny sometimes walks the trails out there. We didn't see any sign of him at all. He's easy to locate when he's traveling in the swamp. He's a noisy walker and he sings to himself all the time. We would have heard him," said Tommy. "Should I take my scooter out towards the dam again just to make sure we didn't miss something? I could be back here in a flash. Maybe Sarah could help you look around here. She's pretty good at finding things."

"Might be a good idea. We were all out at the dam, but we weren't looking for him or for clues then," I said. "We'll keep looking through some of the vacant buildings. Maybe we can meet up in Winter's Pool Hall in about twenty minutes."

"Sounds good. *Tokhi waniphika ni!*" said Tommy as he fired up the old scooter. It coughed twice and then kicked in. I sure hope it didn't conk out tonight. I'd get Dad to look at it tomorrow. Tommy needed wheels.

"Hey Cinnamon. What was Tommy saying to us?" I was pretty weak when it came to the Lakota language.

"I think he said *good luck*. We'll need it," said Cinnamon as she headed towards the next empty building. I wonder if she was worried about bloodsuckers in these old buildings. If they were around, we'd need more than good luck. I turned on my flashlight even though it was light out and we were still outside. Can't be too careful.

"You need to save your batteries," Little Mouse said. "If you have trouble seeing, you can hold my hand."

There was no way I was going to hold the hand of a girl half my size and years younger, unless she was scared. I check with her when we got inside the next building. If there was even a glimmer of fear, I'd be there for her and for Cinnamon.

We decided to check out the old elevator across the tracks and end up back at the pool hall. The elevator was a huge, ugly building with very few windows. Great! More dark rooms. Harvesting grain was big business back when the trains stopped for daily pickups. Now, like many buildings, it was just another shell waiting to be torn down.

The door wasn't locked so we were able to walk right in. We didn't need my flashlight either. There was plenty of sunlight coming through the back of the building where much of the wall had fallen away.

"Nothing here," said Cinnamon. "Let's take a quick peek downstairs. I don't like being here at all. The roof's not safe."

We took three steps down into another pit of darkness. Instant sweaty hands. Where did that scream come from? Could it have been me? A little hand reached over and grabbed mine just before I hit step number four. "Come on Rocky," said Little Mouse. "I'll be your eyes."

She had to be scared. I know I was. I imagined myself screaming. "I can do this!" I whispered to myself. I turned on my flashlight as quick as I could with one hand. I couldn't let go of Little Mouse. She needed me.

We got to the bottom and looked across a huge, empty room. No furniture, no caskets, no crypts, and no Lenny. This room was clear. We could move on to the next fun-filled building. We raced back up the steps and on to the street. Ned was patiently waiting for us in front of the building. I had tried to get him to come into the building with us, but he knew better. Dogs are smarter than humans, most of the time.

"You can let go of my hand now, Rocky," said Little Mouse.

"Okay! Just wanted to make sure you were safe."

"Yeah, that's what I thought," she said.

Out of the corner of my eye, I thought I saw Cinnamon wink at Little Mouse. I think she was on to me. I'd have to prove I was brave in the next building. I tried to get everyone moving back towards the pool hall.

"This is the old post office," said Cinnamon. "Mr. Potts had to move to the new one across the bridge. He's been trying to keep this one going, but the government is shutting it down. It still looks good."

The door to the old post office was open as well. As I turned the knob I said, "I'll handle this one."

"Very brave of you, Rocky," said Cinnamon as she flicked on the lights.

"All clear. We can move on." I was back in control.

We made our next stop at Winter's Pool Hall. As we walked through the swinging doors, it was evident that this was the place to meet many of the locals on a Wednesday night. My first days in Old Town had passed so quickly, but if I was counting right, this was my third night in this booming metropolis.

It was a packed house, at least for this pool hall. Three men were sitting at the bar talking to Willie the Wanderer, four more were playing cards at a nearby table, two were playing pool, and some older guy was talking to Tommy. Okay, how did Tommy get here so fast and without us seeing him or hearing the scooter? That thing was too loud for us not to notice it. My new friend was amazing.

"Hi everyone. I just got here and was filling Grandfather in on Lenny Odetts. Rocky, come on over and meet him." I could see the pride in Tommy's eyes. Old Man Winter was a Skunk Hollow legend.

I grabbed Cinnamon and whispered in her ear, "How come Tommy called him Grandfather. Anyone can see they're not related."

"Mr. Winter raised Tommy's father. In a way, they are related."

"Oh," I said shuffling over to the table, not really understanding.

"*Tunkasila,* this is *le mita kola,* Rocky Malone."

"Well hello young man. Tommy has told me a lot about you. It's a pleasure to finally meet you." Mr. Winter stood up to greet me. Instead of shaking my hand, he put both his hands on my shoulders and looked into my eyes. "I sense an inner strength in you, Rocky. Thank you for helping our family."

"I'm honored to meet you. I was hoping Tommy and Sarah would like me and would soon call me friend," I said. It wasn't a great greeting, but I think everyone recognized my sincerity.

We all sat at Mr. Winter's table. I threw out a couple of quick questions before turning to our search for Lenny. "Mr. Winter, I've heard people in town call you Old Man Winter. Why is that? You have really long, white hair and carry a pretty cool cane, but you don't look that old."

"Thank you Friend Rocky. I've seen many winters, eighty-three in fact. My hope is to see many more. I was called Young Man Winter before my father was called to his maker. After that, I became the eldest Winter."

"Oh! I love your cane. Could I look at it?"

"Of course. This staff was made and given to me by my blood brother, Henry Two Feathers, years ago when we were both young men. It's my most cherished possession. It will be Tommy's some day."

Now it all fit. I could see why Tommy called him Grandfather or *Tunkasila* in Lakota. They were related in a way that most people could never understand. Tommy was so lucky to have Mr. Winter for a grandfather.

Charlie and Sam arrived and pulled up two more chairs. Seven people packed around a table that normally seated four. It reminded me of the crowded lunchroom at my old school, except these were people I wanted to be with; these were my friends.

Mr. Winters looked across the table at the bar. "Willie, my guests seem to be a little thirsty. Would you bring over six root beers?"

"Sure thing, Boss." Willie still had his slow drawl, but his delivery was fast. We were all sipping in a matter of minutes. Maybe it was the frosted mugs that made this root beer the best I had ever had.

"Let's talk about Lenny and what I can do to help. Tommy filled me in a little bit, but let's see what we know so far."

Mr. Winter seemed really interested in helping us. Cinnamon filled the group in on all the details from seeing Miss Odetts to our search of all of Old Town. I was glad she took the lead here. She was a natural when it came to talking to people and remembering details. I liked to write things down to help me remember.

"I guess our next step is to figure out why Lenny is missing," said Mr. Winters. "We'll need to search for clues, and be good investigators by watching and listening. With everyone's help we'll be able to put the pieces together."

I wonder if Mr. Winter had a subscription to my crimefighter magazines. He sure knew the right steps to solve a mystery. We talked a little longer and then decided to move on to the rest of the vacant buildings. Twilight was coming soon and it would be difficult to see anything inside an unlit building after the sun was completely gone.

"Kids, I don't get around very well anymore. Maybe it's best if I stay here and keep my eyes and ears open. Can you check in with me tomorrow?"

"We will Grandfather," said Little Mouse as we all moved away from the table and out the door.

"Thanks for the root beer and letting me hold your staff, Mr. Winter." I said as we left the pool hall.

"Any time and you're welcome Friend Rocky." All the others chimed in with a thank you as well. Little did I realize that from then on, root beer was "on the house" for the six of us. I could make this a regular pit stop, especially on hot days. Speaking of pits, I still wasn't too sure about Willie. It just felt like there was more to him than meets the eye, even one that wanders.

We visited all the other vacant buildings in less than fifteen minutes. It was an easy assignment with twelve pairs of eyes on a mission. We thought it best to meet as early as we could tomorrow morning at the tree stand. Cinnamon and I would talk to our parents at the hotel before heading up to fill Miss Odetts in on our search. "Bring anything along you think will help, and pack a lunch. We'll probably have to eat on the run." I was pretty sure Lenny wouldn't be back tonight.

When we pulled up to her house, Miss Odetts was sitting in favorite rocking chair out on her porch. We decided Cinnamon would be the one to talk to Miss Odetts about our search. I really didn't know Miss Odetts. Cinnamon decided to tell her who was looking for Lenny and where, rather than a straight "We can't find him" comment. If she knew the whole town was still looking, it might be a little less stressful.

After Cinnamon's summary of the search, I offered something that always seemed to help me in stressful times. "Miss Odetts, my mother always gave me a warm cup of milk when I had trouble sleeping. If you have some milk, I can heat up a cup for you."

"Thank you Rocky, but no. I think I'll just sit out here on my porch and watch for Lenny. Lenny and I always watched sunsets." Even though the sun was gone and night had set in, I could see the tears trickle down her cheeks. I had to find Lenny. This just wasn't right.

We both gave Miss Odetts a small hug and quietly stepped off the porch. We were now really exhausted and had to get back to the hotel and our beds. Tomorrow would be here all too soon.

As we rode by my dad's garage, I thought about the pit. Maybe Lenny had fallen into that cold, black path to the underworld, or worse yet someone or something dragged him down there. "Cinnamon, we have to make one more stop." Was that me talking? Am I nuts? Where's this newfound bravery coming from? It was after dark, I'm exhausted, and I'm thinking about checking out a big hole in the ground. I need to have my head examined, but not by a blood sucking vampire.

"Okay, but don't you think your father looked there?" asked Cinnamon. "We could check it out tomorrow morning."

"He could have, but if he hasn't, I won't be able to sleep tonight. I sure don't want to come back after midnight. We'd better do it now."

We pulled up next to the big double doors. Both were closed and I was sure I couldn't lift one to get it open. Any hope of having light in there from the full moon was completely gone.

"We'll have to use the office door on the right side of the building. Watch your step. There's lots of junk lying around here." I thought I needed to warn Cinnamon, even though I knew if someone was going to trip over something, it would be me. The ground and I had become good friends the last couple of years. Mom says it's just a stage I'm going through. I was sure I'm just kind of a klutz.

We made it around the building and through the front door without incident. What a relief! It was a junkyard jungle out there. My trusty flashlight was beginning to dim, but I was sure I had a few more minutes of light. We could make it to the pit and back out the door in under a minute if nothing slowed us down.

We carefully walked through the building to the far stall. The infamous pit looked bigger and deeper than what I remembered from my first visit. Maybe it was my flashlight, casting weak shadows with a slowly diminishing beam.

"Shine your light down there, Rocky. I think I hear something." Cinnamon had reached the edge of the pit; I was a reluctant few feet behind. I sent the beam into the pit, sweeping it from left to right.

"Nothing there Cinnamon. This place is gonna give me major nightmares. Let's get out of here."

"Not so fast. We need to see this end of the pit as well. Move around to the side."

I did what she asked; I sent my now very weak beam into the corner closest to the door just as the light flickered and then failed. I shook the flashlight a little to see if I could draw out enough light to get us back outside. It popped back on just long enough to shed some light on two probing red eyes gazing back at us from the middle of the pit.

"Holy turnips!" I yelled, bolting toward the door. "Come on Cinnamon! It's coming after us!"

Cinnamon must have seen it too. We both scrambled out the door and into the night. We sprinted to our bikes and blasted down the street. A quick right on Old Town Road and we'd be safe. The hotel was just a block away. " We can make it. Just a few more feet." We didn't even stop to put our bikes away. Putting a bike away is hard to do when you're running for your life. We both stumbled through the hotel door and dove for the big couch in the lobby.

"What was that?" we asked each other as we all caught our breath.

"I don't know, but I know I'm not going back there." I saw no reason to give my body up this early in life. "I think I'm going to sleep in my parents room tonight, just in case."

"In case of what, Rocky."

"In case it followed us here. Could be outside right now."

"If you're trying to scare me, stop it. I saw those demon eyes looking at us. It was so creepy," said Cinnamon. "We need to tell someone."

"Sorry Cinnamon. I'm not much help right now. That . . . that thing is giving me the heebie-jeebies."

"Me too. Let's go see if our parents have any more news. We can tell them what we saw in the pit. Maybe there's some kind of explanation."

"Sounds like a good plan. Do you think they'll believe us?" I tried hard to get back into my investigator mode, but I was having trouble getting past *Step #2: Record and examine all the facts.* I hope my parents could come up with some facts. Otherwise, it was going to be a long night. I'd make sure I had new batteries for my flashlight, and Ned was going to have to sleep on my bed. I really didn't want to sleep in my parents' bedroom. I'm too old to do that unless they wanted us all together.

Day three in Old Town had finally come to an end. I couldn't believe how much had happened already in this "quaint little burg." I met some amazing people, made some new friends, explored some old buildings, got a new bike, learned a new skill, and maybe found a vampire.

I think I'll check the windows to make sure they're locked. Can't be too careful, even on the third floor. I really hope I can get to sleep. "Come on up here with me, Ned. Such a good watchdog."

Chapter Seven

Breakfast on Wednesday morning was oatmeal with raisins and brown sugar, orange juice, and cinnamon toast. Mrs. Brickle told me to "Eat lots, Rocky. It'll stick to your ribs." I couldn't imagine how that would look, but two helpings of oatmeal and three pieces of toast seemed to do the trick. Couldn't feel any change in my ribs, but my stomach had grown.

"Where's Cinnamon?" I asked as I cleared my dishes to the kitchen.

"She told me to tell you she was off on some errands and she'd see you later," said Mrs. Brickle. "Did you get enough to eat? We're having catfish tonight. Hope you like it."

"I've never had catfish, but I've loved every meal you made so far. Can't wait to try it." I wondered why everyone in this town somehow got around to talking about catfish. "Thanks for breakfast. Ned and I are headed up to see my folks at their new place. See you later."

I would stop by to check on my parents on my way to the tree stand. I was pretty sure the red-eyed monster was gone for the day and they were safe, but I wanted to be positive. Dad was probably already in the pit checking things out. I heard my mom say, "Buzz always meets things head-on." That was my dad.

I hope Dad took my advice from last night and brought some wooden stakes with him. One well-placed stake through the heart would turn any bloodsucker to dust in seconds. Hunting them was best done during daylight hours while they were asleep in their coffins. I'd never actually seen it done, but my friend Ernie had a magazine once that showed you exactly how to do it. I wasn't interested at the time, but now think I should have read it more carefully.

Ned and I stopped by the house first. I was hoping they were in the house and not the garage. Both were in the front room scraping off old paint and wallpaper. What a dirty, never-ending job. I was glad they had decided I should spend the next couple of weeks meeting new friends and exploring the "neighborhood" before school started. "There will be plenty of work for you down the road, Rocky." I could wait.

"Any news about Lenny?" I asked as I entered the front room.

"Hi Rocky. Not much this morning," Dad said. "Eddie Brickle was going to ask his teammates at morning football practice. Most of those kids are from New Town. Maybe someone saw Lenny over there."

"I'm heading off to see if any of my friends heard anything. We plan on following any leads so I won't see you until later today."

"By the way Rocky," Dad said, "I took care of your red-eyed monster."

"Wow! That fast. Did you use a wooden stake? Did it try to bite your neck? Vampires can be very dangerous, even during the day. Sunlight also works to kill them."

"Sorry Rocky. It wasn't that exciting. We had a big Norway rat setting up house in the garage. I used a gopher trap to catch him. He won't bother anyone any more."

A rat? I couldn't believe it. Maybe it was a huge vampire rat. No ordinary rat could have scared me. This was a mega-rat looking for blood. Maybe Dad was really a vampire hunter and he was just downplaying this to keep me from stressing out. Yeah, that had to be it.

"Okay Dad. If you're sure the pit's clear, I'll let Cinnamon know. I can still get some stakes and go down there with you one more time if you want."

"All clear Rocky. In fact we're filling the pit with sand and concreting it over this afternoon. I'd hate to see anyone fall into it and get hurt."

Right! Dad was going to seal the crypt forever. Even the strongest vampire wouldn't break through concrete. My dad was a genius.

"Thanks Dad. See you Mom. I'm blowing this pop stand." I heard that someplace. Sounded like a good exit line.

"Bye Rocky. We love you." My mother really was a gem.

I was glad I was paying attention when Cinnamon took me to the tree stand on our tour. I almost missed my turn off Skunk Hollow Road, but remembered the tree with the split trunk at the beginning of the path. The path wasn't visible at all from the road, thanks to that big old tree. Anyone on the road would never see the path.

I jumped off *Phantom*, found a good place to hide him, and went the rest of the way on foot. Ned was excited about all the new smells of the forest and somehow seemed to sense where we were headed. Ned got to the stand way before me.

"Hello Ned," I heard Little Mouse squeak. Both Tommy and Little Mouse were up in the stand hard at work.

"How long have you two been here?" I called from down below.

"We like to start the day when the sun comes up. Not sure of the time." Tommy was grinning again. "Wait a minute, I'll let you up."

I looked around for the ladder, but didn't see it. Just as I was about to head into the brush to find it, the ladder slid into place. Tommy had rigged up a rope and pulley to draw the ladder up and down.

"I got this stuff at the sawmill. Thought it might come in handy."

"What a great idea," I said as I stepped onto the first rung.

"When we leave, we can tie the rope off behind the tree. No one will see it." Tommy's invention was a great addition to the stand.

"I hope Cinnamon is okay with this change to the stand." I had remembered how important this place was to her.

"I'm fine with it," said a third voice from above. Cinnamon was here as well. I thought I was moving pretty fast this morning. Guess not.

"Hi up there. This is a great tree stand. Thanks for letting us use it, Cinnamon."

"Glad it's getting some use. Come on up and see all the changes." Cinnamon sounded so excited. I was sure any addition would be great.

I took in the last two rungs and stepped onto the wooden floor. I couldn't believe all the stuff they had added. " How did you get all this up here?" A card table, four chairs, a rug, two railroad lanterns, and a big corkboard, complete with thumbtacks.

"Pretty easy when you have a pulley, some rope, and some good help," said Little Mouse. "The rug was my idea. It was just taking up space in our attic."

"Must have been tough getting it all out here," I said with more than just a little curiosity.

"It took two trips with my scooter and my *travois*. We had a little trouble with the rug though. It's pretty big, even rolled up."

"Okay, what's a travois?" I was betting on some kind of sidecar. I'd seen pictures of them in magazines.

"A travois is something my ancestors used to move their belongings from one village to another. It's two long poles and a net tied together and then dragged behind a horse. I don't have a horse so I use my scooter."

"Tommy lets me ride on the travois some times. Its lots of fun, except on dusty gravel roads," said Little Mouse. I could picture her bouncing along behind the scooter yelling "Faster Tommy, faster."

"Where did these lanterns and the table and chairs come from?" I asked.

"Little Mouse spotted them last night in the old feed store. Tommy and I went there right away this morning to pick them up. That building is going to be torn down and no one wants the stuff. We'll put it to good use. Just needs to be polished up a little." Cinnamon was beginning to sound like my dad and his fixer-uppers.

Everyone was saved from my next hundred questions because new voices yelled up to us from the ground. "Hello up there, can we come up?" Sam and Cryin' Charlie had arrived with more supplies.

Charlie brought tons of lined and unlined paper, notebooks, pencils, and even some markers. "The post office always has stuff like this around. My dad was happy to get rid of it. I also brought some fudge."

Now we're talking! Fudge was an essential tool in every good investigation.

"I brought four things that I know we can use and I can get lots of snacks at our store whenever we need them," said Sam. This girl knew the way to my heart – food.

"I brought a magnifying glass, two spy glasses, and a book," Sam announced.

"The magnifying glass and spy glasses are great, but what are we going to do with a book?" I was confused.

"Read it, Gumball. What do you think? I know it will help us a lot. It's the Sherlock Holmes mystery I've been reading. This is my second time reading it."

I wish Sam would come up with another nickname for me or just call me Rocky. Gumball just wasn't doing it. And what's with wearing a dress in the woods? Sam wants us all to read a book? She can't be serious; it's still summer. I have to admit, I am curious about how Sherlock Holmes solved mysteries. Maybe he read my crimefighter magazines.

"This is a great start everyone," said Cinnamon. "Let's have a piece of fudge and then talk about what we know about Lenny. Rocky will help us get organized so we can solve this big mystery. What do you think Rocky?"

Now we're talking. "Uh huh," I mumbled as I stuffed my mouth with a big piece of fudge.

We all sat cross-legged in a circle on the big rug. We decided not to use the chairs until we had a chance to remove some of the rust. I explained the seven steps to solving a mystery again and then we got down to filling each other in on what we had seen or heard about Lenny last night and this morning. We started using Cryin' Charlie's paper, pencils, and markers right away, and in less than an hour had our new cork board filled and neatly organized with facts, clues, and observations. We were well on our way to solving this first mystery, or so I thought.

Everyone had already heard most of the information we posted, but a few things provided us with some leads worth pursuing. Charlie had run into Gorgeous George Stanley in the fudge shop early this morning. Usually George never gave Charlie the time of day, but today as they passed each other in the doorway of the fudge shop George threw a comment Charlie's way.

"Hey, Crybaby! Heard your old friend Lenny the Loser got himself lost big time." George didn't bother waiting for a comment from Charlie. He bowled his way through the door sending Charlie sprawling.

"How did George know about Lenny? He wasn't in Old Town last night. I thought I'd better add this to our list of questions." Cryin' Charlie had the makings of a good investigator."

"Great job Charlie. You didn't get hurt, did you?" Cinnamon was always concerned about others.

"Not a bit, but Mrs. Peabody thought I was hurt because it looked like I was crying. She gave me all this fudge for free." Cryin' Charlie had a talent that reaped great rewards.

"I found out something this morning too," remarked Little Mouse. "When Tommy was making his first trip to our fort, I stayed at the pool hall to talk to Grandfather. He wasn't there yet, so I talked to Willie."

"This isn't a fort, Little Mouse It's just our meeting place. We'd need to get some cannons for this to be a fort." At least that's the protection I thought good forts needed. "What did you find out from Willie?"

"Willie told me about his being a hobo and all and how Grandfather helps a lots of hobos; he gives them food and jobs when he can. That's how Willie got started," said Little Mouse.

"That's great Sarah, but what does that have to do with anything?" asked Tommy.

"Wait a minute. I'm not done. Willie said that a guy named Hobo Jack stopped in to see Grandfather. He's always looking for handouts, but not this time. Seems Hobo Jack had a big wad of money and was fixing to catch a train to California to go to Disneyland. He just wanted to pay Grandfather back for all his help."

"That's not so strange, that's just being nice," remarked Cinnamon.

"That's what I thought too, except Willie asked Hobo Jack where he got all the money. Hob Jack said it was a *sworn secret,* whatever that is. It sounded pretty mysterious." Little Mouse might be on to something. I wrote it down.

"I saw Mr. Jingles walking out of the pool hall this morning," interjected Sam. "He said that he was having a wildlife picnic with Cinnamon and Rocky. Mr. Jingles wants to have the picnic tomorrow if it's possible. Says he has something to show you. He also said Charlie, Tommy, Little Mouse and I could come as well."

"Seems like everyone knows we're trying to find Lenny," I said. "How did he know we were working on this together?"

Tommy figured it out right away. "I'm sure Grandfather talked to him about how we were working together to find Lenny. Grandfather and Mr. Jingles are very good friends."

"Is everyone up for a picnic tomorrow? I'll bike over there when we leave the stand," said Cinnamon.

We all agreed to take Mr. Jingles up on the offer. I was ready for some more chokecherry juice and goat cheese. The rest of us didn't have any news updates. I didn't think reporting on my breakfast conversation with Mrs. Brickle would make our list and both Tommy and Cinnamon had been busy moving supplies. I was sure we'd have more clues later in the day. We all broke out our lunches and had our first meal together in the stand.

We threw everything out on the table and shared whatever we had. Most had PB&Js and some fruit. Tommy brought some smoked pemmican. He told us it was something his ancestors made and called *wasna*. Of course, this city boy didn't know what it was or if something that old should be eaten, but decided I should have a taste. I became an instant pemmican fan.

Cinnamon laughed. "Is there any food you don't like, Rocky?"

"I don't care for Brussels sprouts, poached eggs, or prunes, but that's about it." I'd even eat those if I was hungry enough.

After lunch we decided to expand our search and also start

talking to people. Charlie and Cinnamon would go together to New Town to talk to the merchants and homeowners. Charlie was always touring the city delivering packages for his dad and everyone knew Cinnamon. Tommy and Little Mouse volunteered to talk to the local farmers. Tommy wasn't much of a talker, but Little Mouse could make up for that.

That left Sam and me. Oh boy! Paired up with Sam. This might be a long afternoon. We'd start out at Miss Odetts house and then go anywhere even the smallest lead would take us. I'd have to figure a way to get her to be nice to me before we got to Miss Odetts. That could be a challenge since it seemed like every time I opened my mouth, she blasted me. It wouldn't look good if I just stood there and she did all the talking. I really would be a gumball.

We decided to meet back at the stand at 5:00. That gave us four hours of investigation. I was hoping someone would *catch a break*. That's my mystery solver term for finding a good clue.

We all climbed down the ladder and Tommy showed us how to pull it up and tie off the rope. Tommy was really smart. I bet some day he invents something amazing – maybe like that new fad called the Hula-Hoop.

"Before we take off we need to have an official greeting to let each other know all is safe and it's okay to talk." We were going to be doing a lot of digging and we sure didn't want any bad people listening in.

"What if we howl like a wolf?" said Little Mouse. She howled at the top of her lungs. I had to cover my ears.

"No, that will just draw attention to us. It has to be something that is more like a greeting," said Cinnamon as she uncovered her ears.

"How about blowing our noses?" Cryin' Charlie pulled out his handkerchief.

"No, no offense Charlie, but one runny nose is enough," said Sam as she pushed her glasses up on her nose. "Maybe we could use a sign instead of words. I know two easy ones. How about a hand under your chin and out if it's safe to talk and swing your hand and arm away and down from your heart if it's not."

"That's a great idea Sam," I remarked, and I really meant it. I didn't ever run across hand signals in my magazines. I wonder if she read it in that book she brought along? Maybe this Holmes guy knew sign language. I could have been wrong, but I thought I saw Sam smile at me.

We all practiced the signals a few minutes so that we were all doing them the same and then moved on to our afternoon assignments.

Chapter Eight

Sam, Ned, and I were headed to the Odetts' house. Before we arrived I thought it best to fill Sam in on what I planned to do there. I thought it might be a tough sell since we really hadn't hit it off well. We pulled our bikes over on a small grassy area about a half-mile from the Odetts' house.

"I thought your hand signals were great, Sam." It's always good to start with a compliment. Girls like that.

"You should thank Tommy. He knows all the Native American signs. He taught me a lot of them. I don't talk to him like you do, but he and I still communicate. It's pretty fun when we aren't close together."

Ned and I communicate but he doesn't talk. I guess that's kind of like sign language. I was developing a new appreciation for Sam. There was a lot more to her than just a pretty dress. I hope that she and Tommy would teach me some more signs.

"When we get to Miss Odetts', I'd like to have her show us Lenny's room. She says nothing is missing, but maybe we can find something that will give us a clue about what happened. We have to be careful about what we say or do. She's awfully scared and sad. We'll need to convince her that we're doing our best to find Lenny and anything she can remember will help."

"That sounds like a good plan. I'll help any way I can," said Sam. She sounded sincere. There wasn't even an "Of course, Gumball" comment in our conversation. Maybe I was off the hook, at least this afternoon.

When we arrived at the Odetts' house we found Miss Odetts rocking back and forth in her chair on her porch. I had my suspicions that she spent the whole night in her rocking chair. "Miss. Odetts, are you okay?" She had this faraway look in her eyes and she barely acknowledged that we were on the porch with her.

"Where's Lenny?" she whispered. "He needs to come home. I hope he's not in danger."

"Miss Odetts, it's Rocky and Sam," I said standing directly in front of her so she had no choice but to look at me. "We're here to help find Lenny." I knew I was repeating myself from the night before, but I thought she might want to know we were still on the case.

"Oh thank you. Someone told me that the whole town is looking. Do you think they found him?"

"Not yet Miss Odetts," said Sam, "but with everyone helping out, we will find him."

"Sam's right Miss Odetts, but we need you to stay strong. Have you eaten anything or slept at all since last night?"

"No, I don't think so. I can't stop worrying about Lenny."

"We need to get you something to drink and some food. Can I look in your kitchen?" I asked. I knew some food was bound to help; it always helped me.

"I made some cookies," she said. "Help yourself."

I went to the kitchen and found some bread and jelly as well as cookies and lemonade. Maybe Miss Odetts would eat a sandwich. I made up a plate and brought it out to her. While I was in the kitchen, Sam had been trying to talk to her with limited success.

"Thank you," said Miss Odetts as I handed her the sandwich and cookies. "I guess I am hungry." As she nibbled on the sandwich, I could see she was slowly starting to regain some strength, at least mentally.

"Everyone is working so hard. How can I help?" she asked weakly.

"When you're finished with your lunch, maybe we could check out Lenny's room. I know you said he left all his clothes and didn't pack any food, but maybe something in his room might give us a clue."

"That would be fine. Have you tried my cookies? I have plenty in the kitchen. They're Lenny's favorite."

"We'll try one if you promise to eat all of your lunch." Sam was also concerned that the last two days had really taken its toll on Miss Odetts. Food and rest had to be a top priority.

Miss Odetts ate her entire sandwich, two cookies, and a full glass of lemonade. After handing me the plate and glass she announced in a much stronger voice. "Let's go find some clues in Lenny's room. It's upstairs."

Lenny had a huge number of "treasures" he had managed to collect over the years. "Lenny has lots of collections," said Miss Odetts. "He's always picking up something that reminds him of where he's been. Here's his baseball card collection. They're all Chicago Cubs players. We went to a game in Chicago once."

Miss Odetts showed us tons of collections. Rocks, feathers, poker chips, pennies, animal pictures, model cars, matchbooks – Lenny had a little bit of everything. I could spend days just digging through his stuff.

"What's his favorite collection," I asked.

"Oh that would be his Mickey Mouse figures. He keeps them in a cigar box under his bed. He takes them out every night before he goes to sleep. We took the train all the way to California last summer. Lenny loved the train trip and Disneyland."

"Could I see them?" I asked. I had seen the Mickey Mouse Club on Ernie's TV last summer. I liked watching a few Mouseketeers like Annette Funicello . . . who didn't? My favorite guy was Cubby O'Brien. Although most of what the Mouseketeers did on the show was silly, lots of people watched it every week anyway.

I looked under the bed, but there was no cigar box and no Mickey. A collection was missing along with Lenny. This had to be an important clue.

"Oh my! Lenny will be heartbroken. That box of toys is his favorite collection. I can't believe someone took it," said Miss Odetts.

"Have you had any visitors other than us since Lenny left?" I asked.

"No, just you two and that cute redhead Cinnamon."

"Do you think Lenny might have taken the box with him when he left?" asked Sam.

"He might have, although I've never seen him with that box outside of his room."

I wrote a few notes in the small notebook Cryin' Charlie had given me this morning. I didn't want to forget any of our observations. Just as we were finishing the investigation of Lenny's room we heard a loud knock at the front door.

"Miss Odetts. Are you home?" bellowed a very familiar voice. There was no mistaking that voice. It was the voice I had heard in the theater.

I gave a quick don't talk sign to Sam as Miss Odetts moved down the steps to answer the door. I had to come up with a quick plan to find out what Slim Stanley was up to. I leaned over and whispered in Sam's ear, "I'll go down with Miss Odetts and pretend to leave. You stay up here and listen. I think he's up to something and we need to know what."

Sam's eyes were as big as her glasses, but she nodded yes. It might have been better to have Tommy or Cinnamon hiding instead of Sam, but all good investigators had to learn about working undercover.

I walked down the steps and into the front room just as Miss Odetts opened the door for Slim Stanley. "Thanks for the cookies Miss Odetts. I'll see you later. Hello Mr. Stanley."

"Good bye Rocky. It was nice to meet you," said Miss Odetts. "He's such a nice boy, don't you think?" Miss Odetts didn't even mention Sam. With a little luck, this instant stakeout might work.

"Yeah sure," said Mr. Stanley. "Say hello to your dad for me. Is that your mangy mutt on the porch?"

"My dog's name is Ned, and he's not a mutt." I really didn't like this guy, and I was sure Ned felt the same way. I wish he had tried to pet Ned. That would have been funny.

Sam stayed in Lenny's room directly above the front room. As luck would have it, she could hear every word through an open heat vent in the floor. If she crouched down she could even see what went on below her. I crossed my fingers and retreated to our new house to keep a lookout for Stanley's exit. He had to pass by the house on his way across the bridge. In less than five minutes, he drove his big Caddy past the front door.

Less than a minute later, Sam followed on her bike. Since she had no idea where I had gone, she was heading to the picnic area under the bridge. Good thinking Sam! Ned and I ran out the door, jumped on *Phantom*, and caught her just as she got to the bridge.

We walked down the path together and sat across from each other at the picnic table. I could tell she was eager to fill me in on the conversation.

"Rocky, I was so scared. I kept thinking Miss Odetts might remember that I didn't leave with you. What would that guy do to me if he found out I was listening in?"

Sam was definitely shaken. I decided I needed to calm her down. When Little Mouse had grabbed my hand in the old feed store. I calmed down right away. It was worth a try. I reached across the table for Sam's hands. As soon as our hands touched, Sam looked into my eyes and immediately relaxed. No icy stare.

"You did great Sam. You are amazing. As soon as you're ready, tell me what that big Slime had to say."

Sam took a couple of deep breaths and then relayed the conversation almost word for word without notes. She was good. I bet she could memorize poems after reading them just once. What a talent! That was a skill I'd probably never have.

Sam told me that Mr. Stanley said he was really sorry about Lenny and offered to help Miss Odetts any way he could. He said that he had "lots of connections" and he'd check with everyone. Miss Odetts thanked him for stopping by, but Mr. Stanley wasn't ready to leave.

Sam continued, "He said some things that were kind of confusing at first." He said 'Miss Odetts, have you thought anymore about our recent conversation? I think it's a perfect time for you to move to my new apartment building in New Town. This place is too much for you to handle right now and Lenny's disappearance isn't helping.'"

Slim Stanley went on with a voice that sounded more hostile. "My offer still stands. I'll take this old house off your hands and move you into a brand new place. With this place as a down payment, you should be able to handle the monthly payments with no problem."

"No thank you Mr. Stanley. This is our home."

"You need to think about it Miss Odetts. You're alone now. Lenny may not be back."

Miss Odetts barked back in an icy voice "Good bye Mr. Stanley."

"I came downstairs after I knew he was gone, gave Miss Odetts a hug, and told her to stay strong. She knew I heard the whole conversation. Her last words to me were that she'd never give up her house, especially to the likes of Slim Stanley."

"Great detective work Sam!" I said with enthusiasm. "It really sounds like Slim Stanley is trying to force Miss Odetts out of her house and make money at the same time. He's one cruel beast. I'll bet he knows where Lenny is. We have to find a way to uncover his plan."

"I'm with you Rocky. That guy gives me the creeps. Where to now?"

"Let's head over to the schoolhouse. I have an idea."

I had the feeling she was ready to curl up in her overstuffed chair with a good book, but would follow my lead if I asked. As I let go of her hands and got to my feet she said in a soft voice, "Thanks Rocky. I'll try to be as strong as you on our next assignment."

Me? Strong? I would have been shaking like a leaf if our positions were reversed.

We decided to stop by the pool hall to see if Old Man Winter knew anything about Slim Stanley's attempts to buy out Miss Odetts. I thought we were getting close to establishing a motive in our mystery. I was sure we could get some valuable information from Mr. Winter since his family and the Stanleys had long histories in Skunk Hollow.

"Rocky, as long as we're close to my house, I'd like to stop and change out of this dress. I ripped a hole in it on Miss Odetts' floor register."

"Sure thing," I said. "I'll meet you in the pool hall. Where's your house?"

"We live above the store, Gumball. Wasn't that obvious? I'm always there."

Sam's confidence was back as well as her sharp tongue. Boy, I just couldn't get a break. I needed to figure out what I was doing to push her buttons. Sometimes girls just confuse me. Maybe my mother could give me a few first hand pointers being a girl and all. It was worth a try.

Sam parked her bike in front of Torgeson's and I rode up the street to Winter's Pool Hall. The pool hall wasn't busy at all. Just one customer sitting at the bar.

"Ned, stay outside. Hello Willie. Hi Little Mouse. What's going on?"

"Oh not much. Willie and I are talking about what it was like being a hobo. Grandfather is upstairs taking a nap and Tommy took his scooter out west of the tracks to talk to a few farmers. He'll be back soon."

Little Mouse didn't miss much. I was sure she was pumping Willie for information about Hobo Jack. I decided it was better to let her get what she could from Willie without me meddling in.

"Would chew like a rutbeer? It's on ta house." Willie the Wanderer hadn't forgotten Mr. Winter's instructions.

"That'd be great. Can I get a cup of water for Ned?" I was always ready to sip an ice-cold root beer and Ned looked thirsty too.

"Anyhow, dat's whats I know 'bout Hobo Jack. He's long gone an we probly won't sees him for a couple months." Willie sounded like he was telling the truth and why would he lie to Little Mouse. Willie had to know that Grandfather expected the truth from everyone at all times.

"Hey Little Mouse. I'm meeting Sam here in a few minutes and we're heading out to the schoolhouse. Do you want to come along? You might find something we overlooked."

"Sure, but I'll have to walk. I don't have a bike. Willie, will you tell Tommy when he gets back?"

"If you can handle it, you can ride with me. *Phantom* can handle two people."

"I'll give it a try. It's not that far. If it gets to be a problem I'll walk."

Just then Sam burst through the swinging doors holding on to a big floppy straw hat complete with a flowery headband and of course she had some kind of sundress to match – lots of bright colored flowers and ribbons. How was she going to ride a bike in that get-up? To keep peace I decided to keep my comments to myself. Smart move Rocky!

"Sorry I took so long. I had to stick these flowers into my hat."

"You look great," said Little Mouse. "I love summer flowers."

"Me too," I added trying to sound sincere.

There were those piercing green eyes again. Cold as ice.

"Sure Rocky. Let's go before you trip over your tongue."

"Little Mouse is coming with us. She might find something we overlooked."

I gulped my root beer down and followed two headstrong girls out the door. I sure didn't feel like a super crimefighter at the moment.

I sure hope I don't get the hiccups or a stomachache from drinking too fast. Sam would really be on my case. At least Ned would be sympathetic.

Little Mouse crawled up on the back rack of *Phantom*, put her hands on my hips, and we headed south on Old Town Road toward the school. I was a little wobbly at first, but in a short time got the hang of a second person on my bike. I could feel Little Mouse's fingers claw into my sides when we started out, but her grip eased as I became more confident. By the time we reached the school, I was an old pro.

Sam actually had more trouble than we did riding her bike. Between wrestling with her big, floppy hat and keeping her dress out of the chain and spokes, I wasn't sure what was funnier. I kept my comments and my eyes to myself for the most part. I knew I was a slow learner and had to take a peek now and then. Sam reminded me of Lucy on that funny TV show. The big difference was I didn't dare laugh. Watching *I Love Lucy* I would laugh until my sides hurt. Sam was just as funny in her getup, but I had to hold it in. Wish I had a camera.

As we pulled up to the school we noticed a bike already in the bike rack. Ned spotted it too and let out a low growl. "Everyone be very quiet. You too Ned. Let's not just rush in."

I wasn't sure who owned the bike, but it looked familiar. Maybe it belonged to Gorgeous George or one of the Slimes. We'd need to be careful. Ned had sensed something wrong and I trusted his instincts. I flashed everyone our signal for quiet, carefully parked *Phantom*, and eased around the corner of the school to the front door.

I signaled Sam and Little Mouse to follow making up signs as I went. I really needed to have Tommy and Sam teach me more Lakota signs. They'd come in handy right now. Both girls figured out what I was trying to tell them and followed a few yards behind. Ned just sat down next to our bikes and watched the show.

I peeked in the door and saw George's friend, Clyde, digging through the teacher's desk at the front of the room. He was so busy he didn't see or hear us. What in the world was he looking for?

Clyde was talking to himself as he dug through the desk. I could hear every word and decided to let him ramble on. " I know it's here someplace. I've got to find it. George'll kill me if I don't get it back to him."

I signaled Sam and Little Mouse again. This time I put my hand over my mouth to tell them not to say anything, and then cupped my hand around my ear to tell them to listen carefully.

Clyde continued his rant. "Why didn't I just tell George I lost it? He'd be mad, but get over it. Telling him I left it out here was a big mistake."

Just then Clyde stopped digging and put his head up. "Who's there?" he barked in his best tough guy voice.

"I am," said Sam as she blew by me in a flurry of blond hair, flowered dress, and floppy straw hat. Within seconds she was right in front of Clyde inches from his face. "What are you doing here Clyde? Are you the one who tore up the school? You're in big trouble now."

I had a quick flashback to my first meeting with Sam and knew that Clyde had to be sweating big time. I was sweating just listening to her put Clyde in his place. This wisp of a girl could be intimidating.

Clyde was caught off guard, but not for long. "I'm in trouble? Are you kidding? Get out of my face Four Eyes before I hurt you big time."

"Oh Clydiekins. Are you missing something? Maybe like this pocket knife I found?" How did Little Mouse get by me without me seeing or hearing her? And where did she find that knife?

"Give me that knife, you little half-breed." Clyde was livid.

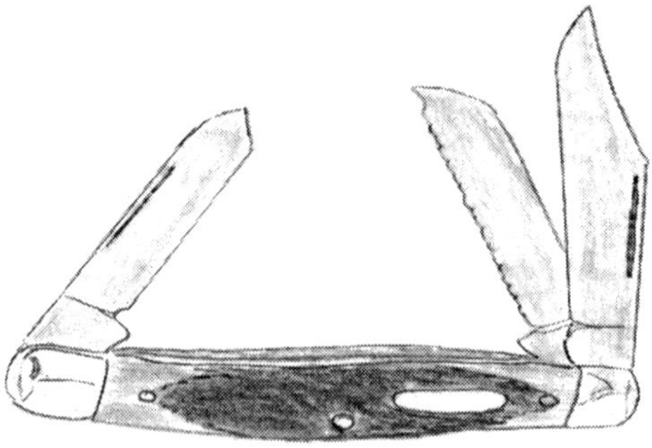

"I'm Dakota Oyate, as if you cared." (She told me later Dakota Oyate meant Dakota people.) "And you still haven't answered Sam's questions. We're waiting." Little Mouse kept her distance, but took on a stance that had to mean she was ready for anything Clyde could dish out. Clyde had crossed the line and Sarah wasn't about to back down.

Great! I had two girls confronting Clyde and what had I done? I was supposed to be leading this group and so far I had taken a back seat. Guess it was my turn to get into the action. "Well Clyde, we're waiting," I said as I moved toward the front of the classroom and the desk.

"I don't answer to you three. I'm out of here and you'd better watch your back," squealed Clyde in his semi-threatening pig grunt.

"You'd better reconsider. Wouldn't want to be in your shoes going out that door. I'd like to offer you the chance to explain what's going on here." Clyde was hiding something and we had him on the ropes.

"Right. You weenies don't scare me," said Clyde as he headed for the door.

"Weenies? I thought we were worms? Fine, come on back when you have something to tell us. Have a nice afternoon."

Clyde walked out the door and disappeared around the corner.

"Are you just going to let him go?" asked Sam. "I'm sure he knows something about Lenny."

"He'll be back before you can count to ten," I said with confidence. "Ned, herd."

Little Mouse smiled and started counting backwards. "Ten, nine, eight, seven . . ."

Clyde burst through the door. "Okay, okay! What do you want to know? Just call off that wolf."

Ned casually walked in a few steps behind Clyde and sat down just inside the door. I swear Ned had a grin on his face. Maybe he was part boarder collie. He sure knew how to herd animals.

"Okay Clyde, tell us what you know. We're all ears," I said.

"The knife's not mine. It's George's. He let me use it to carve my name in a desk. He was done with his carving."

"That's defacing property Clyde, but go on," I stated.

"That's all there is. I just came back to find the knife. It must have fallen out of my pocket."

"What does that message on the chalk board mean? See you later alligator?" Sam asked pointing to the board.

"I don't know. I didn't write it."

"What do you know about Lenny disappearing?" I asked.

"Nothing. Just know he's gone. Everyone knows that."

"When did you find out?" I figured George had told him. I just needed to narrow down the time.

"Right before we came out here on Tuesday. George told Freddie and me that Lenny was taking a trip, and we could all go out to the old school and have some fun. No one would be around to stop us."

"What a bunch of losers," said Sam. "Lenny takes pride in keeping this place nice for everyone. Do you like destroying nice things?"

"We didn't do that much. Just messed things up a little. No real damage. We could have done a lot worse."

"Oh that was kind of you. Thank you for not completely destroying the school," said Sam sarcastically.

"You're welcome. We're actually pretty good guys," said Clyde. What was really sad was I think he believed he was a good guy.

"You just don't get it Clyde. If you robbed a bank and just took a little money, they'd still lock you up. You're still a crook," said. Sam.

"I ain't no crook."

"Is there anything else you can tell us?" I asked.

"Nothin', except George is going to be looking for you after this."

"You might consider not talking to him about our conversation. He might not look too kindly on you telling us about his part in messing up the school and what he knows about Lenny." Could be in your best interest to just tell him to leave us alone." I was sure Clyde didn't get what I was telling him, but it was worth a try. I didn't want George after me.

"Okay, can I have George's knife back now?" Clyde was eager to have this conversation over and be on his way.

"No, we're keeping it for insurance," I said. "Ned, you can let Clyde leave." Ned got up, shook his head, and slowly moved away from the door.

Clyde sprinted past Little Mouse and Ned and was gone in seconds.

"Bye Clydiekins. Don't be a stranger." Little Mouse makes me laugh.

"That was brilliant Rocky. I can't wait to tell our team," said Sam.

I wasn't completely sure what I had done that prompted praise from Sam, but I'd take it. "We need to head back to the tree stand. We told everyone we'd meet there at 5 o'clock. I do have one more thing to do before we go. I need a pencil and some paper. I think there's some in the desk. Do you think we can find where George carved his name?"

"It's right here on this desk," said Little Mouse. I wasn't sure how she found it so fast, but she was great to have on the team.

Carved into the top of the desk was *GS WAS HERE*. I did a quick pencil rub and then compared the letters to the writing on the chalkboard. Perfect match – five letters were identical. George had to be the author of both. We also had the time they were in the school and proof that George knew Lenny was missing before most everyone in Old Town. It was a good day for investigations.

We straightened out desks and drawers, closed up the school and got back on our bikes.

"Tally ho," I barked as we moved out onto the dirt road.

"Tally ho?" asked Little Mouse. "What does that mean? I don't get it."

"Oh, never mind. Let's go."

Chapter Nine

I knew it was going to be a long, slow trip to the tree stand. Little Mouse was small and light, but my legs were burning from the added weight. Sam was still struggling with her dress and hat. I forgot about laughing at that sight. I had to concentrate on getting us to our destination before I was completely exhausted.

Little Mouse was concerned about Sam and her dress getting caught in the spokes of her bike. "Hey Sam. Do you want to stop off at your house and get some blue jeans?"

"I . . . I don't have any jeans," said Sam as she struggled with her dress, the tears now rolling down her cheeks. "I'm not much of an outdoor person so I just have dresses. This is the second one I've ruined today."

"My mother can sew up your dress. She's really good at patching and sewing things. If you want I'll ask her to make you an outfit that I know you'd like and it'll be good for biking."

"That would be nice Rocky, but just fixing the tears in my dress would do."

"Let's stop on the way to the tree stand. I'm sure she's back at the hotel by now." I knew my mother could solve Sam's problem with bikes and dresses.

We made it back to the hotel without any more tears or spills. My legs were pretty sore carrying Little Mouse, but I decided not to complain. We'd gathered quite a bit of information, and I was eager to find out what everyone else had uncovered. Maybe we could put the pieces together and locate Lenny.

We parked our bikes and headed into the hotel dining room. I was thirsty and was hoping to find some cold water. Mrs. Brickle must have heard us coming because she met us with a big pitcher of lemonade.

"Thanks Mrs. Brickle," I said between gulps. "This sure hits the spot."

"Your welcome Rocky. Cinnamon and Charlie are out back in the shed looking for some tools she says she needs. She'll be here in a few minutes for some lemonade."

"Are my parents back yet?" I have to see if my mother can fix Sam's dress."

"Not yet. So sorry you tore your dress Sam. How'd it happen?"

"Oh, I just got it caught in my bike chain. I ruin more dresses on that bike. I hope she can fix this one. It's my favorite."

I wasn't too optimistic. The dress would need some major repairs and a good scrubbing. I hoped mom knew how to get grease out. That bike chain did a real number.

Cryin' Charlie and Cinnamon joined us at the dining room table for some lemonade. I helped myself to another glass. All I needed was a cookie or two and I'd be all set until dinner.

"Boy do we have a lot to tell you," said Charlie.

"Not now," said Cinnamon. "We need to wait for Tommy."

"Tommy thinks I'm at the pool hall," said Little Mouse. "Maybe I should walk back there and get him."

"I'll call the pool hall to let him know you're here," said Mrs. Brickle.

"No need," said Tommy as he walked through the hotel door and into the dining room. How does he do that? No one told him we'd be here. It must be strong Lakota medicine.

"Would all of you kids like to stay for dinner?" asked Mrs. Brickle as she refilled lemonade glasses. "We're having South Dakota catfish. It's one of Eddie's favorites. I can call your parents to let them know."

"Sounds like fun. We have a lot to talk over Mom," said Cinnamon. "Would it be alright if we had a big table to ourselves?"

"Of course. We'll set two tables, one for you six and the other for the adults. Eddie's going to miss his favorite meal tonight. Seems some girl invited him over for a barbecue. What's a mother to do?"

We all got excited about Mrs. Brickle's Dakota catfish. New to me, but I couldn't wait. So, what else is new? I think I should maybe own a restaurant when I get older, or maybe I could just hang out here.

We had about an hour until dinner so after phone calls to parents we all gathered in Cinnamon's room. I had not seen this part of the hotel before, so I was all eyes. Cinnamon led us down a short hallway past their living room, dining room, and kitchen. There were four bedrooms in the back. Not as big as the hotel rooms, but plenty comfortable.

Eddie's room was packed with trophies and sports equipment. As we walked by I got a whiff of that old gym locker smell. I wondered if all athletes were given a deodorant that smelled like that. I'd probably say no thank you if they offered me some.

Cinnamon's room was all decorated in red and orange. Someone had painted a sunrise on one wall complete with birds and orange tinted clouds. Even the curtains sparkled with glints of orange and red. It would be fun to wake up every morning to such a cheery room. Cinnamon had a big, round table covered with maps and drawings in one corner. We got some folding chairs from Mrs. Brickle and with a little maneuvering we were able to all sit around it.

"Let's talk over what we know about Lenny," I said trying to take charge in my super crimefighter voice.

"That's a great idea Rocky." Sam chirped. "Who wants to start?" Maybe I wasn't a gumball any more. I took Sam's comment to be her vote of confidence in my leadership skills. There was hope for me yet.

For the next hour we filled each other in on everything we had seen and heard. Cinnamon tried to write down the things we thought were important, and then we worked on creating some kind of time line. By 6 p.m. we had a pretty good idea how the pieces fit. We still didn't know where Lenny was, but were sure the Stanley family was really up to something. We piled all of our notes together and headed to the dining room for dinner. I lead the charge.

"Hey, let's figure out a name for our team at dinner," said Little Mouse. We all agreed as we trotted into the dining room.

"No one eats without clean hands." The voice of my mother checking in again. Like a group of clumsy puppies we all skidded to a halt, did a turnabout, and headed for the bathroom. Twelve hands trying to wash in one sink. What chaos! I guess everyone was really hungry.

As usual, dinner was amazing. We ate and laughed and ate some more. In between mouthfuls of food, we tossed around possible names and outfits for our team of super investigators. We finally decided on Little Mouse's idea. "How about *Ocheti Colapi*? It means seven friends."

"Seven? I only count six," I mumbled with tons of catfish plugged into both cheeks.

"We have to include Ned," said Tommy as he scratched Ned's ears under the table. "He's earned his spot on the team many times over." Everyone cheered for Ned. He put his head down and pretended to be asleep. Good old Ned. No big deal for him.

"I think I have an idea for our logo. I'll draw a picture after dinner. We could all put it on our favorite colored T-shirt."

"Cool!" I said thinking that maybe *hot* would have been the better word. Everyone nodded so I must have guessed right.

"I don't have any T-shirts," said Sam.

"No problem. I have tons. Lots of green ones that I never wore. That's your favorite color, right?" Cinnamon to the rescue again! I could have given her one of my old white tees, but I didn't think that would go over too well.

Once dinner was over, we cleared our plates, thanked Mrs. Brickle, and headed back to Cinnamon's room for some more planning, I'd only been in town a few days and already had more friends than I ever had in Chicago. What a super week. Seven friends who loved solving mysteries.

Cryin' Charlie came up with a name for Mr. Brickle's tree stand. He thought it would be more official if our meeting place also had an official title. "HQ. That's short for Headquarters." Good call Charlie.

Now we were really official.

Cinnamon's logo came out great. It was a simple Dakota sunrise with the number 7 placed in the emerging sun. We all decided to bring our favorite colored tee to HQ in the morning and we'd spend some time drawing them out. I thought I'd ask Cinnamon to do my shirt. I had no artistic talent at all.

I was pretty sure tomorrow would be another exciting day in Old Town. Who would ever believe that? Not me five days ago. This town and my new friends might just work for me.

Mrs. Brickle came around and broke up our party just before nine. "Time to head home kids. You all need to get some sleep."

We said our good-byes and headed off to get some much-needed shut-eye. (That's detective talk for sleep.) As Tommy headed for the door, he turned and held up both hands chest high, five fingers on one hand, two on the other, joined together as seven. I signaled back. "Ocheti Colapi" he said. We were *Seven Friends* out to solve some Skunk Hollow mysteries.

Chapter Ten

We had planned to meet at HQ at 10 Thursday morning. Sam and Little Mouse had stopped by the hotel early to work on T-shirts. After picking out some smaller sizes for Sam and a few even smaller ones for Little Mouse, they carefully transferred the new logo onto each one. To complete the new look, Cinnamon had given Sam some of her outgrown blue jeans as well.

Dad had agreed to take a look at Tommy's scooter in his new garage early that morning. After Tommy dropped his sister off at the hotel, we made our way up to Malone's Small Engine Repair. It took Dad about twenty minutes to have Tommy's ride purring like a kitten. "Tommy, if you take care of your ride, it'll take care of you." Dad liked to say that about cars, trucks, and now even motor scooters.

"Thanks Mr. Malone. I will."

"See you later Dad. You're the best." And then we were off to join the team at HQ. That's Headquarters you know.

One by one, the girls popped into the stand to display their new T-shirts and logos, Cinnamon in bright red, Little Mouse in yellow, and Sam in a very bright green. They all looked great but I figured I would keep my mouth shut and let Tommy throw out the first compliments.

Sam pulled herself up the ladder, marched across the floor, and parked herself about six inches from my face. "Hey Rocky. What do you think of my new outfit?"

No help from Tommy this time. I was on my own. I had to think of something quick. Grasping for a word that I figured would fit the occasion I blurted out "Smashing!"

Sam tilled her head slightly to the left and glared back at me. Oh oh! Here it comes.

"Smashing? Smashing?" Sam didn't sound like she was asking a question. It sounded more like she was going to level me in my tracks. "Is that supposed to be a compliment? You really are a gumball."

Cinnamon laughed. "Good one Rocky. You really know how to impress a girl."

I just couldn't get a break. I thought *smashing* was a great word. I had heard some cool older guys back in Chicago say that about good stuff all the time. Girls! Who can figure them out?

"Okay. The shirts look great. Can you help us with ours?" Cryin' Charlie was eager to get his T-shirt designed. He had picked out a black one from his closet. Tommy's was brown and I had decided to go with a basic white because that's what I had in my closet. Cinnamon had even thought about Ned. She had drawn our logo on some orange material and attached it to Ned's collar. He looked pretty cool. I think guys are *cool* and girls are *hot*, but maybe it's best to keep that thought to myself.

I brought along a couple of white T-shirts just in case I messed up the design. I'd add a little color in my logo to spice it up. My design would be *smashing*. I, of course, kept that comment to myself. No need to push Sam's buttons again.

Once we finished our shirts and passed around compliments about how good we looked in our colors and designs we took out our notes and put together what we knew about Lenny's disappearance. In a matter of minutes we had dated and organized everything on our corkboard.

We put all the facts we had uncovered in order on the left and started a list of unanswered questions on the right. I saw this setup once in one of my Crimefighter magazines. It was really steps two and three in my seven steps to solving a mystery. I'm pretty sure it's what police detectives use when they are working on a case. I was positive every detective read Crimefighter magazine. Why else would the front cover of every magazine say "*Endorsed by Detective Bill Perkins.*"

I didn't know Detective Perkins personally, but I knew he was probably just about as famous as Sherlock Holmes or even the Lone Ranger.

This was our list of known facts:

1. Slim Stanley was looking for something in the old theater.
2. George and his Slimeballs are hiding something.
3. Hobo Jack had lots of money and was heading to Disneyland.
4. Lenny and his box of treasures disappeared on Monday.
5. All the vampires in the old garage are buried in concrete. (I added this one a little later.)

Questions still unanswered:

1. Why is Slim Stanley so eager to buy Miss Odetts' house?
2. Where did Hobo Jack get his newfound money?
3. Was anything hidden in Skunk Hollow?
4. What did Mr. Jingles know?
5. Where is Lenny?

We finally decided it was time to close up HQ and head out to our picnic with Mr. Jingles. He had moved the date up so we were all sure he had some important information that would answer some of our questions and maybe give us some help in finding Lenny.

"With a cloud of dust and a hearty *Hi-yo Silver, Away!*" I yelled out as we mounted our bikes. Even Ned gave me an odd look on that comment. "Oh, never mind. Let's roll."

With four bikes, one scooter, and a trusty dog, Seven Friends headed north to the barn and my first ever wildlife picnic. And we did kick up some dust on the way. Maybe somebody would notice the cloud of dust we left behind. Where's Ernie when you need him?

Mr. Jingles had set up two large tables for our picnic. One table was covered with all kinds of food and drinks and the other was set up for seven hungry people. The goats had all decided that the food was probably for them. As we arrived Mr. Jingles was desperately trying to chase the goats away. His booming voice and gyrating arms had little or no effect on the goats who must have thought it was a great game to run in, around, and over the tables.

We all jumped off our bikes and after about fifteen minutes had the goats corralled in a small pen next to the barn. Ned was a great help rounding them up. I swear he's part sheep dog. After giving them a big bunch of sweet clover, the goats finally settled down to eat and we were able to start our picnic. We had really worked up an appetite. I couldn't wait to dig in.

"What are we having today?" asked Cinnamon. "I recognize a few things, but I've never seen most of what's on the table."

"Everyone grab a plate and I'll fill you in as you fill up," said Mr. Jingles. "Feel free to try anything. I won't feel bad if something doesn't turn out to be your favorite."

I don't think I'm a picky eater. I'm willing to try just about anything after somebody else tried it, but a few of the dishes didn't really look like food. Maybe I'll let Sam go ahead of me. She could be the guinea pig. No sense in me barfing if I didn't have to.

"Hey Sam, why don't you go ahead. Ladies first and all that."

"Why thank you Rocky. There's hope for you yet."

I was pretty sure Tommy knew what I was up to because he was grinning again. I quietly slipped to the back of the line. Pretty smooth Rocky. I would only sample what Sam took. Now that's a good plan.

"Okay kids. Here's what's on the table. We have clams, snails, and catfish from the lake; mushrooms, assorted berries, nuts and quail eggs from the woods; frog legs and cattails from the swamp; and Cinnamon's favorites, chokecherry juice and goat cheese. Let's dig in."

We all filled our plates and took a spot at the other table. I sat opposite Tommy and Charlie. I was pretty sure they wouldn't care if I had poor manners when I wolfed down my food. (I still had my doubts about some of the stuff, so I did keep a close eye on what everyone put in their mouths.) In a few short minutes it appeared that just about everything had been sampled and I started *packing my cheeks*. That's what Dad said when Mom put a great meal in front of us. I had to admit everything was amazing. Even though I started after everyone, I managed to pack my first plate into my mouth in record time. I was ready for seconds in short order.

"Help yourself to . . ."

Mr. Jingles didn't even get a chance to finish his sentence before I was filling up again. Good thing my mother wasn't around. She'd have a few choice words for my lack of manners.

"What's this stuff that kinda tastes like corn?" I asked as I grabbed a few more pieces.

"That's steamed cattail."

"What about this stuff that tastes like chicken?"

"I call that swamp chicken. It's grilled frog legs."

I decided to stick to the nuts, berries, and cheese on my second plate. We all ate and laughed and ate some more. Food was the topic of the day and I filled everyone in on some of Chicago's best. Pizza was at the top of my food list. Tommy's favorite was Mr. Jingles' campfire stew. We all got invited back to try some, but I decided that whatever day was planned I'd be busy with something else. I was pretty sure I wouldn't like rattlesnake meat or whatever else got thrown into the pot. Maybe my new friends were just teasing me. Who eats rattlesnake anyway?

Chapter Eleven

After everyone finished eating and we cleaned up the tables, Mr. Jingles invited us to sit out on some log benches behind the barn near the lake. Tommy and I took out our slings and practiced throwing some crab apples into the lake. It was great watching a bunch of geese race after each throw as if each apple was some great prize. Crab apples make my lips pucker. I wonder if ducks can pucker their bills?

Tommy could throw his apples way out into the lake. Mine landed quite a bit shorter, but the effect was pretty funny. The geese raced back and forth from deep to shallow water. Everyone tried to guess which goose would reach the next apple first. My favorite goose always seemed to come up short. I always want to cheer for the underdog, so of course I picked the runt of the litter. I'd make sure she got an apple before we stopped, even if it meant throwing one close to her. Could be a little dangerous since I'm not too accurate with a sling. I might need Tommy's help to make sure she got a crab apple.

"Hey Rocky! Don't worry about hitting any geese. I don't think you could hit the barn door if you tried."

Guess who said that, and I wasn't trying to hit a barn door. Where does she come up with these ideas? Barn door, really? The barn was behind me.

Once Mr. Jingles let his goats out of their pen, he joined us by the lake. As we gathered around the log benches, Mr. Jingles said he wanted to share some things he had discovered that might help uncover some of the mysteries we were working on. He told us that he and Lenny were good friends and he hoped no harm had come to him.

"Lenny and I have really connected over the years. He and I spend many hours and days fishing, picking berries, mucking through the swamp, and chasing goats. Most recently he asked if I would read some of the books from his mother's collection. As you know, he loves books and "teaching" at the old schoolhouse, but he always had trouble reading. We spent many nights right here by a campfire reading some great stories. His favorite is *Huckleberry Finn*."

"I read that," I said trying to sound intelligent. Does everyone know that Mark Twain's real name is Samuel Clemens?" Sam rolled her eyes.

"It's one of my favorites too," Mr. Jingles continued. "Anyway, Lenny brought several boxes out here to read. Said he'd like to store them here in case we finished one and wanted to start another right away. I put them in a cool, dry place for safekeeping but had only opened the first box. When Lenny went missing, I decided to look in the other boxes. Not sure why I thought I'd find something, but it was worth a try."

"What did you find?" we all asked almost in unison.

"The first box was filled with books by famous authors, the second was filled with music and plays, and the third had an old diary and several ledgers. I think they hold some well kept secrets. We just need to sort some things out. The diary is pretty worn and brittle, but I was able to read most of it. From the initials on the cover, I think it belonged to Beauregard Puce. If I'm correct from his last entry, he's the long lost brother of Julian Odetts. That's Miss Odetts' mother. She owned and performed in the old theater in Old Town before Slim Stanley got his claws into it."

"Can we take a look?" I quickly asked. "I promise we'll be very careful with it."

"Sure can. I'll go get it and meet you at the table. We can all take a look without handling it too much. It's pretty fragile."

We all jumped up from the log benches and scrambled around the barn to the tables again. The goats thought it was a game and ran with us. I, of course, tripped on a branch and fell face first into some mud. Two goats immediately came to my rescue and licked my face as I was trying to stand up again. I was having some trouble getting to my feet. Goats, mud, and me don't mix too well.

"Hey Rocky. Are you washing up after lunch or just making some more new friends?" Sam never missed a chance to throw a zinger my way. "Do you need to hang on to my hand?"

"Sure," I said sheepishly as I put out my hand. That got her flustered. I could tell because she was blushing as she turned and ran to the picnic table. Finally, score one for the Rock.

We all gathered around the table to look at the old, leather-bound diary. The cover was worn and torn in several places, and you could tell even before opening it that a few pages were loose. It had a small leather strap attached to the cover, but it had seen better days. Mr. Jingles carefully opened the diary up to the first page.

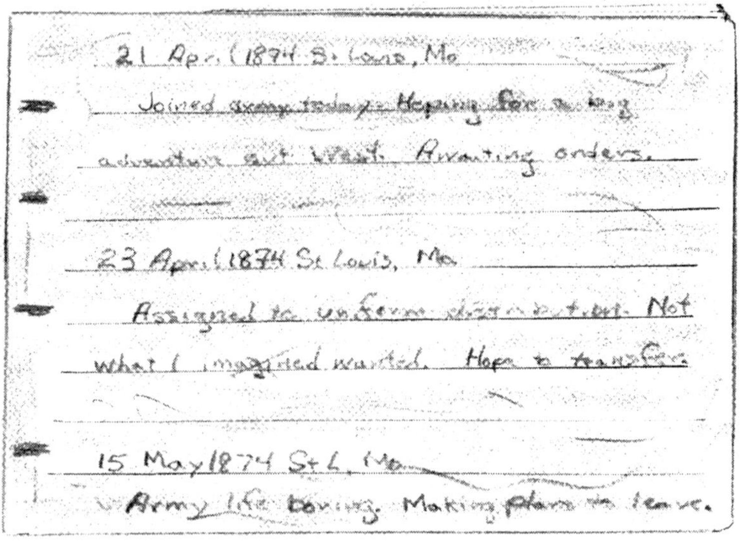
21 Apr. 1874 St Louis, Mo
Joined army today. Hoping for a big adventure out West. Awaiting orders.

23 April 1874 St Louis, Mo
Assigned to uniform distribution dept. Not what I imagined wanted. Hope to transfer.

15 May 1874 St L, Mo
Army life boring. Making plans to leave.

"Thanks Mr. Jingles," said Cinnamon. "Even though it's old, it might help us with some of our questions. Do you think we should talk to Miss Odetts about the ledgers and diary? We should stop by her house on the way home."

"I don't see much here that can help us," groaned Charlie. "It's just an old diary and it's hard to read all the words."

"Even though it's hard to read, I think this diary tells us quite a bit," said Mr. Jingles. "I read through most of the entries last night and I'm pretty sure Old Beauregard's diary did end up with his sister in St. Louis."

"She brought it back here when she came looking for him. She decided to stay in Skunk Hollow and she and her husband started the theater in Old Town. When she passed away years ago Lenny and his sister inherited all the property including the Grand Theater. I think Lenny removed these boxes from the theater before Mr. Stanley took over and then brought them out here for safekeeping."

My head tried to soak it all in. Rocky Malone, Super Crimefighter, is on the job. "Wait a minute, are you saying that the books were stored in the old theater until Lenny brought them out here? Lenny must have known something was up."

"What's a ledger?" squeaked Little Mouse.

"A ledger is a book to keep track of what you buy and sell, or the money you make. My parents keep one in the store. I've even helped with the ledger for the store inventory." I knew Sam would be good with numbers. People that wear glasses often are. That's what I've heard anyway.

"Right you are, Sam," said Mr. Jingles.

"Hey Cinnamon, remember when Slim Stanley almost caught us in the theater? Do you think he was looking for the ledgers or the diary? Why would he care about a bunch of old books unless they held some valuable information? Maybe we're on to something."

"Didn't Slim Stanley purchase the theater from Miss Odetts just this summer? He wants to buy her house too. He has to be looking for this diary." Cinnamon's brain was "firing on all eight cylinders". I heard Eddie Brickle say that about his cool car. I thought it could apply to smart people as well.

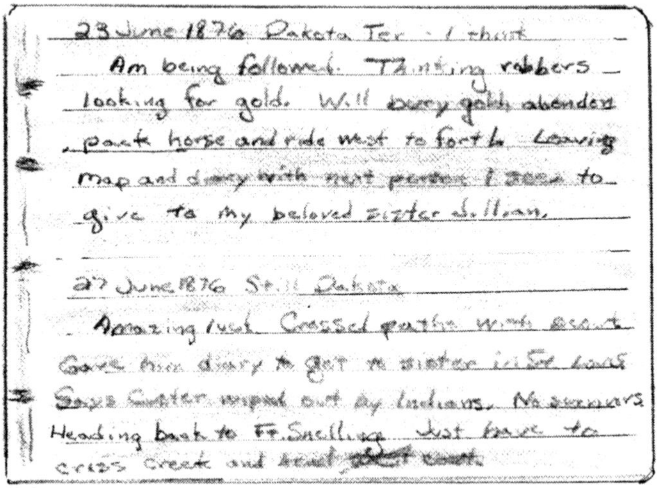

"Right again," said Mr. Jingles. "The last two entries in the diary might be what all these mysteries are about." Mr. Jingles carefully turned the old diary to the last page and read the last two entries.

"Beauregard buried bags of gold? Did he come back for them? Is there a map with the books? What else is in that diary? Do the ledgers have any clues? Is Slim Stanley a criminal?" The questions were coming fast and furious. Ned was the only one that stayed calm and didn't ask any questions. I'll bet he could help us find the gold, even without using our steps to solving a mystery. He was a pretty smart dog.

"Let's go back to our lists and see if we can fill in some blanks. Did someone bring a notebook with our lists?" In our hurry to get to the picnic, I, of course, had forgotten mine at Headquarters.

"I brought mine," said Sam.

"Me too," everyone else chimed in.

"Don't worry Rocky. I picked up your notebook on the way out. Figured you might want it." Tommy *saved my bacon* again.

"Thanks Tommy." At least I had my pencil stuck behind my ear.

I took a big breath to keep myself calm and flipped open my notebook. I didn't need my voice to crack right now. I needed to be in control. Mom says my voice crackles because it's changing. I think it happens when I get nervous or I need a drink of water. No water handy so a big breath will have to do. "Okay, lets fill in some blanks based on what we've learned. Let's go through our facts and questions one at a time to see if we can *draw any conclusions.*" That's the Rocky I know. Move over Dick Tracy. Rocky Malone is on the case.

"Slim Stanley must have figured out Miss Odetts' mother was related to Beauregard Puce. That's why he was looking for the ledgers and diary in the old theater," said Cinnamon with confidence." We all agreed.

"But why does he want to buy her house?" Sam quickly chimed in.

"Maybe he doesn't," I said. "He needed a reason to get into her house to find the ledgers and the diary, since they were no longer in the theater."

"Hey, I bet I know," said Cryin' Charlie. "He needed to get Lenny out of the house. He created a distraction so Miss Odetts wouldn't realize he was snooping around. He could even offer to look for clues just like we did. Only he'd be looking for ledgers, diaries, and maybe a map."

"That sounds like Slimy Slim. He's always up to something. My dad was right about not trusting him." For the first time, Tommy was angry.

"If he hurt Lenny, I'm going to make him pay." Now Little Mouse was angry and I had no doubt she'd find a way to make Slim Stanley pay big time if he really did hurt Lenny.

"We're all sure what Mr. Stanley was looking for. Are we sure that he had something to do with Lenny's disappearance?" asked Sam. "Charlie's idea is a solid one but let's stick with the facts." I was positive Sam had been reading my Crimefighter magazines. She sounded just like a detective in my latest issue.

"Okay, here's what I think," said Cinnamon. "Based on what we found on the blackboard at the school, George and his slimy friends knew about Lenny's disappearance before anyone in Old Town. That's a fact. Lenny was missing on Monday. That's a fact. Hobo Jack had lots of money and was headed to Disneyland in California. That's another fact."

"Someone was seen jumping into a boxcar late Monday. I bet it was Hobo Jack, and I bet Lenny was on that train too." Tommy was putting it together as well.

"I bet Slim Stanley paid Hobo Jack to take Lenny to Disneyland. Hobo Jack convinced Lenny to hop the next box car passing through Old Town, but Lenny wouldn't go without his Disney treasures."

"Lenny loved Disneyland and loved to travel," said Mr. Jingles. "It would be quite easy to convince him to go. Charlie's theory is sounding pretty good. We need to explain this to Miss Odetts. She's so worried about Lenny and I'm sure this information might help her."

"Okay, so where's the map? Stanley doesn't have it and it's not with the diary or ledgers." I was drawing a blank.

"I think I know," said Little Mouse. "It's in Lenny's treasure box. Lenny kept it where he knew it would be safe."

No Lenny, no map, no gold, but things were coming together. We were after all Seven Friends, Old Town's super mystery solvers, and we were on the case.

Chapter Twelve

It was late afternoon when we finally left Mr. Jingles' wildlife picnic. We had not really solved everything, but we had some pretty solid information that we knew would give Miss Odetts some hope about Lenny, and we wanted to warn her about Slim Stanley's possible plans. Just wish we had a little more proof.

Tommy and Little Mouse said their good byes and flew off on their scooter. Sam and Charlie were expected home early so that left just Cinnamon and me to talk to Miss Odetts. We had our notebooks filled with facts and theories. She wouldn't be thrilled to find out Lenny might have hopped a train to Disneyland, but at least he wasn't injured or killed. We would leave those comments out of the conversation.

We jumped on our bikes and took off down the road. On the way I asked Cinnamon if she knew Elvis' song "Hound Dog." She said she didn't, so I started singing it to her in my best choir voice.

"You ain't nothin' but a hound dog, cryin' all the time . . ."

"Thanks Rocky, I'm okay without the music." That song sounded great when I was sitting in the bathtub. Maybe it needed just a little more work before I sang it in public.

Just then, who should appear, but good ole' hound dog George Stanley. He was alone on his bike heading toward the old barn and Mr. Jingles. "Out of my way turnips, and keep that mutt away from me. I've got an important message to deliver to the goatman."

"What message is that?" Cinnamon asked in her unusually calm voice.

"It's for me to know and you to find out," George grunted.

"Okay Cinnamon. Let's find out." I said looking over at Cinnamon. "George, would you like your knife back? Clyde gave it to us for safe keeping."

"Clyde gave it to you? No way! Yea, I want it back. Give it."

"Not so fast smooth talker." I guessed that comment would be way over his head. "We want to work a trade for some information. What's the message you're delivering, and one more question, what's your father up to? It's time to spill the beans. "

"No deal. When my dad finds all the gold he'll be taking over everything in Skunk Hollow. I hope he levels Old Town, you with it."

Bingo on question number two! "Okay George, no message, no knife." A little more pushing and I'd have that message out of him too. I had to be careful though. He really couldn't do anything to me or to Cinnamon, not with Ned around. But who knows what he'd do if he got really mad. I liked my face too much to push him over the edge.

While I was thinking things through, Cinnamon jumped in. "Why don't you give us the message and we'll tell Mr. Jingles? I wouldn't want to be around him if it's bad news. He's really big and can get awful scary."

George's beady eyes opened really wide. Her comment had hit pay dirt. "Well, I guess that'd be all right. No skin off my nose. My dad says that there's a new ordinance in Skunk Hollow. Goats are no longer allowed on the streets or sidewalks. Now, where's my knife?"

"Sorry George. We're in such a hurry. We just can't deliver that message to Mr. Jingles or give you the knife right now. You're on your own. Toodles!" I really wanted to see George deliver his dad's message, but we needed to move on.

Cinnamon and I got back on our bikes and pedaled to Miss Odetts' house, laughing all the way. "Toodles?" chuckled Cinnamon. "Rocky, you crack me up." Ned had to be grinning too. I could almost picture George and his bike twisted up like pretzels and delivered back to Slim Stanley on a cart pulled by several goats. What a stitch!

Miss Odetts was sitting out on her porch again. "Hello children. My, it's busy out here tonight, everybody coming and going. You'd think this was Saturday night."

"Hello Miss Odetts. We just talked to Mr. Jingles and we have some news." I was happy Cinnamon took the lead. I'd ask her later about what went on around here on Saturday night.

"Oh my! What did you find out?"

We filled Miss Odetts in on everything we knew and all the ideas we had. Although she was still worried about Lenny, she did seem relieved.

"Land sakes! I knew that Slim Stanley was up to no good. It's time to put an end to his shenanigans," said as her eyes narrowed.

I was seeing a new side of Miss Odetts and I was excited, but I had no idea what "shenanigans" were. Watch out Slim!

"If you kids have a few minutes, I think I can help you uncover some of the mysteries you had about the old diary."

"We just have to be home for dinner at six, so we have a little time." My stomach was telling me we had about an hour. I hardly ever needed to look at a clock to know what time it was. My stomach always let me know.

"Good. I think I'll start with my uncle, Captain Beauregard Puce. He was originally from St. Louis, Missouri. As a young man, he was eager to see the world. He didn't have much money so he enlisted in the army hoping to travel out west to seek his fortune. By some twist of fate he ended up at Fort Snelling in Minnesota at the time Col. George Armstrong Custer was passing through. Although he never met the man, he volunteered to return some gold Custer left at the fort. Beauregard was given a promotion and sent out on a mission. He left Fort Snelling with very few skills to help him survive the journey. He hoped to learn on the way. This was a big mistake."

"I didn't see all of that in his diary," I said. Now I was really paying attention. "How do you know all of this?"

"Beauregard and my mother Julian were very close. Beauregard lived with my mother and my father, Leonard Odetts, until he left for Minnesota and they sent letters to each other until he went on his mission."

"Now I get it," I said. "What happened next?"

"Somehow Uncle Beauregard vanished, but his diary ended up with my mother in St. Louis. She was convinced she could find him if she just followed the clues in his diary. After many discussions, she and Leonard packed up their belongings and headed north. Her trail ended in Skunk Hollow. My parents made their living in the theater and were quite successful in St. Louis. When they got to Skunk Hollow, they built this house and the Grand Theater. When they passed away several years ago, the theater just sat empty. They also built another house west of town by the tracks. It was too big for Lenny and me, so we moved back here. I sold the theater to Slim Stanley just a few months ago. He told me he would clear everything of value out of it, and I needn't worry about anything. I didn't even think about all the files and books they had in the theater office."

"Now the interesting part. Lenny had decided he wanted some of the old books. He gathered them up, along with the diary, and kept them hidden in our basement. A few weeks ago he decided to bring his books out to Mr. Jingles to read. I didn't pay much attention, but knew Lenny loved books and Mr. Jingles was willing to read to him. Lenny must have known that the books would be safer there."

"Did you ever read the diary?" asked Cinnamon.

" Oh yes, many times with my mother and with Lenny. The last page was a map supposedly leading to the gold Beauregard was carrying. It was so poorly drawn, my mother, my father, and I could never figure it out."

"The map's missing from the diary," I said.

"Oh I know. Lenny asked if he could keep it with his treasures. To me, it was just a worthless piece of paper, but to Lenny it held a secret that he alone would discover. He's like his uncle Beau. Always looking for an adventure."

We chatted a few more minutes and then headed back to the hotel for dinner and maybe some cards. I thought I could teach Cinnamon how to play Old Maid or Crazy Eights if I could find my decks. Dad liked to play Pinochle. I never got the hang of that game.

This had been a long and exciting day. Hope Lenny comes home soon and I hope he has the map. I'll bet I can figure it out and it won't take me fifty years. Just another easy mystery waiting to be solved by ace detective Rocky Malone. Of course it would be Lenny's gold, but he'd probably give me a finder's fee. I'd buy some new blue jeans.

Dinner was great, as usual. We had some kind of casserole Mrs. Brickle called "Tater Tot Hotdish." I only ate two helpings because I needed to save room for cookies and ice cream I heard we were having later. Mom always said, "Don't eat so much junk food Rocky. It'll spoil your dinner." I ate less dinner so I wouldn't spoil my junk food. It was a good plan and I was sticking to it.

Cinnamon and I set up our card game at the dining room table just in case other people wanted to play. No one was interested, so we just taught each other some of the card games we had learned. I was pretty good at Slap Jack. I think I owe Gerty the quickness I had in my hands. I felt bad about slapping Cinnamon's hands though. We only played a couple of rounds and then switched to Old Maid and a game called Memory. Cinnamon was great at both. I was toast. (That was another line I picked up in Chicago. It was better than saying I was the big loser.)

"That was fun Rocky. Let's get some ice cream. Is strawberry okay?"

"You bet it is. That's one of my favorites."

"I think you'd say that about any flavor."

"Sure I would. Ice cream's the best thing since sliced bread." As we ate our ice cream we talked about Lenny, the diary, Slim Stanley, and the gold. "I'm sure it's buried somewhere around here. We just have to help Lenny find it before Mr. Stanley."

"Do you think he's seen the map?" asked Cinnamon.

"I think he knows it exists because he's been snooping around a lot, but I don't think he's seen it. He'd be digging holes everywhere by now."

"I wonder what Miss Odetts is planning? Did you see that look on her face when we told her about Hobo Jack getting money to take Lenny on a trip to Disneyland?" Whatever was going to happen we both agreed we wanted to be there to see the fireworks.

Nine o'clock rolled around pretty fast and we both decided it was time to get some much-deserved sleep. Ned and I headed up the stairs to our third floor room and Cinnamon made a beeline for her room.

"See you tomorrow Rocky."

"Right on Cinnamon."

"Brush your teeth Sweetie."

"Yes ma'am." Mom was always reminding me to brush, or was that Cinnamon calling me Sweetie? No, it had to be Mom.

Chapter Thirteen

Something cold and wet was scraping across my cheek. Great! It was Ned waking me from a fantastic dream. I had just captured nine bad guys and was taking them all to the county jail. Crimefighter Rocky Malone was the town hero again.

"Ned! Cut it out. I'm sleeping in today."

"No you're not Rocky. This is a workday. We're one week away from our grand opening and you need to help mow the lawn and clean the patio this morning. Let's get crackin'."

"But Dad . . . tomorrow's my birthday. Can't I celebrate by sleeping in? Mow the lawn? That's not a lawn, it's a jungle."

"Nice try, Buddy. Everybody's helping today. No exceptions, no deals. Wear some old clothes. You're going to get plenty dirty."

"What's for breakfast?" At least I could look forward to another great meal from Mrs. Brickle.

"Bran flakes and coffee." Your mom, Mrs. Brickle, and Cinnamon went to Milbank to shop. We're on our own for a while."

"Now there's a good start to the day. Maybe if I pout some more Dad will make some eggs. Who am I kidding? Dad's favorite breakfast was bran flakes and a cup of coffee. That stuff tastes like cardboard to me. And coffee? Not my cup of tea. Maybe I could sneak a few cookies and a glass of milk before we headed up to the garage.

We worked all morning chopping, trimming, mowing, and bagging. I'd never mowed a lawn before, but once I got the hang of it, it was kinda fun. I didn't let Dad know that though. He might expect me to do it all the time. Cleaning up the patio was next on the list. It actually looked pretty good once we swept away all the anthills and hosed it down.

"Great job Rocky. Let's clean up."

I thought that meant we were finished, but I was wrong. Cleaning up meant throwing all the brush and clippings in the back of the pickup and hauling it out to a landfill. We drove out Old Main, crossed the tracks, and headed west. We stopped at Winter's Pool Hall for root beers and then headed back to the hotel for lunch.

"If the women aren't back from shopping, I'll make you my specialty," Dad announced as we jumped back in the truck. I picked up a few supplies over at Torgeson's Mercantile. They've got a little of everything over there."

Oh no! Dad's specialty was beans and fried Spam sandwiches. I really hoped the women were back.

"Beans and Spam build character. Did I ever tell you that Spam and beans kept us going in the war? You just wait Rocky. It'll grow on you.

"Yes Dad. I know the story." I had no doubt that that stuff would grow on me, probably into some kind of oozing blob. And beans building character? Beans just built up a lot of gas in me.

"By the way Rocky, I ran into your friend Samantha at Torgeson's Mercantile. She was running the cash register at the front counter. She's quite the cutie with those little horn-rimmed glasses. Says she's got some interesting news and will stop over later if you're around. I told her you'd be at the garage all afternoon."

Great! That meant more work. I wonder what Dad had in store this afternoon. Maybe I could slow things down a bit by eating slow. What's the rush getting back there anyway? Problem was trying to eat my lunch slow. I was much better off gulping it down.

"Hey Dad! I tried to give Ned some of my lunch, but he just sniffed it and walked away. What does that tell you?"

"It tells me your dog has no taste."

We finished lunch and headed back to the garage. Dad drove his pickup and I hopped on *Phantom* hoping that I'd get a break later on in the day. Maybe I could ride over to New Town and get us some fudge. It wasn't that far and I was pretty sure I could make it across the bridge without getting run over. *Phantom* and I were like a blur when we needed to be.

Dad had decided to paint the entire inside of the garage in a half a day. Was he kidding? That place was huge.

"We're whitewashing everything from top to bottom Rocky. I have big rollers, big brushes, and some sawhorses. We'll knock it off in no time."

Dad was right. It went really fast because every wall was already somewhat white. Dad put down lots of newspaper and cardboard so I could really just slop it on and it looked pretty good. In less than three hours we were working on the last wall and bearing down on the office. Unfortunately, I was also covered head to toe in whitewash.

"You should see yourself Rocky," teased Dad. "I don't think you missed a spot on your entire body."

"Rocky, is that really you under all that paint? I thought maybe Casper the Friendly Ghost had come to haunt us."

"Hi Sam. My dad and I were just finishing this wall. Want to help?"

"And end up looking like you? No thank you. I'll just sit and watch for a while." Sam was wearing her Seven Friends T-shirt and jeans. No dress today. Thank you Cinnamon! You couldn't tell what I was wearing.

"Rocky why don't you wash up and take a break. I'll finish up here. There's a hose out back. Maybe Samantha can hose you off."

"That I can do," said Sam as she quickly jumped off the chair Dad had given her to sit on. I think she sounded a little too eager.

"I think I can do it myself. Besides, I don't want to get paint on you. Maybe my dad can help."

"Sorry Pal. I need to keep going here. Looks like you have all the help you need.

"Come on Rocky. Let's find that hose. I promise I won't hurt you. It's only water." Yup, she was on a mission and I was her next victim.

We went around the back of the garage and found the hose right where I left it when I cleaned the patio. "We should make sure the paint runs off into the sand over by the garage. I'll just stand right . . ."

I didn't even finish my sentence before the water hit. "Boy this is fun," laughed Sam. "Now stand still so I can get every square inch. You're a complete mess. When I'm done, you'll be completely clean, top to bottom."

Sam was enjoying this way too much, and I was stuck. I couldn't run away. How would that look? I could see the headlines: *Painted boy escapes deadly garden hose and small girl with glasses.* I just had to endure the pain and humiliation.

After about fifteen minutes of torture I finally passed Sam's inspection. I never knew getting sprayed by water could hurt so much. "I got most of it Rocky. Now let's sit in the sun while you dry off and I'll tell you about our friend George Stanley."

"Can't wait to hear it Sam. George and I are becoming good buddies you know."

"Yea, I can tell by the sweet names he calls you. You're his favorite. Anyway, I was biking to the post office for my dad and happened to run into George just as he was crossing the bridge. He was trying to ride his bike, but it looked like he'd run into a tree or something. The bike was in pretty bad shape."

"Was this right before dinner last night?" I asked.

"Yes it was. Just about five o'clock. I had to hurry before the post office closed. He yelled at me and told me to get out of his face. He's not a very nice person Rocky. I wasn't any where near his face, nor would I want to be."

"You can say that again. I think George found out that Mr. Jingles has a temper." I told Sam about meeting George and the message he had to deliver to Mr. Jingles.

"I wish I could have been there. It would have been fun to see George's bike airborne."

"Me too Sam. Can't wait to tell the others. It's about time George got some of his own medicine."

"I have to get back home for dinner. I'm cooking tonight. Will I see you at the bandstand later?"

"It's a date."

"No, it's not Rocky. I don't date."

"Umm . . . I didn't mean a date, I meant I'll just . . . oh, never mind."

"Bye Rocky."

Sam left me standing on the back patio, one foot planted on wet concrete, the other again in my mouth. That girl really makes me sweat.

I headed back inside to see if Dad needed a little more help before dinner. Mom was busy cleaning out our "beach house" next door. She had gathered another pickup full of junk to go to the dump. I hadn't been in the house for a few days and I was amazed to see how much they had done inside. I was hoping I didn't have to whitewash this place too. I had my fill of paint for a while.

Finally the pickup was full and Dad and Mom headed to the dump. I grabbed *Phantom* and headed back to the hotel. Even though Sam had cleaned me off pretty good, Mom said I needed to take a bath, put some clean clothes on, and get ready for dinner. "In that order?" I asked. "I can't wait for a real home-cooked meal. No offense Dad."

"None taken. My cooking just needs some time to grow on you."

I rushed back to the hotel, scrambled up the stairs, blew into my room, laid out some clean clothes, and headed to the bathroom. I could move pretty fast when the smell of food was in the air. My bath took a little longer than expected; I discovered several patches of white paint in my ears, hair, and even some private parts. Not sure how that happened.

Dressing for dinner is always an easy task for a guy. Jeans, T-shirt, shoes, socks, and don't forget clean underwear. I could do the whole clothes thing in under two minutes. I never understood why it takes girls so long.

Dinner was great of course. Baked chicken, mashed potatoes, gravy, peas with baby onions, and some kind of pudding for dessert. Mrs. Brickle called it bread pudding. Whatever it was, it was now my new favorite.

"Thanks for the great meal Mrs. B. I was looking forward to this all day." I glanced over at Dad to see if I had made him feel bad, but he was busy wolfing down his second plate of food. I was pretty sure Mom was not thrilled with how we both were packing it in.

"Remember that this is Saturday night in Skunk Hollow. Everyone heads over Central Avenue and the park to listen to music, play some games, and visit stores. Everyone will be there." Cinnamon sounded excited about showing me Skunk Hollow at night. I was hoping the street lights were all on. Hanging out in the dark doesn't excite me much.

"Who's playing music tonight." I thought maybe I could bring my harmonica. I'm not very good, but if asked I'd give it a shot.

"We never know who will show up," said Cinnamon. Sometimes we have guitar players or blues singers from the city. We've had the school band and choir around holidays. Eddie and his friends often bring their 45s and plug in a big old phonograph. It's a blast."

"We're doing that tonight," Eddie announced over his third helping of potatoes. Man, that guy could eat.

After dinner was finally over we all helped clean up. It didn't take long with two families "rolling up their sleeves." I think my dad has as many lines as I have, maybe more.

"Rocky, would you and Cinnamon like to pick out some spins to play tonight? It would help a lot. I need to wipe down my wheels before heading to the strip."

"You bet," I said. I guessed spins were records, although I had no idea why Eddie wanted to wipe wheels or drive to a strip.

Cinnamon caught my look of confusion. "I'll fill you in later Rocky. Let's head to Eddie's room to look through his records."

Looking through Eddie's records was great fun. Eddie had plenty to choose from. Of course there were a lot of Elvis tunes and some by the Platters, Diamonds, and Bill Haley and the Comets. We picked out several rock & roll tunes, a few sappy love songs, and some that would make our parents happy. Mom loved Pat Boone and the McGuire Sisters. Those records had to be gifts. I couldn't see Eddie buying songs for old people.

We made our way to Eddie's car with the records just as he was finishing up. "Thanks kids. Would you like to ride to New Town with me? I'm leaving pretty quick.

"Sure would," I said jumping into the back seat of his '49 Chevy Coupe. Now that was a great set of wheels.

"You do need to tell your parents your leaving, and you can sit in

the front with Cinnamon."

"Way cool, I'll be right back," I said as I scrabbled out and headed back into the hotel.

I heard Cinnamon's comment as I bolted through the back door. "Just a little excited, aren't you?"

I was back in the car before the hotel screen closed. "All set, and yes I am. Let's rock 'n' roll." There, I used my favorite line before anyone else made a comment. Way to go Rocky!

As Eddie's car eased across the bridge, I hung on to the armrest and pretended to look out the window. I actually had my eyes closed and my fingers crossed. I was sure falling into the creek wouldn't be fun or cool.

We finally made it across the bridge and Eddie headed to the park and the bandstand. Eddie parked his car next to several other cars belonging to his friends. It had to be a car show with all the polish and chrome.

"Hey Eddie, I bet you're going to win."

"Win what Rocky?" asked Eddie as he killed the engine.

"The show of course. When does it start?" Now I was confused, but that was nothing new for me. I must have missed something.

"I don't think there's a show here tonight Rocky," said Cinnamon. "We're just getting together to play some music."

"Well if there's no show, there should be. Look at all these cars?"

"Did you think this was going to be a car show?" asked Eddie. "That would be fun, wouldn't it?"

"You bet it would, and you'd win hands down." I still planned on checking out all the cars. Some day, I'd be graduating to four wheels and it was always good to plan ahead. I knew I wouldn't be getting an old pickup. That would be years off and *Phantom* was still the best ride around, even on two wheels.

"Rocky, you are so funny," said Cinnamon. "Let's go help set up the music. I want to look at some of the records Eddie's friends brought.

The bandstand in the park was pretty cool. I was surprised I hadn't seen it when we first came across the bridge or when I visited the fudge shop. It was practically across the street in the city park. I really needed to be more observant and not so concerned about that bridge.

"This was one of the first buildings on this side of the bridge,"

said Cinnamon. The people of Old Town built it before there even was a New Town. It's one of the traditions that brings everyone together, even though some in New Town want it gone. They'd just a soon the Old Town people never crossed over."

"You mean like George Stanley and his clan of thugs?" I asked.

"You've got that right Rocky," said Cinnamon. "I'm sure they'll be here tonight looking for trouble. Just stay close to your friends. They're all chickens when they're outnumbered."

"Sounds good to me. Hey look, here comes Tommy and Sarah on their scooter." I was excited to see them, even though we'd been with them yesterday.

"Hello Tommy and Little Mouse," I yelled even though they were probably too far away to hear me. Tommy looked our way as he got off his scooter. He briefly held his hands over his head with seven fingers pointed to the sky, Seven Friends coming together once again. Little Mouse jumped off the back of the scooter and darted across the park to the bandstand, arms, legs, and long, brown hair flying in the wind. She moved so fast and so effortlessly, she was almost a blur.

"Wow Sarah! You really have some wheels," I said as she put on the brakes.

She scrunched up her face and said, "I don't have any wheels Rocky. That's Tommy's scooter."

"He just meant you were fast," said Cinnamon.

"Then why didn't he say that? Does everyone in that big city you come from talk like you? You'll have to teach me that language."

"Okay, but it's just English," I said. I wondered if I was beginning to sound like Willie the Wanderer. Now that was a confusing language.

Sam and Cryin' Charlie showed up a few minutes later. Sam was all decked out in a flowery summer dress with shoes and hat to match. I took the silent approach. It's always better to say nothing than try to talk with a foot in your mouth. Anyway, she looked pretty good. Charlie had on plaid shorts, a white button-down shirt and a pair of wide suspenders. The shirt was too small and the shorts way too big. I don't think Charlie worried about looking good.

"Most of my clothes are dirty, but I found this in my closet. What do you think? Pretty sharp, right?" asked Charlie as he did a slow spin."

"I think you need to have Sam help you with your wardrobe."

Everyone laughed, including Charlie. He didn't mind being teased by his friends.

"We're picking out some tunes to play tonight, Cinnamon announced. "I'll bet everyone can find at least one favorite to play in all of these 45s."

"I'm going to look for Fats Domino," said Charlie. "My dad knew him in New Orleans."

"Well, *Ain't that a Shame*," I said to be funny. Only Charlie got it.

"I like *Rock Around the Clock*," squeaked Little Mouse.

"That's in here someplace. It's one of Eddie's records. I like Bill Haley and the Comets too, but Elvis is my all-time favorite singer. Here's *Jailhouse Rock*." That's numero uno among crimefighters like me.

"I can't decide between Jerry Lee Lewis or the Crewcuts," said Cinnamon holding up two records. "I just know that there's going to be *A Whole Lot of Shakin' Going On* tonight."

Remembering George Stanley's barb about worms, Tommy and I both shook a little like worms on a hot sidewalk. Everyone laughed until Charlie took out his red bandana to dry his eyes and blow his nose. Then we laughed at the moose call. This was going to be a great Saturday night.

We finally got back to the records and it was Sam's turn to pick. "I'm not sure we'll find any, but I just heard Buddy Holly sing *That'll Be the Day* on American Bandstand. It's a new show on afternoon TV. Buddy Holly's amazing and he wears neat glasses just like me. If we can't find that then see if you can find Roy Orbison.

"Hey, that guy wears glasses too. I bet you also like Ray Charles," I teased.

"Yes, I do," said Sam. "Do you have a problem with that?"

"No problem here. Glasses are the cat's meow. I was thinking about getting a pair myself." How do I get into these conversations?

Tommy couldn't decide for a long time but finally settled on

Folsom Prison Blues by Johnny Cash. Now, that's good music. "I hear the train a comin'. It's rolling round the bend ..." I sang in my best choir voice.

Cinnamon cut me off. "Maybe later Rocky."

"Yea, much later," Sam added. "Like after we all leave." Everyone laughed again. I wondered if my voice had cracked or something. Around the house, Mom always called me her little warbler. She recognized true talent. At least we weren't talking about glasses anymore.

One of Eddie's friends was in charge of playing the records and she told us she'd for sure play our picks. "You guys have good taste in music. Don't be afraid to come up and dance with us a little later."

That's not happening, I thought as I made my way down the bandstand steps. "Oh sure. See you later."

The rest of the night was pretty uneventful. We listened to music, wandered the streets of New Town, got some fudge, and watched Eddie and his football buddies try to dance with some of the high school girls. That was even funnier than our worm impressions. We sat in the grass and tried to sing along when they played the songs we picked out.

"Maybe we should form a band," said Cryin' Charlie. "We've got some pretty good voices. Rocky, you could play the drums."

"That'd be cool. Do drummers sing?"

"Not so much," Charlie replied.

"Oh, I get it." Everyone laughed again. I did too. It was fun to hang out with all my new friends, and I didn't even mind being teased. Deep down, I knew I would eventually be the lead singer if we did form a group. I was just waiting for that perfect melody beyond the bathtub.

We never crossed paths with George and his buddies the entire night. They had to be up to no good to miss all of the action on Saturday night. Might be good to look into it tomorrow.

The music ended with a slow song by the Platters, *Only You.* Cinnamon tried to get me up on the bandstand, but I convinced her that my dance skills were much worse than my singing skills. That got me off the hook, but I did have to promise to let her show me a few steps before next Saturday rolled around. I couldn't believe that in one week I was getting hugs, holding hands, and now dancing with girls. What's happening to me? Good thing they were all just friends. My friend Ernie was never going to believe any of this. I needed to write him a letter.

Chapter Fourteen

Today's my birthday! September 1st, the best day of my life. I was hoping to celebrate by sleeping in and then opening a ton of presents. But no, we had to get all dressed up and go to church. We didn't even know where a church was in Skunk Hollow. Mom had heard that one of the oldest churches in the Dakotas was somewhere around here and she thought it would be fun to try it out.

I didn't have any church clothes to wear, so maybe I could just stay home. What's this? Mom borrowed Eddie's old black confirmation suit and I would look "just dandy" in it. Where did Dad come up with that comment? I didn't want to look dandy.

Of course, the suit was about three sizes too big. I had to roll up the sleeves and the pant legs. Help, I drowning!

"A few stitches here and there and you'll look like a perfect little gentleman." Mom did some amazing things with a needle and thread, but this was hopeless. There was no way out. I was going to church in a suit that made me look like I was one of the Marx brothers. Groucho, Harpo, Chico, and here comes their little brother Rocky.

"I did get you a birthday present when I was in the big city Rocky. You can open the box right now." Maybe Mom got me something I really needed. I ripped open the box eager to see my first birthday gift.

"They're called white bucks. I was told they're the latest rage in Hollywood."

Mom got me white dress shoes? I couldn't believe it. I hope she didn't expect me to wear those things to church. If she had to get something for my feet, why not blue suede shoes. They were the real rage.

"Try them on Rocky. They'll look great with your new suit." I was doomed. Hope nobody sees me in this get-up.

"Good morning Rocky. Don't you look . . . interesting."

"Please Cinnamon, help me out here." Somebody had to step up and tell my mom that this was not the image I needed out in public, even if it was Skunk Hollow.

"I got you a gift too, but I need to wrap it. You'll have to wait until tonight."

"I'm sure I will love it Cinnamon, but you didn't have to get me anything." I'll bet dollars to doughnuts she got me something I could use. Right now, black shoe polish would be a great gift.

"I guess as long as we're handing out birthday presents, you might as well open this one too." Dad tossed me a brown paper bag sealed at the top with masking tape. He wasn't good in the gift-wrapping department. "I know you can use one of these."

Oh great. Dad was always giving me tools and hardware. He probably used the discount coupon he got when he left the hardware store in Chicago. The bag wasn't very big or heavy so my guesses were a tool belt, some paint brushes, or maybe a hardware store apron. This was supposed to be my lucky day! "Thanks Dad. Should I open it now or save the surprise for later?"

"Everyone is dying to see what your old dad got you. Go ahead and have at it Rocky."

I opened the bag slowly, expecting to be disappointed, but what Dad had given me for my birthday was a brand new Cubs baseball cap straight from Wrigley Field. Now that's a birthday gift! Sometimes Dad was amazing. "When did you get this?" I asked cramming my new cap onto my head. "This is the best."

"Glad you like it Rocky. I drove over to Wrigley Field a few days before we left. Had to drop off a few tools for the equipment manager. We managed to work a little trade. He says that this cap was worn by the Cubs shortstop, Ernie Banks. We

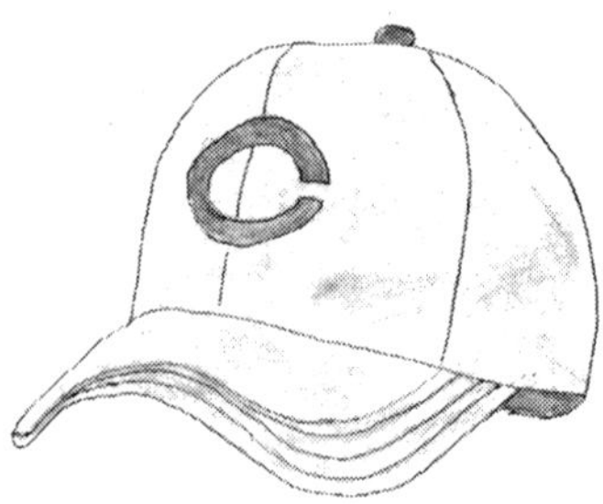

only got to a couple of games in Chicago, Rocky, but I knew the Cubs are your favorite baseball team."

"Ernie Banks? Wow Dad! He's their top player. I can't believe it. I'm never taking this cap off."

"Oh I think you will," said Mom. "We're headed for church in just a few minutes and you will not be wearing that cap."

I loved my mom, but she sure knew how to *rain on my parade.* (Another great line I'd have to use some time. I really need to write some of these good lines down. Where's my notebook?) I bet the minister would understand me wearing my Ernie Banks cap in church. If it was his cap, I bet he'd even wear it during his sermon.

Cinnamon had invited all Seven Friends over to the hotel for popcorn and TV at seven thirty Sunday night. She said she started doing this a couple years ago to get Old Town kids together. I figured it was going to be a surprise birthday party for me. I did my best to play along.

"What shows are we watching?" I was hoping it wasn't Ernie's favorite, *Howdy Doody Time* with Buffalo Bob. That puppet gave me the creeps.

"Oh, we only get a couple channels. Sometimes we watch Jack Benny at 7:30, the Ed Sullivan Show at 8, or General Electric Theater at 9. Some guy named Ronald Reagan hosts that. It's a pretty fun night. Mostly we laugh and talk and forget all about what's on TV."

"I'll have to eat a light dinner to save room for the popcorn," I stated matter-of-factly. I was thinking we'd probably have birthday cake and ice cream. She couldn't fool me with this Jack, Ed, and Ronald stuff. I'm way too smart for that. Birthday party all the way!

"Okay then. See you tonight, said Cinnamon. We're visiting relatives in the next town after church. They don't have kids, but lots of animals. I really love the little pigs and the donkeys."

"Donkeys? I thought they only lived in zoos. Can you ride them?"

"Not these. They're pretty small. Let's go out to the Anderson farm some day after school next week. You need to see farm animals up close, city boy. I'm sure you can ride a horse out there if you want."

"I'm game." I was always up for a new adventure into the wild. Horseback riding though? No chance on that happening.

After travelling over endless dirt roads and passing through a lot of farmland, we finally ended up at the church. The church was nothing like what I had expected. All the churches I had seen in Chicago were big, beautiful buildings filled with statues and stained glass windows, and were surrounded by well-maintained grounds. This church had none of that and less.

"Are you sure this is the right place? This building is even older that Old Town. I'm pretty sure no one uses this any more."

"This church is a big, rich piece of Dakota history," said Mom. "I was told that it was built by settlers and Indians way back before South Dakota became a state. I wouldn't be surprised if some very famous people attended services here. Let's go inside and meet the minister."

There were a few cars parked next to the church so just maybe there was going to be a sermon. As we walked through the front door a man that had to be somebody important greeted us.

"Welcome to our church. I'm Jonathan White Cloud. If you have any questions please ask. The church is yours to worship as you see fit."

"Come to think of it, I do have a couple of questions," I said as I removed my baseball cap. "First, are you the minister? Second, when does the service start? And third, why does this church have a dirt floor?"

"Good questions young man," he said as he shook each of our hands. "I'm not the minister, nor is there a sermon here today. We do have sermons, gatherings, and weddings here quite often, but not today. Families belonging to the Santee Sioux tribe built this church in the 1870s. I'm a descendant of the original builders and come here often to pay my respect to my forefathers. We try to keep the building looking like it did when it was built. That's why there is a dirt floor. If you look at the walls, those are hand-hewn logs that are close to one hundred years old."

"I have a good friend, Tommy Two Feathers. Are you related? He says he's Lakota." Mr. White Cloud looked like Tommy, only older. Tommy would be thrilled if I told him I met his cousin.

"I don't believe we are related. I do remember meeting a Daniel Two Feathers once. His family was originally from the Black Hills."

"That's right. I think he told me that." I was ready to talk about some real history. Maybe Mr. White Cloud knew about Custer, Sitting Bull, and maybe Beauregard Puce.

"That's enough questions Rocky," said Mom tugging on my jacket sleeve. "Thank you so much for your warm welcome Mr. White Cloud."

Mom decided that we would stay and have our own little service with time to worship and reflect. She asked Dad and me to think about three things to be thankful for and three things to pray for. "And Rocky, do it silently."

"Got it Mom." I could dash of a few quick prayers, a couple of thankfuls and I'd be out the door in five. We had places to go and birthdays to celebrate.

After fifteen minutes, I was still working on my list. I should have brought my notebook. I finally decided on my three prayers. I prayed for Lenny's safe return, my parents' success in starting a business, and world peace. I figured world peace was a safe bet. That's on everybody's list

I really struggled with my top three thankfuls. Finally I settled on being thankful for all my new friends, my new bike, and free root beer at Winter's Pool Hall. I had lots of others, but Mom only asked for three.

When we were ready to leave, Dad gave Mr. White Cloud a few dollars to help keep the church going, Mom gave him a little hug, and I told him it was the best church service I had been to in a long time. My parents gave me a funny look, but I really meant it. I could see why people wanted to preserve this place.

After church we decided to stop for Sunday lunch at a local greasy spoon Dad had seen on the way. "As long as we're all dressed up, why not do a little lunch?" he said. "We can celebrate Rocky's birthday in style." Right, Dad. I knew where I wanted to go, back to my room to change into some real clothes. I hoped they were all strangers in the cafe. I really didn't want to be seen by anyone I knew in this get-up, white bucks and an oversized black suit. What kid wears that stuff anywhere?

The cafe really was a greasy spoon. We literally slid into a booth with somebody's half-eaten breakfast still on the tabletop. "This looks good. Too bad we already had breakfast," announced Dad as he checked out each plate.

Was he kidding? I'm always up for food, but was thinking I might just have to pass on lunch. My stomach was already rebelling. Just as I was about to suggest we try another cafe, a waitress appeared ready to take our order. At least I think she was a waitress. She was wearing an apron and had a pencil behind her ear. Beyond that, I wasn't sure. She didn't look like anybody's grandma, that's for sure.

"What'll ya folks have?" she asked in a kind of Willie the Wanderer drawl.

"Not this," I said pointing to the half-eaten food on the table. "Do you have a menu?"

"Cain't you read boy? Iz right up der above da counter."

I looked up and sure enough, there was the lunch menu scratched out in chalk on an old blackboard. Today's menu: Hamburger, ½ Chicken, Spam sandwich, and Chef's special stew.

That's it? I sure wasn't going to try the stew. They could throw anything into that pot. I guess I'll have a burger. I already knew Dad would go for the Spam and Mom will ask for a salad. It's not on the menu, but every cafe I've ever been to always has salad.

"I guess I'll have a burger. What does that come with?"

"Comes with a plate. Everythin' else iz xtree."

"I'll just have a root beer."

"No root beer. Coffee, tea, er milk."

"He'll have milk," said Mom, "and I'll have a salad with tea. What kind of dressings do you have?"

"French."

"Then French it is," said Mom smiling her best Sunday smile. She was amazing. Nothing ever got to my mother.

"And I'll have the Spam sandwich with fries and coffee," said Dad. "You don't find Spam on menus very often."

"No fries. Da deep fryer's broke. I'll bring ya chips instead."

"That's fine. Thank you."

The waitress scurried off to the kitchen without even a hint of clearing our table. "She must be busy," said mom as she got up from the table. "I'll take care of these dishes."

"Mom, we're the only ones here. I'll bet she's on her way out back to smoke."

"Now Rocky. How could you say such a thing?" Mom asked.

"Oh, probably because I saw her pull a pack and some matches from her apron as she went into the kitchen." Even when I was hungry, my crimefighter mind was observing the surroundings.

By the time Mom had the table cleared, dishes stacked, and everything wiped down our waitress appeared again. "Jus' comin' out ta clear da table. I sees you got there before me, ha, ha. Yer food will be up in a minute."

Twenty minutes later the food arrived. My burger was burnt to a crisp, Mom's salad was not much more than wilted lettuce and Dad's sandwich was, well Spam. Not an A-one meal in my book. Mom and I nibbled at our food. Dad inhaled his. Five minutes later we were already to leave.

"That hit the spot," said Dad. "I think I'll leave a tip."

"I think I'll leave a tip too. My tip is to never eat here again."

"Now Rocky. Think of all the children in China going without food."

"Let's send them this stuff. Bet they don't eat it."

"I'd like to stop at the garage on our way home," said Dad. "We only have five work days left before we open the doors, and I'd like to make a list of things that need to be done. But before we do that, how about stopping at the fudge shop, birthday boy?"

Now we're talking my language. We should have skipped that greasy spoon and headed right to the fudge shop. Now, that's my kind of lunch.

"Looks like someone was busy last night," Dad said as we pulled our pickup next to the curb in front of the garage. Someone had moved a ton of rusted-out metal, parts, and motors from the junk pile next to the garage and placed it in a big heap in front of the garage door.

"I'll have to thank who ever did it. They saved me lots of time carting that stuff. It'll be really easy to bring it inside or toss it in the pickup for a quick trip to the junk yard." Dad could always find a way to make things look better than they actually were.

I had already figured out who had built the mound of junk in front of the garage. It was easy to see why George and his buddies weren't around the bandstand last night. They were busy leaving their mark on Dad's new business. I couldn't wait to let George know that by moving the junk from the side of the garage to the front he had saved Dad, and more than likely me, several hours of work. It was going to be fun watching George boil. I had to find a way we could all watch him unravel right before our eyes. I'd see what everybody wanted to do at the so-called TV night tonight.

Chapter Fifteen

All our friends arrived at the hotel just as we finished cleaning up dinner. Cinnamon washed the dishes and I wiped. Our parents were thrilled when we volunteered for cleanup and they quickly decided to get out of the hotel for a while. They didn't seem very interested in watching TV with us. Mrs. Brickle suggested a walk down Old Town Road and Big Island Trail all the way to Snakebite Falls. Mrs. Brickle was excited to show my parents the old school, Backman's Swamp, and the bathhouse next to our swimming hole.

"Now you children have a great time but don't get too crazy. Remember Rocky, you're a guest here."

"Yes Mom, I remember," I said even though I knew TV time was going to turn into a wild and crazy birthday party. Let the fun begin!

"Okay everybody," said Cinnamon as she turned on the TV. "Our first show is Jack Benny. He's pretty funny. Who wants popcorn?"

What? We're actually going to watch TV? Where's the surprise party? I really thought we'd have cake and ice cream. Oh well. It's been a long day. Maybe I should kick back and watch the tube. I can always eat some popcorn. "I'll take a bowl, Cinnamon."

"Me too," said everyone else as they all picked a comfortable spot in front of the TV.

"Sam and Sarah, can you help me with the popcorn?"

"I've got to go to see a man about a horse," announced Charlie.

"Me too," said Tommy as he jumped up to join Charlie.

"What man and what horse?" I asked.

"Rocky, we're going to the bathroom," said Tommy.

"I knew that. I'm okay for now." And they think I say funny stuff. Just as I got comfortable in front of the TV, I heard some shuffling behind me.

"Surprise! Happy Birthday Rocky!" my friends all yelled.

"Let the party begin. Cake and ice cream for everybody," Cinnamon added.

"Let's sing Happy Birthday," said Sam. "Rocky, you just listen."

"Okay, I can do that, although I do sing a pretty mean birthday tune." My new friends hadn't forgotten me. I've only been here for a week, but I think Skunk Hollow is growing on me. Dad will be thrilled.

"We got you some gifts too. Do you want to open them?" asked Sarah. She was as excited as I was.

"Thanks you guys. This is the best ever surprise party. Well, actually it's my first surprise party. I once thought I was getting a party at school, but it never happened. My parents always took me out to dinner, but that was never a surprise. For a party town, Chicago wasn't it for me. Once I had . . ."

"Gumball, be quiet and open your presents."

"Okay Sam, I can do that."

"Rocky, open my gift first," squeaked Sarah. "I made it just for you." Little Mouse was so excited she practically sat in my lap as I opened up her gift. "I made the wrapping paper too. Do you like all the animals and symbols?"

"Wow Sarah. This is really neat." She had painted two beautiful feathers and attached them to a bound leather base.

"I wanted you to have these because you are like another big brother to me. I might start calling you Rocky Two Feathers. They're not real eagle feathers though. I hope you don't mind."

"I love them and every time I look at them I'll think of you." I could see that Sarah was really proud of her work, and I wanted her to know I really appreciated her effort.

"That's really sweet Rocky," said Cinnamon. "I can see why your mom calls you Sweetie."

Okay, now I'm embarrassed.

"I made something for you too," said Tommy. "Didn't wrap it though. I just tied it up in this old sock."

I decided to smell the sock to make sure it was clean. If I didn't pass out, I'd untie the knot. Everyone was laughing but it doesn't hurt to be careful around dirty old socks. Mine didn't always pass the sniff or the touch test. That's when you looked for a clean pair. I do that with underwear too. Just not around girls.

Tommy had carved the image of a bear into a polished gemstone. "This is stone is called a cat's eye. Just keep it in your pocket and it will bring you good luck and clear thinking. The bear symbolizes strength."

"Thanks Tommy. This is neat. How did you carve a bear into stone?"

"Our family has done stone carving forever. My dad taught me a few years ago. I'll show you some time if you want."

"You bet," I said as I stuffed the cat's eye into my pocket. I could already feel good luck heading my way.

"Now it's my turn," said Sam handing me a box covered in pink and green flowers. It was just about the right size for a book. Maybe she got me a Sherlock Holmes book. I'd be okay with that. I'd read it when school started. I carefully opened the box.

"It's a matching brush and comb set. I hope you like it," said Sam.

"Of course I do. It's just what I needed. Thanks Sam." A brush and comb set? What guy has those? When I have bad hair days, I just cover my head with a baseball cap. A Cubs cap, now that was a great hair-grooming gift.

Sam was all smiles. "You're very welcome Rocky. I have a set just like it at home. It was something I knew you could use. No offense."

"Yea, my hair's always a mess. These will sure help."

"Here's my gift Rocky," said Cryin' Charlie. "Didn't think about wrapping it."

"Wow Charlie! This is really great, a notebook with a leather cover and a place to put my pencil. I can really use this when I'm solving mysteries and writing notes to people. Look it has my initials on it. Did you do that?"

"No I asked Tommy to do that. He's pretty good at that kind of stuff." Tommy just smiled.

"One last gift Rocky." Cinnamon handed me a soft packaged wrapped in red paper, of course.

I tore open the gift and found a navy blue t-shirt decorated with Cinnamon's 7 Friends logo in a rainbow of colors.

"I found this yesterday when we went shopping. I had to work fast to get it done for today. Hope you like it."

"I sure do Cinnamon," I said pulling it on over my ugly white T-shirt. "Hey, you guys are the best of friends. I really wasn't expecting any gifts, but these are all really cool. Thank you. I mean, when you think about it, having good friends is . . ."

"That's enough gushy stuff Birthday Boy," said Cinnamon. "Let's play some games. How about Twenty Questions? Rocky can go first."

I played Twenty Questions a lot with Ernie, so I new I could stump them. "Okay I'm ready."

"Is it alive?" asked Little Mouse.

"Yes, that's one"

"Is it an animal?" asked Charlie.

"Yes, that's two."

"Is it your pet?" Asked Cinnamon.

"Yes, that's three." These guys have played this game before.

"It can't be Ned. That's too obvious. Is it Gerty?" asked Sam.

"Yes, and that's four." I guess I made that too easy for them. Maybe I should have picked a president or something nobody eats, like a turnip.

Everyone got a turn and most made it to at least fifteen questions. We couldn't solve Sarah or Charlie's words. Sarah's word was *chokecherry* and Charlie stumped us with *mockingbird*.

"Before we start another game, maybe we should talk about getting together at HQ tomorrow. We'll need to plan what to do next about Lenny, the Stanleys, and the lost map." I was having a great time at the party, but didn't want to give up on the mysteries we were working on. A good crimefighter never lets a case grow cold.

After talking it over, we decided to meet after lunch. That would give us all a chance to sleep in a little, catch up on stuff around the house, dig for some more clues, and run the errands we all knew our parents would ask on a Monday morning.

Just as we were ready to start another game, my parents and Mrs. Brickle stepped into the dining room. "We're back kids," said Mrs. Brickle. "It's getting pretty nasty outside. I think you all had better plan on spending the night here in the hotel. I don't want any of you travelling home in a storm. I'll try to reach your parents."

"Yahoo! An all-night birthday party! This is going to be grrrrrreat!"

"Dream on young man," said Dad. "Bed time's 10:30 and that's only because it's your birthday. Irene and Mrs. Brickle, either of you want coffee?"

After a few minutes of whimpering, we all settled down and played our next birthday game. The game was called Charades. Sam suggested we pit the boys against the girls. It sounded like a great match-up, but the girls seemed to be able to read each other's thoughts. Charlie, Tommy, and I didn't even get one right. After about fifteen minutes I suggested we try something else. Charades wasn't my cup of tea.

Chapter Sixteen

I have a great idea," said Cinnamon. "It's a perfect night to tell some ghost stories."

"That sounds like fun," said Cryin' Charlie. I have a doozie that will make your hair stand on end."

"I've got one too," offered Sam.

"I'm in," said Tommy. "I'm always interested in the spirit world."

"I vote for a little more TV," I said sheepishly. "We could save the scary stuff for a picnic on a nice, sunny day."

"Oh come on Rocky. It'll be fun. Besides, we shouldn't watch TV during a storm. It's dangerous."

Cinnamon was right of course. I didn't want to get electrocuted, but I didn't want to be thinking about ghosts and vampires all night either.

"How about telling jokes or singing some songs? I've got some good ones."

"Nice try, but you're outvoted this time," said Charlie. "I'll start."

"Wait Charlie. Let's turn out all the lights and I'll get my flashlight. If I put it upside down on the floor, it'll look just like the embers of a campfire. The thunder and lightning outside will make it even scarier."

Great. Cinnamon was really getting into this stuff. I'd better get my flashlight just in case. Maybe we could just leave the hall light on. This wasn't how I wanted to celebrate my birthday.

Cinnamon found her flashlight, turned out the lights, and had us all sit in a circle on the dining room floor.

"This story is called *Bloody Bill and the Box of Bones*," said Charlie.

Just then a large lightning bolt lit up the night. The crash of thunder made my teeth rattle. Someone screamed and then it was dark again.

"Thanks for the great introduction Rocky," said Charlie.

Was that me? That's twice in a week. "Your welcome Charlie. Just wanted to set the mood."

"Now, on with my story. Many years ago when this town was just getting started a very bad man rode into town on a horse as black as coal. He was all dressed in black like his horse. Even his hair and mustache was black, as black as the night without stars. He had guns, but his favorite weapons were two giant knives that lay crisscross on his back.

Most of the people in town kept their distance because they knew he was looking for trouble. Bloody Bill hadn't worked a day in his life. He got everything he needed by killing and stealing. If someone tried to stop him, he'd just take out his knives and hack them to pieces."

Another lightning bolt, but I held the scream in this time. This story wasn't that scary and it happened years ago.

"Bloody Bill was leaving a trail of blood all over town. If someone crossed him, he'd first cut off an ear, then a nose. If they tried to fight him they'd lose a hand. If they ran, he'd cut of their legs. The whole town was dying at the hands of Bloody Bill. Then one day a cowboy rode into town looking for Bill. He didn't have any knives or guns, but said he planned on bringing Bloody Bill to justice. The townspeople figured that this cowboy would just be another mark on Bloody Bill's belt. The cowboy told people to let Bill know he could be found at the local saloon washing the dust out of his throat. Bloody Bill arrived at the saloon in minutes with both knives drawn and evil in his eyes. "Hello Bill. It's been a long time and I see you haven't changed your ways. I told you you'd have to pay for your sins." A lasso suddenly appeared in the cowboy's hand and before Bill could even raise a blade he was hog tied and lying on the floor." Charlie took out his bandana, wiped his eyes, and blew his nose.

"Wait a minute. That's it?" I said. That's no ghost story.

"I'm not finished," said Charlie stuffing his bandana back into his pocket. "The cowboy dragged Bloody Bill back out into the street and announced to the gathering townspeople 'Justice has been served, do with him what you will.' Bloody Bill yelled out 'I'll get you for this, all of you, you hear me?' Charlie raised his voice to sound like a caged man about to meet his doom. "The townspeople descended on Bill and using his own knives cut off his ears, then his nose, hands, feet, and finally his head. They took his bones and scattered them to the wind. Bloody Bill had come to a violent end at the hands of the townspeople. Some say his ghost still walks the streets of Old Town looking for revenge and all of his bones. Nights like tonight, if you listen closely, you can hear his bones rattling in the wooden box he carries as he searches for more."

"That's good Charlie, but I don't believe that for a second."

"So okay then, what's this?" Charlie whipped out a bone from behind his back and threw it into the middle of the circle. We all screamed and jumped to our feet as it clattered on the wooden floor and came to rest next to the glowing flashlight. Charlie laughed and said in a very calm voice "It's okay guys. It's just a bone Mrs. Brickle gave to Ned for a treat after dinner tonight."

"Good one Charlie. That sent a shiver down my spine. Okay, I'll go next," said Sam. No shiver down my spine but I almost wet my pants when that bone hit the floor.

"Let's take a cookie break," said Cinnamon. Miss Odetts baked Rocky some chocolate chip cookies for his birthday."

"I'm up for that," I said as I jumped up and turned on the lights. I knew our time in the light wouldn't last, but I planned on enjoying a few moments of calm before another storm hit.

After a short cookie break, off went the lights and we were all back in the circle waiting for Sam's story. "This one isn't as long as

Charlie's but believe me, it's true. This is about the *Witch of Backman's Swamp.*"

"Oh I've heard of her," said Little Mouse. "Lenny told me he saw her out in the swamp."

"I'm beginning to think Old Town is filled with ghosts, witches, and vampires.

"Maybe it is, heh, heh, heh," cackled Sam in a voice that sounded, well, . . . like a witch.

I wasn't really getting into Sam's story. I needed Ned. "Here Ned. Come and be my pillow. That's a good boy." I scratched Ned's ears as he settled in beside me. I didn't really need a pillow. I needed a security blanket. Okay, bring on those nasty witches.

"My story starts a few years back when a young boy came across an old, rundown shack while he was walking through Backman's Swamp. The boy called out 'Is anybody home?' as he slowly and carefully approached the shack. 'Who's there?' croaked a voice from inside the shack. 'It's Robert, Robert Peabody, ma'am,' said the boy. 'Well, come in and set a spell Robert Peabody. You must be tired from your long walk.'"

"Sam, can you talk in your regular voice?" I asked. Sam was trying to talk like a witch, and it was working. My skin was already crawling just with her voice.

"No keep going Sam," said Cinnamon. "The voice makes it real."

"Okay," Sam continued. "Robert was tired and a little hungry so he took a chance and decided to walk into the shack. 'Well hello young man,' said an old woman sitting on a stool near a boiling pot. 'Let me introduce myself. My name is Jezelda and I love to have visitors, especially tender, young boys. Would you like to stay for dinner?'"

Sam was sitting right next to me and gave me a poke in the ribs when she said "tender."

"Cut it out Sam, and I really don't like that voice."

"Back to my story. Jezelda gave the pot a few stirs and cackled again. 'It's almost done, I just need one more ingredient.' 'What's for dinner?' asked Robert. 'It smells really good.' 'Some call it swamp chicken. I hear tell others call it frog leg stew, but I call it . . . YOU.'"

In that same instant Sam jumped up and grabbed me by the shoulders. There was tons of screaming and laughter. I did most of the screaming.

After we settled down again Sam said in a much quieter voice "There's more to the story. It's been said that if anyone goes into the swamp and calls out her name, she turns them into frogs. To this day you can hear the frogs calling for Robert, the Swamp Hag's first dinner."

"I hear that all the time," said Little Mouse. "I thought they were saying ribbitt, ribbitt."

"You mean if I say *Jezelda* I turn into a . . ." Tommy didn't even finish his sentence. He squatted down on all fours and hopped away saying ribbitt, ribbitt on each hop.

"Not funny Tommy." Right then and there I vowed never to eat frog legs again. I didn't believe that story for a minute, but it doesn't hurt to be a little careful.

"Those were great stories. I have one too, and my story is true. I have the facts and an eye witness."

Now we're talking. I love solving mysteries with facts. Having someone actually witness something makes it true. "Go for it Cinnamon. We're all ears."

"I call my story *The Vampire Rats of Old Town* and my witness is, drum roll please, . . . Errrrrocky."

Oh great. Cinnamon was going to talk about exploring the pit of doom in my dad's garage. I'll have to remind her that she was scared too. Dad solved the problem by burying them in sand and concrete. Vampire rats couldn't dig through that, or could they?

Suddenly the lights flashed on. Even that scared me a little, but I thought it best not to scream. "Okay kids, it's time for bed. I've called your parents to let them know you'll all be home after breakfast tomorrow. Girls, you can sleep in Cinnamon's room. Boys, you're upstairs with Rocky. I have plenty of pillows and blankets for all."

"Oh yea! A pajama party," chirped Little Mouse.

"Guys don't do pajama parties. We do sleepovers," I said.

"Sounds boring," said Sam.

"Brush your teeth before you head for bed Sweetie."

Mom did it to me again. Now everyone will be calling me Sweetie. I think I might prefer Gumball.

Chapter Seventeen

Tommy, Charlie, and I had decided to turn my room into a campsite, complete with a tent, fire ring (fake of course), fishing hole, and a trail through the woods. Our imaginations went wild and when we finished we all admitted it looked pretty good. Unfortunately, we were too tired to enjoy it and all fell asleep stretched across a bed completely stripped of sheets and blankets. Monday morning came way too soon.

I think the only reason we even woke up was Ned decided it was time for his breakfast. He made sure he licked each of our faces. "Just pretend you got a good morning kiss from a beautiful girl, " I said to Charlie as Ned slobbered on his cheek.

"No girls I know have tongues of sandpaper," announced Charlie as he wiped his face with his red bandana.

"I know a few," said Tommy in a very serious voice, "but I'd never let them lick my face." That made us all laugh.

"Did you guys know that frogs have really long tongues? They just sit there and grab bugs right out of the air."

"Do you mean like this Tommy?" I blurted out as I hopped on the bed and flicked my tongue. All the time I was hopping I was thinking about Jezelda the Swamp Hag. I was hoping no one said her name out loud. This wasn't the swamp, but I didn't want to take any chances. I wasn't interested in being anybody's swamp chicken.

"Hey, did you guys know that last year some kid at school got his tongue stuck on the flag pole? It was in the winter and the principal had to use hot water to get it unstuck. I heard it was a true story." Charlie was dead serious.

"No way. I heard that same story back at my school in Chicago."

"I heard about that story too," said Tommy. "Someone said it was George Stanley's buddy, Clyde, doing it on a dare."

"Now that I can believe. That guy is a few cards short of a full deck. Should we tell the girls how Ned woke us up and our frog jokes?" I asked.

"I don't think they'd appreciate our humor," said Tommy.

"And I'm not asking to see their tongues. No way!" said Charlie. And then we laughed some more.

"If they ask, let's just say we played cards."

I wondered what the girls talked about last night and this morning. I was pretty sure they didn't make a cool campground or tell jokes in the morning. They were probably brushing each other's hair or deciding what to wear.

We were headed downstairs in short order. I had decided to leave the room decorated camp style. I thought it looked like a pretty great place to spend my nights and I was sure no one in the hotel would be cleaning up after me. This was a guy's room after all.

Breakfast was homemade waffles with maple syrup and fresh strawberries. Mrs. B even had some whipped cream to top it off. We each had two before the girls even made it downstairs.

"Mrs. Brickle, I haven't had a bad meal yet. These waffles are numero uno."

"I think that was a compliment, so thank you Rocky."

"Hi Cinnamon, Sam, and Sarah. How was your pajama party?" I asked.

"It was great," said Sarah. "We talked, played games, had a pillow fight, and tried on lots of Cinnamon's fancy clothes."

"Doesn't sound like fun to me," I whispered to Charlie. I got a cold look from Sam, but I was pretty sure she hadn't heard me.

"What did you guys do?" asked Cinnamon.

"Oh guy things. We made a tent, told some great stories, and played cards for money." Okay, so I stretched it a little. But I couldn't tell them we pretty much went to sleep as soon as the tent was up.

"So who was the big winner?" asked Sam.

"I was," we all said in unison.

"I see," said Sam as she slowly looked at each one of us. I don't think we fooled her at all. Maybe I'll just have another waffle and let someone else do the talking.

"Rocky, Eddie said you should bike up to the football field after breakfast to talk to Coach Nelson. He says you can be the new ball boy on the team if you want. That should be fun."

"Thanks Mrs. B. That would be way cool. I think I can find the field."

"I'd go with you Rocky, but I'm helping my mother clean rooms this morning. I'll draw you a quick map, but it's easy to find."

"Sounds great Cinnamon. Don't bother with my room though. I got it just the way I like it." Maybe I should run back up and check for loose underwear just in case she decided to check on our camp-making skills.

"I'll ride with you part of the way," said Charlie. "I have to get to the post office to help my dad sort mail this morning. Monday is always a big mail day."

"Great. I do need to stop off at my dad's garage to see if he needs anything. Hope that's okay."

"Sounds like a plan. Let's rock 'n' roll," said Charlie. "I can't believe I said that. You're rubbing off on me Rocky."

Yeah, now what do I say? "Well, okay then." Not smooth at all Rocky. I've got to be faster on the draw.

We made it to the garage in record time. Dad and Mom were still cleaning and painting both the garage and the house. I could see the progress, but it still looked like a couple of old buildings covered in white paint.

"Hello Rocky and hello Charlie." Mom had paint in her hair and on her clothes, but was as cheerful as ever. "We're making great progress, don't you think?"

"It looks great Mrs. Malone. I can't wait to see it finished. My whole family is coming to the open house."

"That's great. Rocky, we're going to need your muscle on a few projects.

My mother's idea was to serve lemonade and cookies in the house and out on the patio during the grand opening. She had worked her magic and had purchased a bunch of stuff from a restaurant that had just changed owners in New Town. They were remodeling and wanted to unload everything. Mom said she would take every table, chair and appliance they wanted to toss out.

"I saw some bright and cheery material down at Mrs. Gittemeire's Thrift Shop. I can sew some nice table cloths for the tables in no time."

"How many table and chairs did you get?" I knew who'd be hauling them.

"Twelve tables, forty eight chairs, a refrigerator, a freezer, and a stove. It'll only take you and your dad about six trips with the truck and trailer. We'll try for Thursday. We should be all done cleaning by then."

Six trips across the bridge in a loaded pickup? Is she serious? I figured Thursday was my last day on earth or my first day in the hospital, if I survived the fall. "Yes ma'am. Dad and I can handle it." Maybe we could walk the stuff across. That would be about sixty trips. Piece of cake! I'd talk to Dad later about my idea. I'm sure he knows that bridge is on its last legs.

"Son," Dad said. He always called me Son when he had a special job for me. "You haven't forgotten about delivering our flyers? They're already to go. You can go door-to-door in New Town after you meet with Coach Nelson."

"Okay Dad, but I don't have a basket on *Phantom*. How am I going to carry them?"

"You'll figure it out, and who's *Phantom*?"

"*Phantom's* my bike, remember? I bought it from Eddie with my auction money."

"Oh yeah. Good investment Son. Can't go anywhere without a good set of wheels. Here are the flyers. Now, on your way. Nice to see you Charlie"

"You too Mr. Malone."

I found a plastic bag in the trash and tied it to my handlebars. It wasn't a very good basket, but I figured it would be okay for the trip around New Town.

"Hey Rocky. My dad delivers the mail to everyone in town. I bet we could ride along and drop all those flyers off in no time. Want to stop by the post office after you talk to Coach?"

"What a great idea. Do you think your dad would mind?"

"He won't care. He loves company on his route. Let me take the bag so you don't have to carry them up to school."

"Great. Let's blast off."

"Varoooom!" yelled Charlie. Charlie's a pretty cool tomato.

After tying the plastic bag to Charlie's bike we headed down the road and across the bridge. There weren't any cars around so we made it across without incident. I never feel good about crossing that bridge, but *Phantom* was up to the task and we made it to safe ground in record time. Charlie acted like it was no big deal. He crosses it every day, so he must be used to it. Me on the other hand, bolted across like a scared jackrabbit.

"You're pretty fast on that bike," said Charlie as he pedaled up behind me.

"Yea, I guess I am. I've been working out." Actually, with me, fear equals fast. I'm pretty sure workouts didn't make me fast because I've never really done one. I couldn't say I'm really moving fast because I'm scared to death.

I took the first left off of Central Avenue and headed past the city park to the school. Charlie took a right and headed to the new post office. I was pretty sure I wouldn't get lost since it was a straight shot to the school and I thought I could hear the sounds of a football team practicing. I wasn't sure what they were saying, but it sounded like someone had just done something amazing and everyone was cheering. Maybe Eddie scored a touchdown or something.

I could see the field off to my right and the school off to my left. In just a few days I'd be stuck in that building for hours on end. It looked pretty nice from the outside, but that's how schools are – all pretty with fields and playgrounds to lure you in. Then, once you open that door, bang-zoom your stuck and you can't get out for nine months. I'm already missing the summer.

I parked *Phantom* next to the bleachers and walked over to the team bench where some guys with whistles were hanging out. I guessed that they were the coaches because everyone else had helmets on. "Have you seen Coach Nelson?" I asked the closest coach.

"Well hello young man. You must be Eddie's friend Rocky. I'm Coach Nelson."

"Hello sir. I'm Errrrrocky Malone. Pleased to meet you. How's the team going to be this year? Can you win it all? I went to see a Chicago Bears game at Soldier Field once. We sat a long ways away from the field and the players looked just like ants." Great first impression Rocky. Stutter first, then bore him to tears with trivia.

"Just call me Coach, Rocky," he said. "Do you have a minute to talk about being our ball boy this year?"

"You bet I do. I'm really excited about being the ball boy, whatever he does. I've never been a ball boy before. Thanks Coach Rocky." I couldn't believe there would be two Rockys on the sideline for the Skunk Hollow Raiders.

"No Rocky. Just call me Coach. My first name is Bill, not Rocky."

"Oh, I get it."

"Hi Rocky," said Eddie as he jogged over to get a drink. "I see you've met Coach. Why are you so red? Have you been working out this morning?"

"No, I just rode *Phantom* over here really fast. I didn't want to be late. I could use a good workout though. I'm pretty out of shape."

"You'll get a good workout every game day Rocky, right Coach?"

"Right Eddie. Let's get that scrimmage started and Rocky can see first hand what he'll be doing."

My job was to run our football out on the field every time we were on offense and Eddie was the quarterback. That took a while to figure out. I managed to run it out a couple of times when Eddie was playing defense. After a few tries, I finally figured out that when Eddie called a huddle, we had the ball. I also helped out with water and towels during time-outs and when players were on the sidelines. The scrimmage only lasted a half hour, and by the time it was over, I was exhausted, but I had a great time being out there with the team and coaches. Hope I didn't screw up too much. I really wanted the job.

"What do you think Rocky?" Coach asked. " Do you think you can handle this on Friday?"

"In a heartbeat, Coach. I'll be there."

"Great. The job is yours," said Coach as he reached down and shook my hand. He wasn't as big as Mr. Jingles, but I could tell he was amazingly strong. His grip was like a vice. I'm glad he likes me.

"Try to be here an hour before the game. We'll have plenty to do while the team is getting dressed. I'll ask Eddie to bring you along when he comes. I understand your staying at the hotel while your place is being fixed up."

"Yes sir. The hotel's great. I have my own room and the food's amazing. That Mrs. Brickle can sure cook."

"Okay then Rocky. I need to get back to practice. See you in a couple of days."

"Thank you Coach. I know we'll win on Friday. Eddie's the best." With that brilliant comment I made my way back to my bike and headed down the road to the new post office. I was going to yell out something as I mounted *Phantom*, but all I could think of was 'Happy trails.' I decided it was best to keep quiet and just ride away. Eddie does that when he leaves and that's a pretty cool move.

Just as I was about to cross Central Avenue, good old George Stanley pulled up in front of me. For the first time since I arrived in Skunk Hollow I was on my own. No friends, no parents, and no Ned. What was I thinking this morning when I told Ned to stay at the hotel? I just didn't think it was a good idea to take him to the football field. Now I wish I had.

"Out of my way BB brain. I need to find my Dad."

"Whatever you say George. I don't have time to sit and chat either."

"As if . . ."

"By the way, my dad told me to thank you for moving all of the scrap metal and junk away from the side of the garage. It was so much easier to haul away stacked in the driveway. He says you should stop by some time so he can thank you in person. I think he'd like to give you something for helping out."

"I didn't do that. Did you say he wants to pay me? Not saying I did it, but it took quite a long time to move that stuff. Whoever did it deserves a big reward. I'd be happy to collect it and give it to the guys who worked there Saturday night."

"No reward George. Just a free tune-up on your bike. Looks like you had a few problems lately." I decided it was time to vacate the scene. Exit, stage right. I knew George would never catch me on his beat up bike.

"I'll get you for this Malone. Wait 'til my dad hears about this. You'll be sorry you were ever born."

"Bye Gorgeous, and . . . you can eat my dust." Yes! I faced up to George and survived. Now I just had to make sure Ned never left my side.

I made it to the post office in record time. I was beginning to think I could be blistering fast on *Phantom* any time I wanted. Maybe my nickname should be Rocketman. Move over Superman. There's a new hero in town.

Mr. Potts was packed up and ready to make his deliveries throughout the town. Charlie and I rode along and passed out flyers to just about everybody. Quite a few people said they would be stopping by our Grand Opening.

Some people even asked if they could drop off mowers or chainsaws that needed repairs. I was pretty sure Dad wanted the business right away, so I told them to bring their stuff over any time. Dad could fix anything.

On our trip around town I told Mr. Potts and Charlie about my meeting with George. Charlie laughed and then had to blow his nose. Then I laughed because he was calling moose again.

"You need to be careful around that Stanley kid, Rocky," said Mr. Potts. He's a bad seed."

-GRAND OPENING-

**SATURDAY,
SEPTEMBER 7**

Having purchased and taken possession of Mike's Auto, in Skunk Hollow, we will be glad to welcome old friends and new, old customers and new at this opening date.

WE WILL BE SERVING COFFEE AND LUNCH THROUGHOUT THE DAY

We will also have many worthwhile bargains for you. Having completed our inventory, we will dispose of many odds and ends in TOOLS and ENGINE PARTS, RAKES and SHOVELS.

OTHER ITEMS INCLUDE NUTS, BOLTS, and ODDS & ENDS.

OUR NEW PARTS DEPARTMENT is as complete as we can make it. Come out for a cup of coffee. Let's get acquainted. After several years in the hardware business, I am now anxious to serve all the folks in and around Skunk Hollow.

**HAROLD (BUZZ) MALONE
SMALL ENGINE REPAIR**

"I will Mr. Potts. I just don't like the way he bullies everybody, and I think the Stanleys are doing some bad things around here. I'm going to catch them in the act one of these days."

"Just play it safe Rocky. You too Charlie. I don't want either one of you to get hurt."

"All of our friends are looking out for each other. We won't let anything happen." I gave Charlie our Seven Friends sign from the back seat. I think he saw it in the mirror because he flashed it back over his head.

"Is that some secret code Charlie?"

"Yup it is Dad. Can't talk about it."

"That's cool. My army buddies used signs all the time. Got us out of some pretty tough jams. It's great to have friends you can depend on."

"You bet it is Mr. Potts. Charlie and I are like brothers, aren't we Charlie?"

"We sure are. Sorry, I have to blow my nose again."

We finished delivering flyers well before lunchtime. Mr. Potts asked me to have lunch with them, but I thought I'd better get back to the garage. I was pretty sure my parents had a few more tasks for me and I had to stop by the hotel to get Ned before heading to HQ.

I was back at the garage in a few minutes, just in time for a little picnic. I was hoping for PB&Js or even cheese sandwiches, but Dad had this grin on his face as he put the basket out on the table. "Don't look so worried Rocky. Mrs. Brickle packed this lunch for us."

"Yes!" I blurted as I launched myself into the closest chair. I had a pretty tough morning and I was really hungry.

"She calls these sandwiches Dagwoods," said Dad. "Isn't that a cartoon character that eats these huge sandwiches with a little of everything on them?"

"Yeah, he's in the funny papers every Sunday." My favorite cartoon is still Dick Tracy, although I don't think he has a sandwich named after him. If there was it might be called Dick Tracy's Mystery Sandwich. Guess what's in it? Dad would love it.

I opened up the basket and sure enough, inside were three monster sandwiches, chips, and root beer. Mom was a good cook, but I never got root beer for lunch. If it comes up, I'm voting to stay at the hotel forever. Much less work and great food. Who wouldn't want that? "I hope I can finish this sandwich." Who am I kidding? This Dagwood is history.

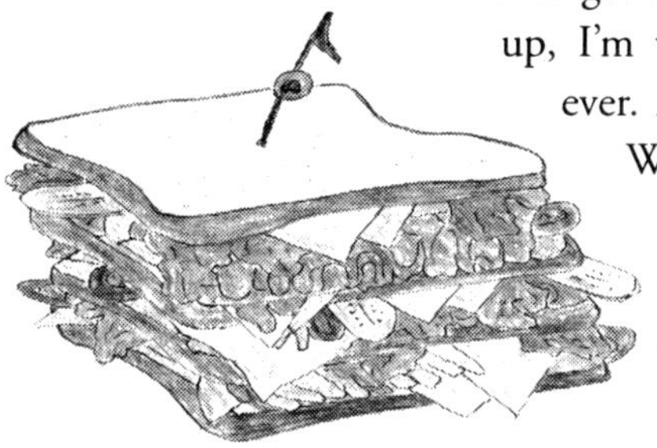

After inhaling the sandwich,

stuffing my mouth with chips, and washing everything down with root beer I was ready to roll back to the hotel to get Ned. Mom asked me to bring the basket back to Mrs. Brickle and to thank her for the terrific lunch. The basket didn't have handles so I had to tuck it under my arm and bike one-handed. That skill needed a little work. I was definitely not Rocketman on the way back to the hotel.

As I turned the corner onto Old Town Road a big, black Cadillac blasted past and just about knocked me over. Mrs. Brickle's basket went flying as I fought to stay upright. Slim Stanley had a grip on the steering wheel and a look in his eyes that told me he was more than a little angry. He yelled something at me as he passed, but his windows were up so I didn't hear him cuss. I was pretty sure he wasn't wishing me a happy birthday. Maybe I'd grab Ned at the hotel and head down to Winter's Pool Hall to see what was cooking. Willie the Wanderer or Mr. Winter would know what pushed Slim's buttons.

Ned was so excited to see me. I don't think he likes hanging out in my room by himself very much. His idea of fun is cruising the neighborhood with me. Can't blame him there. That's my idea of fun too. I thanked Mrs. Brickle for the lunch and headed out the door.

"Would you like a few cookies for the road, Rocky? They just came out of the oven."

Cookies always stop me dead in my tracks. "That would be great Mrs. Brickle. I am kinda hungry."

"Rocky, you're always hungry," yelled Cinnamon from the kitchen.

"Hey Cinnamon. I'm heading down to the pool hall to get the low-down on Slim Stanley. Want to ride along?"

"Sure, but I need to finish up these dishes."

"I'll help you finish up." We had dish washing and drying down to a science and had everything cleaned up and put away in minutes.

"I can help you clean up your room some time too Rocky. It's a disaster up there."

I had no idea what she was talking about. My room was perfect. It had that lived-in, last day of camp look. "No thanks Cinnamon. I have everything organized just the way I want it."

"Okay then. Let's make some tracks," said Cinnamon as we both grabbed another cookie and headed out the door.

"See you Mrs. B and thanks again."

"Be home by six. We're having a special dinner tonight." All of Mrs. Brickle's dinners were special. Of course I'd be there at six ready to chow down again.

We flew down to Winter's Pool Hall, bolted through the swinging doors, and bellied up to the bar. Old Man Winter was standing behind the bar.

"Where's Willie?" Cinnamon asked.

"He's out back talking to his friend, Hobo Jack."

"Hobo Jack is back? Do you have news about Lenny? Was Mr. Stanley here?" I had more questions, but thought it best to just start with three. I was following Mom's suggestion, three thankfuls, and three prayers, now, three questions.

"Have a root beer and I'll tell you all about the good news." Mr. Winter poured us each a frosty mug and filled us in on the morning events.

"I was sitting over at the far table playing a little solitaire when Hobo Jack showed up. Needless to say, Willie and I were both surprised to see him. Just as he sat down at the bar to talk to Willie, Slim Stanley blasted through the doors, arms flying, temper flaring, and bad language flowing. It wasn't a pretty picture."

"That's what he looked like when he almost ran me off the road about a half hour ago."

"Really? That guy's a menace. Anyway, Slim walked right up to Hobo Jack and yells 'I thought I told you to take that crazy Lenny Odetts on a long train trip. I gave you good money to keep him out of my way. Can't you do anything right you bum? You're fired. Give me back my money and get out of town.' Guess he didn't see me sitting at the back table when he spilled the beans."

Mr. Winter said Hobo Jack was feeling really bad about Lenny. They had a great train ride for a few days, but Lenny decided Disneyland was too far and he hadn't told his sister he was leaving. Stanley had convinced Hobo Jack that he was just a good guy and wanted to give Lenny and Hobo Jack something to remember, a free trip to California. Hobo Jack jumped at the offer. Says he'd never held that much cash before.

"He was getting Lenny out of the way so he could dig through the Odetts' house. We know what he was looking for, but Lenny outsmarted Mr. Stanley." Way to go Lenny! I hadn't even met him yet, but I knew he had to be what people in Chicago called *street smart*.

"Hobo Jack brought Lenny back and he's up with his sister right now. Willie is trying his best to console Hobo Jack in the back room. I thought things through and decided to give a friend of mine a call. He's a big city lawyer who would love to see Slim Stanley sweat a little. I think we need to shake things up around here a bit. What do you two think?"

"You're getting a lawyer? I'll be a witness. I say let's lock Slim Stanley up and throw away the keys. They can take his son too. This is way more exciting than old, boring Chicago." I couldn't wait to get on that stand in front of a real judge. 'Rocky, Super Crimefighter, do you swear to tell the truth, the whole truth, and …' Maybe our story would be published in one of my magazines. I need a real courtroom suit, not Eddie's super large confirmation suit.

"That's a great idea Mr. Winter," said Cinnamon. You can count on us to help in any way we can. Rocky, let's head to HQ. We can stop and say welcome back to Lenny on our way."

"You've got it girl." Cinnamon was always as cool as a cucumber. Me, not so much.

Cinnamon and I stopped off at the Odetts' house on the way to HQ. I was excited about meeting Lenny after a full week of searching, listening, and lots of other undercover stuff. His return signaled the end to one of our mysteries, but there were still other mysteries waiting to be solved. I was pretty sure Lenny could help out a lot.

"Rocky, when we get to the Odetts' house you need to promise to hold off on asking Lenny too many questions. I'm pretty sure that he'll share everything he knows in time, but right now he just needs to feel safe and happy. Let's not add to his stress."

"You are right Cinnamon. A good investigator always knows the right time to ask questions. I'll jot them down in my notebook for later. Let's just welcome him home and be on our way. We can talk about what to do next at HQ."

"That's what makes you a good leader Rocky. You understand people."

Cinnamon was much better at reading people than me. I was ready to charge ahead and find out about the diary, the map, removing the ledgers from the hotel, Slim Stanley's devious plan, and tons of other questions I was sure Lenny could shed some light on. I'm thankful Cinnamon's around to keep my mouth in check. "Double thumbs up Cinnamon."

Cinnamon crossed her eyes and gave me that funny smile. She's one amazing friend. I have a lot of friends in Skunk Hollow, and it feels pretty good. I think I'll tell everybody that when we get to HQ.

True to our word, we only stopped for a few minutes. Cinnamon introduced me to Lenny and he gave me a big bear hug. He wasn't at all what I expected. He was a kind of a skinny, bookworm looking guy. He reminded me of one of those scientists who travels through jungles looking for lost tribes and funny insects. Lenny wasn't much bigger than me and his clothes just kind of hung on him. I don't know why I thought of this right then, but he reminded me of one of the lost boys in that movie Peter Pan. I could see why George and his friends picked on him.

"My sister told me all about you Rocky. Thank you so much for looking in on her. I hope we can be friends. Have you seen my school?"

"I'd like to be your friend Lenny, and I love your schoolhouse. We have so much to talk about." Cinnamon gave me the eye. "But not today. We have to be on our way. We'll stop by tomorrow if you're around."

"We'll be here," said Miss Odetts. "It's so good to have Lenny back. Please thank all your friends for helping me get through the week."

"Your welcome and Aloha."

We jumped on our bikes and headed up the road to HQ. "Aloha Rocky? What's up with that?"

"It means hello and good bye in Hawaiian. I was saying both to Lenny. Pretty good, right?"

"Sure Rocky."

Chapter Eighteen

Cinnamon, Ned, and I were the last to arrive at HQ. We had a little trouble all getting up the ladder. Ned had decided he wasn't staying on the ground this time. His climb up the ladder was slow, but he was a dog. They don't normally climb ladders. He finally made it to the top and got all kinds of praise and ear scratches. He took it all in and then curled up on the rug over in a corner.

"We do have a big problem with Ned," I announced. "I knew he could make it up, but going down is going to be a problem."

"No worries," said Tommy. "I'll make a harness out of our rope and have him down in no time."

"Sounds like a plan. Speaking of plans, let's figure out what to do next. Did everyone hear that Lenny is back?"

Everyone was so excited about the news they all talked at once. It reminded me of those big family reunions. Everyone talks and no one listens. I always leave those things with sore ears, but never remember hearing anything other than the first question everyone asks: *So, how have you been?* Don't bother answering. They won't hear you anyway. I just stuff my mouth with food, mumble "Oh fine", and move on.

"One at a time, one at a time," announced Cryin' Charlie over all the voices. "Rocky, you go first."

Finally everyone quieted down and I filled them in on my morning adventures. Cinnamon continued with our trip to the pool hall and the Odetts. Tommy and Little Mouse talked about a conversation they had with their parents about the Stanleys. Sam had ridden up to Mr. Jingles and looked through the ledgers and the diary again, and Charlie filled us in on what he heard at the post office after I left.

"Okay, so what's our plan?" asked Little Mouse.

"I think the first thing we do is find out what Lenny knows about Slim Stanley's plans,' I said. "Based on what we saw in the diary and Sam's research in the ledgers, no one has found Beauregard Puce's gold. It could be still here someplace."

"Slim Stanley has been buying and selling property for quite a while. I think we need to uncover the truth about that too. Maybe we need to talk to Mr. Winter's lawyer friend to see if what he's doing is legal."

"I want to find out if Slime really did torch my grandparents' house and sent them off to see *Nagi Tanka*, the Great Spirit," Tommy said with quiet compassion.

"I want to find a way to stop Gorgeous George and the Slimeballs from picking on people all the time. He hates everybody in Old Town." Cryin' Charlie took out his handkerchief, wiped his eyes, and honked twice. We all shook our heads in agreement. George made all of us miserable.

"Let's have another picnic under the bridge tomorrow," said Cinnamon. " We can invite Lenny. He loves picnics."

"Great! It's my turn to bring the food. I know just what to make," said Sam. "You do like Spam, don't you Rocky? We have a few cans left at our store."

"Not really. That's my dad's favorite but not mine. I can bring my own lunch."

"No, it's my treat. I know you'll like what I make."

My stomach was already churning in protest and I was sure I was turning green. Maybe she was just pulling my chain. I'm never quite sure with Sam.

We spent the next few hours reorganizing HQ. I liked the way it was, but the three girls had us moving, dusting, sweeping, and polishing everything. I voted to keep the rustic look, but that went nowhere. I kept hearing "you'll appreciate it when we're done." This was truly something that I would never understand. Why mess with a good thing?

Tommy had devised a great harness to get Ned out of HQ. Come to think of it, he worked on that harness for quite a long time and got out of almost all the cleaning. No wonder he was smiling all the time I was up to my elbows updating HQ. He definitely knew more about girls than Charlie or me.

We got Ned down with out much trouble. He almost looked like he enjoyed the ride down. After watching Ned, I decided to give the old harness a try myself. It wasn't as fun as I thought it would be. Tommy's dog harness didn't exactly fit me like a glove. After watching my flight, landing, and pinched body parts, everyone else passed and took the ladder.

We had about an hour to kill, so Charlie asked if I wanted to play a little Ringer before heading back. "I'm game," I said. "What's Ringer?"

"Ringer is a marbles game. It's pretty fun. We play it at recess just about every day, except if there's snow on the ground."

I had collected a few marbles in Chicago, but never really played a game. It sounded like fun. The girls and Tommy passed on the game and decided it was time to head back. "See you mañana."

"Don't lose all your marbles Rocky," said Sam as she rode off laughing. I think that was meant to be a joke.

Charlie pulled out a bag of marbles and drew a large ring in the sand. I could tell that this was his game. I told him I didn't have any marbles and he laughed just like Sam. "That's okay. I have plenty to go around."

Ringer was a pretty easy game to learn. In just a few minutes I had learned to *knuckle down*, play my *shooter*, and collect *mibs*. The object of the game was to use your shooter to knock the other marbles out of the ring. Any that were knocked out became yours. You kept your turn as long as you hit at least one out.

Charlie was pretty good and easily beat me every game, but I didn't care. All the marbles were his anyway. I think I got a little better each time we started a new game.

"You'll be a top *mibster* in no time. Who knows, some day you might even be able to beat the school champion."

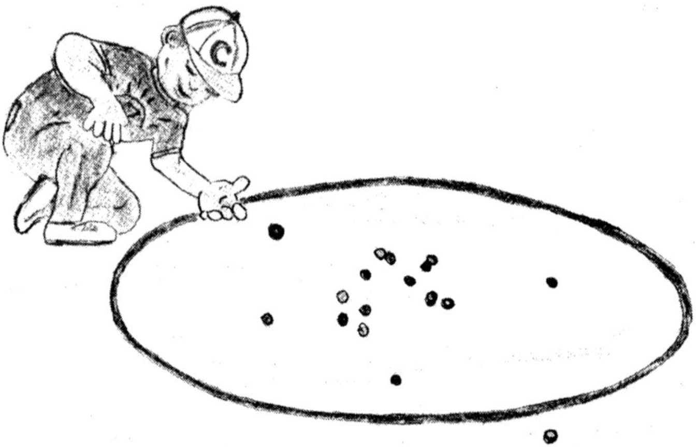

"Who's that?" I asked.

"That would be Tommy. I've seen him run the table many times. Playing him is a sure way to lose all your marbles." This time we both laughed.

I decided to swing by Mrs. Gittemeire's Thrift Shop to see if she had any used cat's eyes, onionskins, or shooters. I did have a quarter burning a hole in my pocket and thought it would be money well spent. I'd probably lose most of them anyway, but a small bag could get me in the games. I needed to push *Phantom* a little. I didn't want to be late for dinner.

I could smell spaghetti sauce and baked bread as soon as I walked through the hotel door. Spaghetti and meatballs was one of my favorite dinners. I hoped Mrs. Brickle cooked a ton because I was really hungry for some good old Italian food.

"Cinnamon, will you and Rocky set the table for seven? I've invited Lenny and Katherine over tonight to celebrate. Eddie's over at his girlfriend's house again. She's cooking him spaghetti as well. I invited both of them here, but I think they have a whole evening planned."

"You bet Mrs. B. We'll have it done in no time. Who's Katherine?"

"That's Miss Odetts," said Cinnamon. "It's great that Lenny's back. I bet he'll have lots of stories to tell."

"Rocky, wash your hands before you set the table."

"Yes ma'am." My mother cared a lot more about personal hygiene than I did. Those were adult words. To me clean was no visible dirt or bad smell. I gave my hands the look and sniff test and decided a little soap might be the right path.

"Let's have Lenny sit between us so we can both talk to him."

"Good idea Cinnamon. I'll have my notebook handy just in case I get a chance to ask him some questions about our case."

"I don't think that's a good idea Rocky. Let's just let Lenny enjoy the dinner. We can ask questions later."

"You're right. Maybe I'll just take a few notes."

Mom interjected "You need to keep your notebook in your pocket Rocky. This is a celebration dinner, not a board meeting."

The Odetts arrived right at six o'clock. Miss Odetts brought dessert, strawberry shortcake with homegrown strawberries and whipped cream. This had all the makings of a triple-A rated meal. All we needed was some frosty mugs of root beer and everything would be perfect. I'd be eating like a king.

"Would you pour the milk for all the kids Rocky? Cinnamon, can you make sure all the adults get coffee?"

Rats! Maybe Mrs. B has some Ovaltine. That stuff can make milk at least drinkable.

"Everyone find a seat," said Cinnamon. "Lenny, will you sit right here between me and Rocky?" We all picked our places around the table and Mrs. B brought out the biggest bowl of spaghetti I think I'd ever seen. "I heard a few people were hungry," she said winking at me.

"Let's all bow our heads and think about something to be thankful for," said Mrs. B I was glad she didn't ask us to think of three thankfuls. I was way too hungry to work on that again,

I was thankful that Lenny was back safe and sound, and I was thankful for this great food. "Through the teeth and over the tongue. Look out stomach 'cause here it comes." I must have said that out loud. Everyone was looking at me. Lenny laughed so hard I thought he'd fall out of his chair. I'd work on being a little more quiet the rest of the meal. I was pretty sure my parents would appreciate that.

Between mouthfuls, Lenny filled us in on his train ride out West. He said he travelled through Huron, Pierre, a place called Wall Drug, and the Badlands. Most of the time they travelled by boxcar with other hobos. Once Hobo Jack was able to get them into a caboose by offering to cook a meal for the people running the train. That didn't last long since Hobo Jack insisted that everyone would love his beans and canned meat surprise. By the time they reached the Black Hills Lenny had decided that he wanted to skip Disneyland and come home. He said Hobo Jack was a good friend and had no problem finding trains going back East.

They had travelled over seven hundred miles on several different trains, but never crossed the state border. Lenny said it was a great adventure but was going to give up hopping trains in the future. He decided cars and buses were the best way to travel on a vacation although some day he thought an airplane ride might be fun.

"What was your favorite part?" I asked. I thought questions like that would be okay. No probing or stressful questions.

"I liked Dinosaur Park in Rapid City. I even got a souvenir to add to my collection. It was a long walk up that hill, but I loved the view and they had a teacher there to tell us all about when dinosaurs walked the earth. I'm going to talk about that in my next lesson at our schoolhouse."

"Can I come? I can't wait to hear all about dinosaurs Lenny." Cinnamon had told me about Lenny and the schoolhouse. I'd probably learn more in that classroom than I would hanging out at Skunk Hollow School.

"You sure can. I'll be up there tomorrow." Lenny was all smiles. I could tell he was excited to be back home and among friends.

"Rocky, can you help me with something in the kitchen?" Cinnamon pushed her chair away from the table and walked into the kitchen.

"We need to get to the school tomorrow morning to erase the board, and fix up what the Slimeballs damaged. Lenny would really be crushed if he found out those punks were messing up his pride and joy."

"Let's do it right away tomorrow. I'm supposed to help my parents again, but they'll understand. Let's see if we can round up our friends to help out. Even if we can't fix everything, Lenny will appreciate our effort."

"Sounds like a plan," said Cinnamon. "Let's head back to the table. Are you ready for strawberry shortcake?"

"I was born ready." Cinnamon gave me one of her goofy smiles.

We laughed, told stories, and talked the night away. Before I knew it I was saying goodnight to everyone and heading for bed. Cinnamon and I told Lenny we'd meet him at 10 o'clock at the schoolhouse. If we got an early start we could round up our friends and have everything back in order before Lenny arrived. I wasn't quite sure how to repair the carvings in the desks though. Maybe Mr. Two Feathers could give us some suggestions. He made all kinds of things out of wood. The sawmill would have to be our first stop.

Chapter Nineteen

I darted out of bed just as the morning sun began peaking through my window. It didn't take me very long to brush my teeth, throw on some clothes, pull on my baseball cap, and slide down the banisters to the first floor. If crimefighting didn't work out for me in later life, I knew I'd make a great firefighter. I was sure I could be ready to fight fires in a matter of minutes and sliding down a fire pole would be a piece of cake. I don't like to be around fires much though. That could be a major drawback.

Cinnamon was already waiting for me in the dining room. "Good morning Rocky. I was worried that you might oversleep. Another couple of minutes and I would have been knocking on your door."

I had a quick vision of Cinnamon knocking at my door and me answering in my red long johns with the butt flap. Not a pretty sight. Maybe I should get some new PJs just in case that does happen down the road. Normally, I don't care what I look like when I'm sleeping, but red flannels and a girl at my door is probably not a good combination. Maybe I should just sleep in my jeans. That would work.

"Are you up for some cereal and toast this morning? We should eat quick and head over to the school."

"I'm up for anything except maybe bran flakes," I said.

"How about Eddie's favorite cereal? He calls it 'the breakfast of champions.' It's not too bad with a few blueberries. How many slices of toast do you want?"

"Just two for starters. I'll eat another bowl of cereal if I'm still hungry."

"You must have a hollow leg to store all the food you eat."

"No hollow spots. Just bones and tons of muscle." I showed her my biceps. "Move over Superman."

"Yea, I can see it," chuckled Cinnamon. "I'll definitely call on you for those heavy lifting jobs. Now finish up so we can get going."

"Okay," I said giving my biceps one more flex. "These babies really pack a punch."

"If you say so." I was pretty sure the smile on her face was one of sheer admiration.

My mother wasn't around so I felt I could shovel the food in pretty fast. Cinnamon didn't seem to care. I think she probably watched Eddie pack it in at the dinner table. He ate more than me, probably to give him that edge he was talking about. "I think I'll have another bowl."

"I'll pack some snacks Rocky. We need to get to the schoolhouse pronto."

"That works for me."

It was a quick ride to the sawmill to see if Tommy and Little Mouse were around this early in the morning. Ned led the way right to their doorstep. My dog must have some bloodhound in him. He's never been to the sawmill before, but somehow he figured out where we were heading. Or maybe he was listening to us talk this morning. Ned is crazy smart for a dog.

Tommy was helping his dad cut some huge logs and Sarah was busy hanging laundry on a clothesline next to the house. Hanging laundry wasn't an easy task for Sarah because of her size, but she had established a routine that seemed to work for her. She had dragged a small stump from the woodpile and placed it under the clothesline where the next piece of clothing was to be hung. Then with two clothespins in her teeth and clothing in her hands, she'd jump up on the stump, throw the clothing onto the line, grab the line with one hand, grab the clothespins with the other and secure the clothing before she tumbled to the ground.

"That was amazing Little Mouse," I said as we pulled up on our bikes.

"Hi Cinnamon and Rocky. What's amazing?" she asked as the next piece went up on the line.

"You hanging clothes," I said.

"You're silly Rocky. How else would I do it?"

I didn't have any idea how I could improve on her routine nor could I ever copy it. I could see the headlines if I ever tried. *Rocky Malone, while attempting to hang clothes in his back yard, becomes Skunk Hollow's first human pretzel. Authorities are working hard to unravel clothesline, pins, and clothing from his body. Rocky couldn't be reached for comment.*

As Tommy joined us, Cinnamon filled them in on our plan to quickly get to the schoolhouse and repair some of the damage done by George and his buddies. Both were eager to join us. I asked Tommy if his dad had anything we could use to repair the gouges in the desks.

"All we need is some sawdust, wood glue, and some stain to match the desks," said Tommy. "It won't dry right away though. We'll have to tell Lenny what happened."

"I'm sure Lenny will appreciate our efforts. He really loves that schoolhouse," said Cinnamon.

After leaving the sawmill we biked to Torgeson's to let Sam know where we were going. She was busy putting our lunch together and said she would join us in a bit. She promised to call Charlie to let him know where we were headed. "Why don't we just have our picnic at the schoolhouse? We'll all be there anyway."

"Good idea Sam. That way we'll have plenty of time to talk to Lenny and he could join us for lunch." I was hoping Sam was okay with making a little extra. If she really was planning on some more Spam sandwiches Lenny could have mine. I'd fill up on Cinnamon's snacks.

We made it to the schoolhouse before nine and quickly made the repairs and cleaned up before Lenny arrived. We thought it best to tell Lenny about the vandals right away. We didn't know how he'd react, but seeing the Slimeball's handiwork, we were all still angry.

Lenny arrived right at ten. "Hello Cinnamon. Hi Tommy. It's nice to see you Sarah. Good day Rocky, and how's Ned today?" I bet if all the desks were filled, Lenny would have a greeting for each person. He's sure a friendly guy.

We all said hi back and Cinnamon filled Lenny in on what had happened while he was gone. Lenny didn't show much emotion, but his lower lip quivered as she showed him the damaged desks.

"Those guys are not nice people," Lenny said as he examined our handiwork. Thank you for repairing everything."

"We know how much you love this school," said Little Mouse. "We couldn't just leave it."

"I'd sure like to find a way to teach those jerks a lesson," said Cinnamon. "They just don't get it." Cinnamon was usually so calm, but this had sparked a fire in her.

"We will," said Tommy.

"I brought my box of treasures," said Lenny. "After what I heard last night, I'm not taking any chances on losing my stuff."

Just then Charlie and Sam showed up. "Hello Charlie Potts. Good morning Samantha," said Lenny. "We almost have a full classroom today." We all greeted each other and helped Sam bring in the lunch she had prepared. I was hungry already, but knew I'd have to wait a while.

"What treasures do you have with you?" I asked. I was always up for a little show and tell. Who knows? Maybe he has Beauregard Puce's long lost map.

Lenny poured out his box on the front desk and talked about each piece in great detail. I learned all about the history of Mickey Mouse, why a rabbit's foot is so lucky, and why you need to throw spilled salt over your shoulder. I had lots of questions for Lenny, but decided to save them until he was done. We could all tell he was excited to share his stories.

"Here's a new treasure I got on my trip. It's a Tyrannosaurus Rex or T-Rex.

It's just like what I saw in the Black Hills. They were the meanest of all the dinosaurs and could eat up to five hundred pounds in one bite.

"Kinda looks like Gorgeous George," squeaked Little Mouse.

"Yeah, but not quite as ugly," said Cryin' Charlie.

We all had a good laugh and then let Lenny get on with his story about all the other dinosaurs he saw. By the time he finished I had decided to convince my parents to go to the Black Hills next summer. I'd tell them I wanted to see the presidents at Mount Rushmore. I was pretty sure dinosaurs wouldn't be high on my mother's list of fun adventures, but she'd be up for a visit to a monument. She likes that kind of stuff.

"Hey, isn't Deadwood out there?" I asked.

"Yes it is," said Cinnamon. "That's where Wild Bill Hickok met his end. Aces and Eights, the Deadman's hand. They say Wild Bill's spirit still haunts the town."

"Guess I'll pass on that trip. Ghosts don't interest me that much." I was hoping nobody wanted to tell more ghost stories.

"Hey, there could be another storm tonight, said Sam. "I have another hair-raiser to share. It's not about ghosts either. It's about trolls."

"I think I have to go somewhere with my parents," I stated in what I hoped came across calm and sincere. "I'll have to pass."

"Don't worry Rocky. I'll talk to your parents. They won't want to be out on a cold, dark, stormy night."

"Thanks Cinnamon. You're a great help," I said and didn't really mean it. I'd have to think of another way out.

"I have one more treasure to show you, but you must promise not to tell anyone. It's my Uncle Beau's map of buried gold. It's pretty much useless, but I know that Mr. Stanley is looking for it." Lenny carefully unfolded the old, torn page from the diary we'd all seen at Mr. Jingles.

"I've been looking for this treasure for years and haven't found anything. Do you see that X on the map? It looks like Uncle Beau buried the gold near an oak tree next to a lake. If this is Skunk Hollow Lake and it's buried thirty feet or thirty paces from the tree, it could be in my back yard, or it could be under my house."

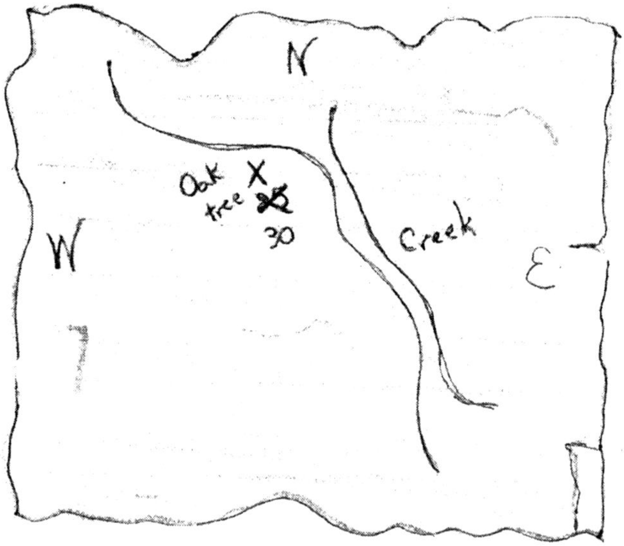

"That shouldn't be so hard to find if it's in your back yard," said Sam.

"Digging under the house might be a problem though," I added. "We'd need a jack hammer for the concrete.

"There are tons of oak trees between the bridge and the end of our property," said Lenny. "The map doesn't tell us how big the tree was or if a treasure was buried thirty feet, thirty yards, or thirty paces away." We were all beginning to see why no one ever found the gold.

"And remember, Beauregard Puce hid his gold over eighty years ago," stated Charlie. Lot's of things change over that much time."

"I have an idea," said Tommy. "Let's take our logging raft on a little trip tomorrow morning. We can go north along the edge of the lake and check out all the old oak trees. Maybe one will stand out and we'll get lucky."

"You have a raft? We could float down the river like Huck Finn and his friend Jim." I was sure Sam would be impressed with my knowledge of Mark Twain's book.

"No river around here Rocky, Just the lake and Badwater Creek," said Tommy. It's still lots of fun though. We could do a little catfishin' if you want. Lots of 'em around here."

"I'm in," said Cinnamon. "Who else wants to go?" Everyone was eager to do a little rafting, including Lenny.

"We should all wear swim suits in case we get wet," I said. "Lenny, wait till you see Charlie's suit. It's a hoot."

"I've seen it. I have one just like it," Lenny announced. We bought them together at Mrs. Gittemeire's Thrift Shop. We could stop in today to see if she has any more on the rack if you want one."

"No, that's all right. I'll stick with my old faded blue. Who's hungry?"

Sam opened up a huge basket loaded with tons of meats, cheeses and tiny little buns. There was ham, beef, salami, pepperoni, turkey, cheddar, Swiss, Colby, goat cheese from Mr. Jingles, and a few cheeses I couldn't pronounce. She also brought pickles, mustard, mayo, horseradish, and my favorite, ketchup. "I baked the buns myself. My parents helped me slice the meat and cheese. Dig in."

Sam didn't have to say that twice. I grabbed a paper plate, loaded up, and chowed down. "Thanks for not bringing my dad's favorite lunch."

"Your welcome Rocky. I guess that's a compliment."

We had pushed the desks into a circle so we could eat and talk at the same time. I let everyone else do most of the talking. I didn't want any of the food go to waste so I went back to fill my plate quite a few times.

"I think we just found another entry into Skunk Hollow's pie eating contest this fall," said Cinnamon.

"There's pie too? Good thing I saved some room. Why's everybody laughing?"

We talked, laughed, ate, and listened to more of Lenny's stories. By two o'clock we decided lunch was over and we needed to head back. It only took us a few minutes to clean up and put the classroom back in shape. Lenny gave us his official thumbs up. We all knew he was happy to be back in his schoolhouse. We decided that 8:00 am was a good time to meet at the sawmill for the raft ride along the shores of Skunk Hollow Lake. I agreed with the time, but would have preferred sleeping in until say noon.

On the way back to the hotel Cinnamon pulled her bike up next to me. "Rocky, Sam and I were talking and we have a surprise for you when we get back to the hotel. We have to hurry a little though. Things start hopping at 3:00 sharp. Are you cool with that?"

"Cool as a mackerel on thin ice." I read that in my detective magazine. They probably had a new card game they wanted to show me or maybe we had to catch some frogs.

We dropped Sam's basket off at the mercantile and continued on to the hotel. Tommy and Sarah headed for home and Charlie road across the bridge to the new post office. Cinnamon, Sam, Ned, and I made our final stop in the lobby of the hotel.

"Quick Rocky. Turn on the TV. It's time for American Bandstand."

I turned on the TV and plunked my tired body down on the couch. "Hey look at all those kids packed together like sardines in a can. What's up with that?"

We watched the whole show from beginning to end. Some of the songs I recognized, but many were new to my ears. Every song had a different dance move. I especially liked the Elvis tunes.

"Off the couch Big Boy. Sam and I are teaching you how to dance."

"Dance lessons? Me? I don't think so."

And within a split second Sam was just inches from my face. Her piercing green eyes froze me in my tracks. "You don't have a choice," she said. And I didn't.

Cinnamon brought out the phonograph and a whole bunch of records. "I picked out a few that I know you've heard Rocky. Are you ready?"

"No." I knew I was trapped, but they were friends and I knew they'd be patient with me. At least Cinnamon would be. The first 45 on the record player was Jerry Lee Lewis' song, *Whole Lotta Shakin' Goin' On*. I had watched Eddie's friends the other night so I just stomped around a little and shook my arms and legs.

"Not too bad," said Cinnamon.

"Yea, that was a good start. Now this next one, see if you can kinda dance to the beat." For Sam, that was almost a compliment.

"This next song is called *Shake, Rattle, and Roll.* Just follow our

lead and clap to the music at the beginning."

I didn't think this was much different than the first except for the spinning around parts. I was getting the hang of it, but after two songs I needed a break. "That's enough for today. I need to check on Gerty in my room."

"Not a chance. Cinnamon, let's show Rocky the Bunny Hop. I think he can do it without falling down."

"The Bunny Hop? I thought we were just going to stick with the shaking stuff."

We tried a few more songs and I even tried to do what they called the Bop. Cinnamon said I wasn't quite ready to bring that one out on stage. I agreed completely. I had a few Tin Man moves that might get a laugh.

"We need to try a few slow ones," said Sam. My favorite *is Earth Angel.* Rocky, you'll be my partner and I'll show you the steps."

Not only were we holding hands, I managed to step on Sam's feet at least a dozen times. I don't think I added much to the song.

Earth Angel "Sorry" *Earth Angel* "Sorry" *Will you be mine?* "Sorry".

By the time the song reached *a vision of your hap-happiness* "Sorry" Sam wasn't happy and was ready to have Cinnamon be my partner.

"I think I'll pass," said Cinnamon. "We'll just go with group and line dances on Saturday night."

My face had to be bright red. I also learned that girls can make you sweat, even when you're not hot. I knew I had two left feet and I probably wouldn't be anyone's dance partner in the near future. James Brown, your job is safe. I'd better stick to singing and solving mysteries. That brings out my true talents. "Thanks for the lessons you two. I need to go up to my room for a while." I thought I could maybe hide out there until tomorrow. Maybe Mom could bring up some dinner later.

"Okay Rocky. See you tomorrow. Really, my toes don't hurt that much."

"See you later alligator," I said as I bolted up the stairs. At least I could handle those steps, even if it they weren't dance steps.

I did manage to make it down to dinner. Hunger won out over embarrassment. Thankfully Cinnamon came to my rescue by giving me a compliment and things were back to normal.

"Sam and I gave Rocky some dance lessons today. He's really doing quite well. Saturday night should be a blast."

Cinnamon really was a great friend. I knew I'd never win a dance contest, but I'd always have a partner if I had to be out on the dance floor. I've been told that dancing is a requirement at weddings and sock hops. I'll try to be busy on those nights.

Chapter Twenty

I went to bed early, but Wednesday morning still came way too soon. Whoever thought up meeting at 8:00 in the morning was Looney Tunes. Something in my head was telling me stay in bed. Someone was pounding on my door and it was getting louder by the minute.

"Rocky, are you awake? Can I come in?"

What's Cinnamon doing up so early? "Yes … I mean no. I'm not …"

Too late! Cinnamon opened my door and stepped inside.

"That was a fun day yesterday Rocky. Just so you know, I'll be your dance partner whenever you want. Oh, you're not dressed yet. Nice jammies. I really like the color. Red's my favorite."

"Thanks Cinnamon. Can we talk downstairs after I'm dressed?"

"Okay, don't be long. Need any help picking out clothes?"

"No thanks. I'm good," I said pulling my sheets around me. Cinnamon turned and headed down the steps. I threw myself back on the bed, covered in sheets. Cinnamon is a good friend, but she's still a girl, and she was in my room looking at my PJs while I'm in them. This isn't good for my ego. I really think I need a sign on my door. Maybe *Do Not Enter*, although that sounds like I have something to hide. I did, my naked body, but Mom wouldn't understand. Maybe *Enter at Your Own Risk* would be good. No, girls like to take risks and they'd come right in. Maybe I should just lock the door. It was a hotel room after all. I'd ask Mrs. B for a key.

We had country-style omelets with toast and jelly for breakfast. The omelets were filled with ham, cheese, potatoes, onions, and peppers. Mrs. B sure could cook. I could have stayed right there and had another one, but we needed to be on the road in short order. I washed everything down with a big glass of OJ, hid a couple of burps, and took my plate to the kitchen.

"That was amazing Mrs. B I'm packed to the brim."

"You're so welcome Rocky. I'll handle the dishes today. Don't want to keep you from your mission."

"Thanks again," I said. I guess we were on a mission. I didn't really think we'd find Beauregard Puce's gold today, but I was going to be rafting for the first time ever. Tom Sawyer, Huck Finn, and Rocky Malone floating down the river on a big, old raft looking for a grand adventure. Maybe I should write a book.

We all met at Two Feathers' Saw Mill at eight o'clock. Tommy had the raft ready to go, complete with poles and rudder.

"Okay," said Tommy. "Climb aboard. Sarah, you take the rudder. Lenny and I will take the poles. Everyone else should sit near the middle to keep it balanced. Everybody can have a turn poling once you see how it's done. The three of us have been on this raft lots of times fishing and floating logs."

I was a little worried that Ned would be a problem, but he jumped right on and parked himself right in the middle of the raft. Cinnamon and Sam seemed pretty comfortable as well. Charlie and I got on last, and we were both a little shaky. "Ready to set sail Captain," I said in my best pirate voice as I found my spot right next to Ned.

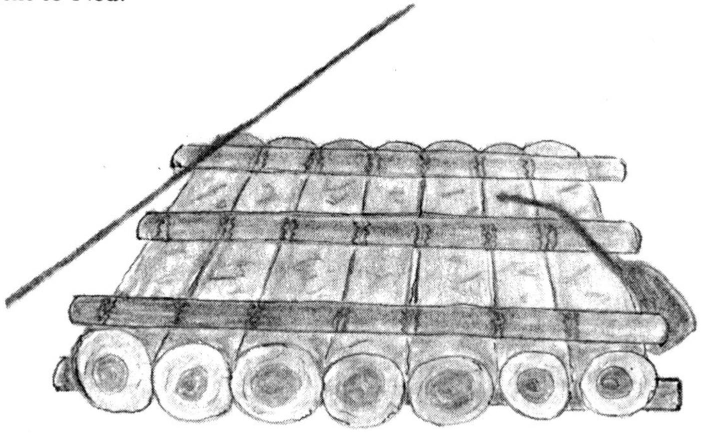

"No sails and no anchor Rocky. We use the poles to move up stream and beach it whenever we pull in to shore."

"Oh yeah. I knew that." Of course, I didn't, but I thought my pirate voice sounded pretty good. "This is the life, sailing the Seven Seas."

Lenny must have liked my pirate voice too. He threw out a few "Shiver me timbers" and "Yo, ho, hos" along the way. This was going to be a great day rafting, looking for treasure, and maybe singing some pirate songs. I wasn't a good dancer, but wait until I let loose on some old songs of the sea.

We moved the raft out to the middle of Badwater Creek and poled upstream under the bridge and into the lake. I didn't like the idea of going under the bridge, but Tommy assured us that it was safe. I wasn't so sure. We could actually touch the beams as we passed under. They looked as bad and weather-beaten under the bridge as on top. The only difference I could see was down here the wood was green and slimy.

The creek opened up onto the lake just a few hundred yards before we reached the lakeside of our house. "Hey look. There's my mom out planting some flowers around the patio. Hi Mom!" I yelled.

"Hello out there. Rocky, you be careful now. Don't fall in. Do you have a life vest?"

"I'm okay Mom. It's really shallow here. See you later today."

"Stop by when you get hungry. We can cook some hotdogs out here on the patio. I'll get plenty for all your friends."

"Thanks Mrs. Malone. We'll be back here about noon," said Tommy. He must have some kind of time schedule for our adventure. Noon sounded great for lunch, but I might get hungry earlier. "Did anyone think to bring some snacks?"

"I brought pemmican," said Sarah.

"I brought some cookies," announced Sam.

"Fudge," said Charlie.

"I just brought my appetite," I announced. "That probably doesn't count."

"Okay everybody. According to Lenny's map we might be near the buried treasure. Let's start looking for big, old oak trees near the water." Cinnamon had good map skills. If anyone could make sense out of that old piece of paper, she could. "Do you have the map with you Lenny. I'd like to see it again."

I remembered everything on the map, but another look wouldn't hurt. Lenny pulled the map from his shirt pocket and passed it around. "It really doesn't tell us much, but just maybe something will click."

Travelling up the shoreline was slow going. I didn't realize how poling really worked until today. We didn't do much with rafts in Chicago. Tommy and Lenny stuck their poles into the lake bottom and walked along the edge of the raft. By pushing against the poles and walking from the back to the front, we moved along only the length of the raft with each trip. I could tell that they had done this many times together. It was a smooth ride and the raft never seemed to stop moving, even when they pulled their poles and walked to the front to start another pass. This might be trouble for me though. I wasn't sure I could even stand up.

"Are you ready to try this Rocky? You can give Lenny a break."

"Sure. I think I got it." I did up until the time I didn't pull the pole out of the water on one of my passes. I fell into the water just like a sailor walking the plank.

"Are you okay Rocky?" asked Cinnamon in a very concerned voice.

"I'm fine, just a little wet. Maybe I can just push from here. I can stand on the bottom."

"Come on back up Rocky," said Tommy. "The lake bottom here is really muddy and lots of weeds. You'll get the hang of poling in a few more tries."

Okay, but what if I don't."

"You'll get wet again," laughed Charlie.

"I can't wait for your turn. Hope you brought a towel."

"Look at that big tree right there," said Sam. "It looks old and dead, but I think it could be the one."

I got really excited. This must be how miners must have felt during the old gold rush days. We've got the fever. Maybe digging for gold was my new career. Another possible news flash in the Skunk Hollow paper: *Rocky Finds the Golden Rock*. It could happen.

The tree was just past our garage very close to Miss Odetts garden by the lake. We all agreed to take a closer look. "This was one of the first trees I looked at years ago," said Lenny. "I gave up on it though. I don't think it's an oak and I think it's too close to the water. Still might be worth another look though."

Lenny and Tommy maneuvered the raft onto shore. I was already in the water so I helped by pushing from the back. We beached it and everyone scrambled off. Since I was in the water, Ned thought he should get in too. When we finally joined the rest of the team, Ned shook himself off and got everybody wet. Good thing we were all wearing swim suits.

Lenny was right about the tree. I'm no expert, but the bark didn't look like the oaks by the hotel and the trunk was practically in the water. Unless the shoreline had changed, we couldn't believe anyone would bury a treasure that close to water.

"We should mark all the trees that are possibilities," I said. "We could come back later and do some pacing and digging at our best sites."

"Good idea Rocky," said Tommy as he pulled out a knife and carved a small 7 on a soft rock near the base of the tree.

"Where'd that knife come from?" I asked.

"Oh, this is a gift from Grandfather."

"No, I mean how did it get here? I've never seen it before."

"It's more powerful Indian magic. I keep it hidden in this sheath strapped to my waist. It's always with me except at school. Knives make teachers nervous."

"They make me nervous too, especially the big, sharp ones. I heard Jim Bowie carried a knife that was over a foot long. Now that's a scary knife."

"This is just a little carving knife I use to sharpen sticks and cut pemmican. It really comes in handy."

"I can see that." Maybe I could ask my dad for a folding pocketknife for Christmas. I asked for a BB gun last year, but Mom took that off my list. She thought I might shoot my eye out or something.

We didn't bring along any tools or shovels to dig around the trees. That would have to come later. Our mission today was just to locate trees that could possibly be the one Beauregard Puce marked on his map. I did bring my notebook along though. I let Cinnamon draw a map of the shoreline and then we'd mark the trees that made our list. I had put my notebook in a plastic bag early this morning. Sometimes I do think ahead.

By eleven o'clock we had poled our way past the path to HQ and could see Winter's Barn on the north peninsula. We were positive that none of the oak trees up this way would make our list.

"I think we should turn around and float back to the Malone's for some hotdogs," said Tommy. We were all running out of gas and snacks so everyone agreed.

"I think I'd like to get off here and stop in to see my good friend, The Goatman," said Lenny. "It's not far from here and I know he'll be happy to see me."

"Sure, but you'll be missing my famous tube steaks," I said.

"Tube steaks?" asked Little Mouse. "I thought we were having hotdogs."

"We are. That's what I call them. It's just a little joke."

"I don't get why that's funny."

"Lenny, could I make a quick drawing of your map before you leave?" asked Cinnamon. "I promise no one else but us will see it, especially Slim Stanley."

"Why don't you just take it with you? I can stop by the hotel later to pick it up."

"That would be great," said Sam. We'll be very careful with it. We know it's one of your treasures."

We said our goodbyes to Lenny and headed back down the shoreline to the Malone patio. Tommy steered the raft into a light current so we no longer needed to pole our way. To pass the time, we broke out two cane poles Tommy brought along and did a little trolling for catfish. We used bits of pemmican for bait. It worked pretty good. I caught my first catfish and man, was he ugly! Tommy said we should throw it back because it was only a couple of pounds. I decided to let someone else try for the big one and took a turn on the rudder. That was much more fun.

My dad and mother had everything ready of us when we arrived. Dad had picked up a wooden picnic table from Tommy and Sarah's dad. "It's just what we need back here when we want to enjoy the view."

I had to admit, it did look pretty good back here. With flowers, plants, a mowed lawn, and a new table, I was beginning to think this might just work for our home.

Dad had built a little fire in a pit he created close to the beach. We each found a long stick and roasted our tube steaks over the open flame. Mom put out all the fixings and I showed everyone how to make up the best Chicago-style chilidogs ever. Everyone loved 'em. We were seven chowhounds.

"We have a special treat for dessert," announced Mom. "I picked up marshmallows, graham crackers, and chocolate bars at Torgeson's this morning. Hope you didn't throw your sticks away."

"S'mores!" exclaimed Charlie. "I'm in heaven." We all scrambled to get our sticks, roasted marshmallows, and ate until we were ready to burst. Now, that's good food. Maybe I could turn this into a little business: *Rocky's Best Chicago Dogs and S'mores. You'll love 'em.*

"Hey everybody," I said swallowing my last piece of chocolate. "I was thinking about the seven steps to solving a mystery and I think it might help to go through them with our maps in front of us."

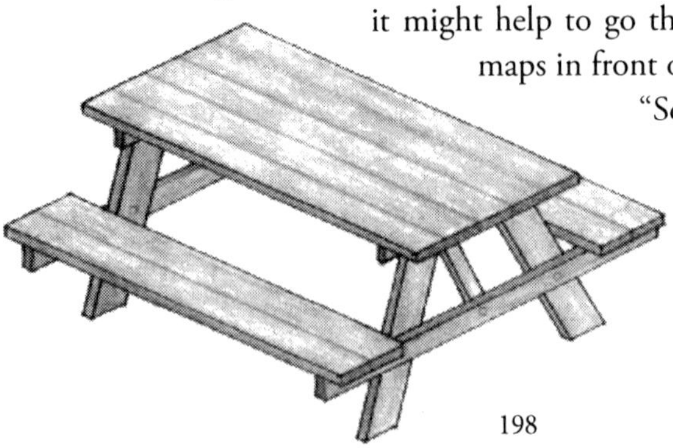

"Sounds like a plan," said Cryin' Charlie. "I'm in."

We cleared the picnic table and all stared at the two

maps in front of us. "First we examine and record the facts," I said.

"From the old diary, we know that Captain Puce had some gold and he buried it," stated Sam to get us started.

"We have his map," said Cinnamon, "even though it's poorly drawn. We know he buried it under a tree near some water."

"No one ever found it," said Charlie.

"Any other facts?' I asked. No one came up with any. "Okay, lets move on. What was the motive?"

"That's easy," said Sarah. "That Puce guy buried the gold because he thought people were trying to steal it from him."

"I know what's next," remarked Tommy. We already did it. Expand the search." We all looked at Cinnamon's map for clues.

I was concentrating on the old map, but it was hard to get my bearings because from where I was sitting, I was seeing it upside down. Then it came to me. "Sam, do you remember Beauregard's last entry? He crossed out west and wrote down east. The map was the next page in his diary."

"That's right, but what does that tell us?"

"He was lost again," said Charlie.

"Right. Now look at the map with the N on the bottom. I think

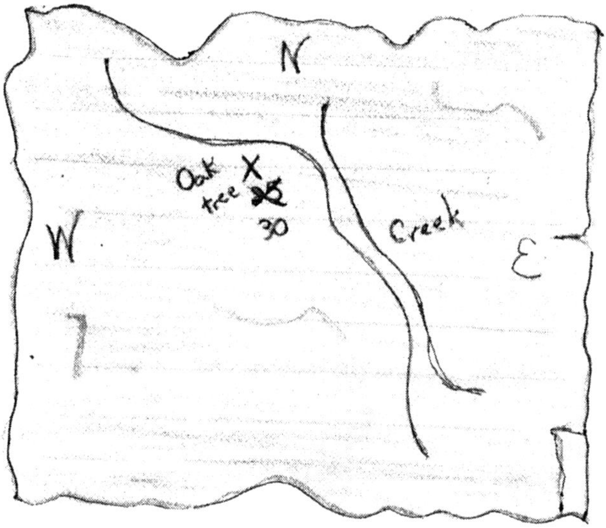

his north might actually be south.

"That could mean he buried the gold on the other side of Badwater Creek," said Sam picking up on my idea. "Puce thought he was on the west side of the creek, but he was actually on the east."

"There's only one tree on that side of the creek," said Tommy. "It's a big, old oak straight across the swimming hole next to Big Island."

"I think we'd better make a trip to Big Island right away," said Cinnamon.

"We could head down there on the raft right now," said Tommy. "We just need to stop off at the mill for some long rope and a few shovels."

"Congrats Rocky. You may have just solved Skunk Hollow's oldest mystery."

"Thanks Sam, but we haven't found anything yet. We're just being good detectives following the clues." I'd take the compliment, but actually it was just blind luck that I was looking at the map upside down. It was a real long shot that we'd find anything, but a true detective follows every lead. If we did hit pay dirt, I might just have to open a detective service. I could still sell hotdogs and s'mores part time.

Cleaning up after lunch was a piece of cake. A little water on the fire, pack up all the leftovers, hose down the table, and wash off with a little beach sand and lake water. Scrubbing with sand was Tommy's idea. He called it nature's cleaner. The chocolate, marshmallow, and chili came off great, but I did smell a little like a catfish when I was done. I probably wouldn't clean up that way if I was planning on going to church or doing a slow dance with a girl.

It only took us a few minutes to get our raft moving again. With a good current and smooth steering, we were at the mill in short order. Tommy ran up to the mill and grabbed some rope, a shovel, a pick, and a few other tools he thought we could use. Seven friends were on their way to find the hidden treasure. Of the seven, only one of us was calm. Ned took his place in the middle of the raft and acted like this whole adventure was no big deal. Everyone else was talking nonstop but no one was really listening.

We traveled around a small bend in the creek and Big Island came into view. The creek split at the island. Off to the left was the swimming hole we were at just a few days ago. I could still feel my hugely successful belly flop. Off to the right on the far bank stood one massive oak tree. I couldn't believe I could get even more excited, but I was. I tried to think of something brilliant to say, but all I could come up with was "Hello Mamma!"

"Funny name for a tree," said Charlie. "But if it is the one, I don't care if you call it Rip Van Winkle."

"Who's that?" I asked. "Must be some local big shot."

"Speaking of big shots, guess who just pulled up by the bath house?" asked Cinnamon as she pointed at a big, shiny Cadillac.

"Oh no!" exclaimed Sarah. "What does he want?"

"I have no idea," Sam said, "but I know we can't show any interest in that tree. He'll figure out that were up to something. Let's not give him any ideas."

"Okay, here's the plan," I said. "Let's anchor the raft in the middle of the swimming hole and pretend we brought it here to swim and dive. Tommy, can we use some of that rope and the pick to make an anchor?"

"Got it."

We maneuvered the raft around, pulled off our T-shirts, and did a few cannonballs off the side. Slim stepped out of his car and moved to the shore.

"Hey, Little Malone," he yelled. "I've been looking for you all day. I saw you go under the bridge a while back and thought I'd catch you down here. Come on over here. We need to talk."

"There's no way I'm going over there," I said just loud enough for all my friends to hear.

"Sorry Mr. Stanley," yelled Cinnamon. "Rocky's not a good swimmer. He needs to stay on the raft."

"Fine. I'll have my say from here. You can all hear this. Malone, since you arrived, you and your little friends have made life unbearable for my son George. He says you call him names, send your dog after him and his friends, and even get people to wreck his bike. I'm telling you, it stops now. If I hear any more reports, I'll be dealing with your parents and then the county sheriff. I got him elected. I can call in a favor any time. Get my drift?"

"Yes sir, but you need to hear my side of the story."

"Rocky," whispered Sam as she grabbed my arm. "He's a bully and a blowhard. He'll never listen."

"I don't need your story. I'm done here." And then the big bully got in his big caddy, backed out onto the old gravel road and sped away in a cloud of dust. I hoped he hit every pothole along the way.

"That was fun," said Tommy. "Remind me to bean George the next time we see him. My sling and I will be ready."

I was shaking like a leaf. "That guy is really scary. I think I'd rather take on a vampire rat."

"Don't worry Rocky," said Charlie. "He bullies everybody. He thinks his kid's an angel. He even tried to bully the principal last year. All he did was manage to get George suspended. She put him in his place."

"Maybe I can talk to her. I could use some help."

"You'll get your chance Rocky," said Sam. "She's your teacher this year."

I wasn't excited about our adventure any more. I just wanted to go back to the hotel, give my mom a big hug, and curl up on my bed with my dog and snake. I had never had an adult talk to me like that. I wonder if I could convince my parents to move back to Chicago. I really didn't want to give up my friends, but this was too much for me to handle.

All of a sudden, everyone was giving me hugs. "We're with you Rocky," said Cinnamon as she hugged me, wet suit and all. "Remember, we're Seven Friends. We stick together."

"I don't think we can go digging around Big Mamma today," said Tommy. "I'm pretty sure George and his buddies were watching us from the weeds over there."

"You're right my brother," said Little Mouse. "I spotted them when Slime got out of his car."

"Nothing gets by you two," I said. "What should we do?"

"We can't go back across the creek with those chumps watching. I think we pull up anchor and walk our raft back to the mill. That's why we brought the rope. I'll tie it to the front of the raft and we'll pull. Sarah can stay on board and keep the raft away from the shore. We'll be back in no time."

"Let's try to come back here on Friday," said Cinnamon. "Rocky has to help his dad move a ton of tables and chairs tomorrow."

"Hey Rocky, want some help?" asked Charlie. "I'm there if you need my powerful muscles."

"That would be great. My dad and I are supposed to be at that restaurant that just sold at ten o'clock tomorrow morning. It's almost across the street from the new post office."

"I'll be there."

It took us a little longer to get back than it did floating down, but it was still easier than poling. There was a path right next to the creek and with six of us pulling on the rope and Sarah steering, we got back to the mill in what Tommy said was record time. Ned even got into the act. I tied him to the front of the rope and let him pretend he was the lead Husky.

"If everyone can, let's meet at 9:00 Friday morning at the schoolhouse," said Cinnamon. In the mean time, think of a way to keep George and his friends occupied while we do some digging."

We said our goodbyes and all headed to our homes. It was almost time for dinner, but I wasn't really hungry. I just didn't think food would make me feel any better.

Cinnamon and I walked through the hotel door and into the dining room. "What's for dinner tonight Mom?" she asked.

"Country-fried steak, mashed potatoes, and buttered corn. Go wash up. We're just about ready."

"That's one of my favorite meals Mrs. B."

"Every meal's your favorite Rocky," said Cinnamon. "I knew food would make you happy again."

We had two special guests for dinner, Old Man Winter and his friend, Uncle Bud McCabe. So this was the big city lawyer. I couldn't exactly put my finger on it, but he was kind of intimidating. He wasn't big, strong, or even handsome, but those eyes seemed to look right through me, and that half smile made me think he knew just about everything about me even before I opened my mouth.

"Well hello Rocky," he said reaching out his hand. "I've heard about you. Seems we have a few things to talk about." He held my hand a few seconds and looked into my eyes. I wasn't scared, but I knew I couldn't tell a lie to the guy. He'd know.

We sat down at the table and Mr. Winter asked if he could say a few words. "Let us be truly thankful for all of our friends, old and new. May we greet each morning with happiness and wonder, and may we go to sleep each night knowing we've done our best to make this a better world. Thank you for this wonderful food Mrs. Brickle. May we begin?"

I looked around to see if anyone else had started eating before I inhaled my food. I knew Mom would appreciate my patience and good manners. I saw Eddie take a bite of his spuds. That was my cue to let her rip.

I didn't pay much attention to most of the conversation. I was busy having a contest with Eddie over who could pack in the most food. There was little doubt who was winning the way food was flying off his plate, but I had to be a close second.

"I just met with Katherine Odetts," announced Uncle Bud. "Seems like our dear friend Slim Stanley has been a naughty boy."

Uncle Bud had my attention. I decided to stop my eating contest and listen in on the conversation. This could be good.

"From what I gather, the aforementioned is making life miserable for everyone in Old Town and I think it's time for a little legal action."

Now we're talking. Let's drag his sorry butt into court and then send him to Alcatraz. I'll be a witness. That's what I was thinking anyway.

"I'm setting up a short meeting with Mr. Stanley tomorrow afternoon at the old schoolhouse. I'm asking a few people from the community to be in attendance as observers. It's time to rattle his cage a little."

"Do you need any of us there?" asked Cinnamon.

"We'll see," said Uncle Bud.

"Who wants a piece of strawberry-rhubarb pie," asked Mrs. B.

"I do," I blurted out. "I've never had it before, but I know it's my favorite."

Cinnamon crossed her eyes and scrunched her face.

"That was a wonderful meal Mrs. Brickle. With your permission I'd like to rent a room for a few nights. Do you have any available?"

"We'd love to have you as a guest. Room number five on the second floor is all ready for you."

"That's my cue to leave," said Mr. Winter as he got up from the table. "See you tomorrow UB. Thank you Mrs. Brickle. Have a pleasant night everyone,"

"Rocky, you look like you still have a few unanswered questions. Would you like to join me on the couch in a few minutes and we can talk things over?"

"You bet! I'll bring my notebook." I pulled it out of my back pocket to show him.

"Great minds think alike," said Uncle Bud as he pulled his notebook from his sport coat.

I was impressed. I wonder if he reads Crimefighter magazines.

"Well young man. What are you concerned about?"

I thought for a while, opened my notebook, scratched my head, and then asked a stupid question, "So why do people call you Uncle Bud?"

"Good question Rocky. Years ago while we were in school together, Thaddeus and I had a small disagreement. I don't remember what it was over, probably a girl. Thaddeus was so irritated with me he shook his finger at me and said 'Don't tell me what to do. You're not my uncle, Bud.' From that day on he and everyone else called me Uncle Bud. I like it better than my given name. It's Horatio, but that has to be our secret."

"My lips are sealed." I wouldn't want that name either I thought to myself.

I decided to share all of the research and discoveries the Seven Friends had been working on since my arrival in Old Town. Uncle Bud was impressed with what we had accomplished in a few short days. I could tell he was quite angry when I told him about my run-in with Slim Stanley. His neck around his collar turned red and he lowered his voice to almost a whisper. "We're going to squeeze that guy, Rocky. You have my word on that as your lawyer."

" My lawyer? I don't think I can have a lawyer Uncle Bud. I don't have any money to pay you. I'm just a kid and I don't get an allowance until next week."

"That's all right Rocky. I'm doing this pro bono for the entire community. Thaddeus and I go way back and I'd do anything for him."

"Okay, last question. Who's this Thaddeus?"

"Sorry Rocky. I thought you knew. Thaddeus is Mr. Winter."

"Really? That's his name? Does anyone else know? I can keep that secret too." I'm starting to wonder if everyone around here has a nickname. I'm going to make a list in my notebook.

"Would you be willing to join us at the schoolhouse tomorrow? I think you'll see some of your good work in action. You must promise me you won't ask any questions though. You'd just be an observer."

"I'll ask my parents, but sure if it's okay with them."

"Great. I've asked the Odetts, Thaddeus, Daniel Two Feathers, and Mr. Potts. Five people should be enough."

"I'll be the only kid? Can I invite a friend?"

"Sorry Rocky. I only need you."

"Well, . . . I guess that'd be okay." I really didn't mean it. My brain was going a hundred miles an hour and my stomach was tied in knots again. I hoped I could get to sleep tonight. This was one rough day. I think I'll go hug my mom.

Chapter Twenty-one

I got to sleep in until 9:00 o'clock and I was sure today was going to be an improvement over yesterday. Wednesday started out great with our rafting adventure, but turned pretty sour with Slim Stanley working me over. I was sure thankful I had my friends there to help me. I'd mention them if we went back to the Indian Church on Sunday.

Hauling tables and chairs wouldn't be exciting, but it was probably just what I needed today. Dad poured me some bran flakes and milk. With fresh strawberries, crushed walnuts, and lots of sugar, they weren't so bad. I didn't want coffee though. I don't think I'll ever want to drink that stuff.

"Your mother and Mrs. Brickle are busy sewing tablecloths. You know how your mother is when it comes to projects. That machine was going at the crack of dawn. She's on a mission."

"Can't wait to see them. Thanks for the breakfast Dad. I almost liked it. I'm ready to start hauling."

"Great Son! I hooked the trailer up to the truck. Hope the bridge holds."

"Dad, I'd like to take my bike. It'll be safer."

"Nonsense Rocky. If we go down, it'd be better to have a hunk of metal around us."

Where does he come up with this stuff? I wonder if Dad took one too many punches in the ring. No point in discussing it though. When either of my parents was on a mission, it was always full speed ahead. I climbed into *Bette Lou* and off we went.

We made the first trip with only a couple of groans from the bridge. Cryin' Charlie was waiting for us at the restaurant door.

"Dad, I forgot to tell you. My friend Charlie is helping us today."

"That's great. Hope he's ready for a workout."

We stepped inside the restaurant and were greeted by all of my friends. "We couldn't let you have all the fun today Rocky," said Cinnamon. "Tell us what to do Mr. Malone. We're small, but we're strong."

"Especially me," said Sarah as she picked up a chair. It was almost as big as her, but Sarah always found a way to run with the big dogs.

Our first load completed in less than fifteen minutes. We stacked twelve chairs in the pickup and three tables in the trailer. "Hey Dad. I think we can do this in four trips."

"That sounds about right, but we'll have to take one more trip after that. Remember, we bought the stove, freezer, and fridge."

"Oh, I forgot. I don't think we'll be much help there Dad."

"Don't worry Mr. Malone. My brother Eddie is stopping by with some of his friends. His practice ends at 10:30 this morning. You'll have some really strong guys to help with all the heavy stuff."

"Great. I have a dolly, but can really use the help getting them in and out of the truck."

Tommy rode back to the garage with us to help unload the first set of tables and chairs. That took a little longer than loading because there were just three of us. Just as we were about to leave, four pickups pulled up to the garage loaded with tables and chairs. "Hey Mr. Malone. Where do you want these," said Eddie as he jumped out of the first pickup.

"Well hello Eddie. This is great," said Dad. "Are these guys your teammates?"

"Best football team around." The guys all got out and shook Dad's hand. I could tell Dad was super excited.

"Little Rocky is our official ball boy this year," said the player they called Meat. "When a teammate needs help, we all chip in."

With all of the football team and my friends helping, we were done in under an hour. My parents were so thankful for the help they invited everyone for lunch. Mom took a break from sewing, sliced up a big ham for sandwiches, and Dad carved up four huge watermelons.

In less than fifteen minutes, all the food was gone and so was the team. I bet that that was just a snack for those guys and they were probably heading home for their real lunch. I know I was still hungry. "Dad, could I borrow a few dollars and treat my friends to some fudge at the fudge shop? I promise I'll pay you back." My cash flow was a little light these days, like zero. I'd need to find a job soon or get a big raise on my allowance.

"We can do one better," said Dad. "Why don't you try some of Miss Odetts' brownies she's baking for us for the Open House. She brought over a batch to sample."

"That sounds great. Can we have the whole plate?"

"Sure, but don't get sick. We have lots to do yet."

We polished off the brownies in record time. I loved Miss Odetts' cookies, but her brownies were chart toppers.

"We know Rocky," said Cinnamon. "Brownies are your favorite."

"How'd you know I was going to say that?" Everyone laughed so hard Cryin' Charlie had to take out his handkerchief to blow his nose. Now that was funny!

My friends all took off for home and I helped Dad polish up the tables and chairs. In about an hour we had them all in place and ready for the new tablecloths. They weren't quite ready yet, but the few that were done looked great.

"Dad, do I have to go to that meeting this afternoon? Don't you need my help for another project?"

"You told Uncle Bud you would. Do you really want to break that promise?"

"No I guess not. He said it was important that I attend. I guess I'll go."

"Atta boy Rocky! You'll be fine."

"Yes Dad."

"Rocky, your mom and I have been pretty proud of you these last two weeks. You've been working hard and really made a difference already here in Old Town. You're really making an effort to make this move work. We want to give you something special for a job well done. We still have a lot to do, but giving it to you now will put a big smile on that old potato face."

All kinds of big rewards exploded in my brain: I'm getting a bigger allowance? a lifetime pass to the fudge shop? a real live BB gun? maybe a kitten? new jammies? a lunchbox for school? new underwear? That's probably it. That's not going to put a smile on my face.

Dad reached in his pocket and pulled out a brand new, never been used, handy-dandy, best ever Swiss Army knife. "You're old enough to have one of these Rocky. I got my first one about the same time. Now go promise your mom you won't cut yourself."

"This is amazing. I've always wanted a pocketknife just like this. You guys are the best parents. I promise to be careful." Dad and I don't hug much, but I gave him one anyway and then ran off to find Mom.

The meeting at the Old Town schoolhouse was set for 3:00 pm. Uncle Bud decided to pick everyone up so we could arrive together before the planned time. He wanted to make sure everyone was in place and ask us all again not to confront Mr. Stanley. That was his job he said with a wink and a smile. That was fine by me.

True to form, his big Cadillac screeched to a halt right in front of the school entrance. Slim Stanley lumbered out of the car and slammed his door like he was angry at the world.

"This better be worth my time, McCabe," he grunted as he walked into the classroom. What are all these people doing here? Looks like an inquisition."

Slim Stanley's entrance didn't bother Uncle Bud one bit. He got up from his chair, walked across the room, and extended his hand.

"Thank you for coming," Uncle Bud said in his best lawyer voice. "I represent these good people and have asked them to attend as observers and clients."

Stanley took no interest in shaking Uncle Bud's hand. "What do you mean you represent them? Am I being sued? We'll see about that."

"Please have a seat Mr. Stanley. This shouldn't take up too much of your valuable time."

"You've got that right mister," he said as he plopped his big frame down in the little chair Uncle Bud pushed in front of him. "I've got places to go and people to meet. Can't run a business standing around talking about nothing."

"Good! I'll get right to the point. As I said a few minutes ago I represent the entire community of Old Town. I have compiled a list of grievances that bear your attention."

"Grievances? These people don't know how good they have it."

"Please Mr. Stanley. Let me continue. I'm not asking you to defend yourself or defend your son. This is just a list of potential grievances that may end up in court. Feel free to take some notes if you wish."

"My son. What's he got to do with this charade?"

"Okay, let's start with your son. You should be aware that he has quite the negative reputation here in Old Town."

"He's just being a boy. I raised him to be tough."

"Tough is one thing, but defacing government property, theft, and vandalism are all illegal in this state."

"My son isn't a criminal. You have no proof."

"Oh but I do," said Uncle Bud as he slid a desk over in front of Slim. "This is some of your son's handy work. I bet we can find several more examples of his handiwork around the town. Enough about your son. There's still time for him to turn over a new leaf. Let's talk about you."

"You've got nothing on me."

"It will be in your best interest to hear me out Mr. Stanley. It never hurts to be prepared."

"Fine, get on with your bogus list."

"These are the issues I'm currently pursuing with my clients." Uncle Bud read every issue and paused briefly after each one. Mr. Stanley was starting to *sweat like a pig*. I wondered if I could take out my notebook and write that one down. I'd never seen a pig sweat, but I bet it would look just like Slim Stanley. Go Uncle Bud. *Cook his goose*! That's another good line for my list. I decided to keep my notebook in my pocket. I could write them down them later.

"Illegal foreclosures and evictions … abuse of your power as an elected official … kidnapping … harassment and verbal abuse of a minor … arson … and my personal favorite, tax fraud."

"I've heard enough! This so-called meeting is over," Big Slim barked as he stumbled out of his little chair.

"Not so fast Mr. Stanley. Aren't you up for the mayor's election again in November? You might want to reconsider. I think you're going to be a very busy man. You won't be running unopposed this time either. It could get awful messy."

"Are you threatening me? You can't prove a thing."

"Oh, I believe I can. My advice is to prepare yourself."

"Why you …"

"That'll be all Mr. Stanley. You're excused. We'll be in touch with you or your lawyer. You do have one, don't you? Have a good day now."

And then it was over. The door on the big Caddy slammed shut and the engine roared as Slim drove away in a big clod of dust and flying gravel.

"That went well, " said Uncle Bud. "Thank you all for helping out. I'll draw up some notes and have each of you sign as witnesses. I think we've got him on the run."

"Uncle Bud, I said. "You're my hero. Do you ever read Crimefighter magazines?"

"Stop by my office sometime when you're in the city. I have some of the very first issues."

"That's way cool."

Chapter Twenty-two

Seven Friends all showed up at the schoolhouse the next morning. I wanted to tell them all about the meeting, but Uncle Bud asked us not to talk about anything until he had "the opportunity to file official documents with the county." I wasn't sure what all that meant, but I promised to keep quiet. I asked if it was okay to tell my friends about seeing Mr. Stanley sweat like a pig. Uncle Bud had laughed and said that was fine. I also had my new Swiss Army knife to show them. That's cool.

Tommy asked Lenny if he wanted to dig for treasure. He was so excited he showed up in an outfit that looked like he was going on a safari. Everybody else was wearing swimsuits and T-shirts. We all figured we'd have to swim across the creek with our tools because we wouldn't have the raft today. Tommy said he'd go back and get it, but we all decided that would take too long.

"There is a path that goes all the way around the island," said Lenny. We'll have to walk across the top of the dam, but it's pretty safe."

"What do you mean pretty safe?" I asked. "On a scale of one to ten, how safe is it?"

"I think about a three. That's a good number, don't you think."

Now I was worried. "A three? Is it dangerous?"

"Only if you fall."

"Great! I feel much better now."

"Okay then. It's settled. I'll lead," said Lenny. "I know the way."

We all grabbed our tools and the snacks we brought just in case it took most of the day. I told everyone I needed to be back by at least 3:00 because Coach needed me to help get ready for the big game.

"I'm coming to watch you," said Little Mouse.

"You won't see much. I just carry water, footballs, and towels."

"Will you be out on the field?" she asked.

"During time-outs and breaks."

"Good. I'll cheer really hard for you when you're out there. I hope you win."

I decided to move on to another subject. I didn't think Sarah really understood my role on the team, but it would be fun to have someone cheer for me.

The path around Big Island wasn't what I'd call a path. There were branches, logs, and rocks all over. Sam, Charlie, and I had a tough time staying upright. Cinnamon and Lenny struggled just a little. Tommy, Sarah, and Ned acted like it was just another stroll in the park – smooth, effortless, and fast.

When we got to the dam, I saw why Lenny thought it was a three. The dam was completely covered with slippery, green moss. Water from the creek was spilling gently over the top. If you could walk across without falling, you'd only get your feet wet. If you slipped, you'd end up on some jagged rocks several feet below. I thought I'd give swimming another try.

Tommy took the lead and showed us how to use our tools for better balance. I had my dad's crowbar, so I didn't think that would be much help. Everyone made it across with no problem, except Sam and me. We finally decided to crawl along on our hands and knees. Ned did it that way, and he made it back and forth at least five times waiting for us to get up the courage. At least I had Sam for company. What's that line? Misery loves company. I hope the rest of the path looks like a nice, wide, blacktopped highway.

We finally ended up in front of the old oak tree on the far side of the creek. I sat down in the grass next to the tree exhausted from the walk around Big Island. I wasn't going to be much help digging for gold. Maybe a snack and some water would help. I pulled out a banana I had packed in a bag I had tied to my waist. It didn't look like a banana any more. It look more like the moss I'd just been through. I didn't care; I ate it anyway.

Tommy brought a whole bunch of pemmican. He passed some to everybody and told us it would bring back our energy. I love that stuff so I took a big piece.

"What should we do first?" asked Charlie way before I was ready to move.

"Let's just sit a few more minutes to talk about a plan. Lenny, can you spread the map out here on the ground?" I pointed to a spot right in front of me. That way I didn't have to move very far.

"The map has an X and a 30 on this side of the tree," said Cinnamon. "We need to figure out how far 30 is."

"I think we should measure out thirty feet, thirty yards, and thirty paces from the tree," I said. "Those can be our starting points.

"The tree is much bigger now. It's just about six feet across, " said Tommy. I think we'll need to subtract a few feet from the thirty."

"I'd be willing to bet Beauregard didn't have a tape measure or ruler with him," said Sam. He's probably measure with his own feet."

"I don't think he'd measure in yards. That's pretty hard without a tape measure. And remember, he was trying to get away quick. My guess is feet or paces."

Lenny hadn't said a word, but looked like he was really concentrating. "My mother told me long ago that I looked just like Uncle Beau. Maybe I have his same shoe size."

"It's worth a try," I said. "Lenny, start at the base of the tree and step off 27 of your feet. We'll mark an X on that spot."

"Do you think that's where the gold is buried?" asked Little Mouse.

"We couldn't be that lucky. Once we have our spot, we'll make a big arc that same distance from the tree. We don't have to go all the way around since the map shows us there is water on one side."

"I get it. Good thinking Rocky," said Cinnamon. "We can do the same with paces."

"Okay, how do we figure out what pace to use?" asked Sam. "Every person has a different pace. I remember that from our mapping unit in school last year."

"I just thought of something. A pace is two steps. If Beauregard just used steps we will need a third arc."

"Maybe Lenny not only looked like his uncle he walked like his uncle," said Charlie.

"That's a stretch, but we have to start somewhere," said Tommy.

We had a plan and Lenny would be our measuring stick. I grabbed my dad's crowbar and scratched the arcs into the dirt. In less than an hour we had our X's marked and our three arcs drawn around the tree.

After looking it over we all agreed that thirty paces was way too far away. We decided to narrow our search to the first two arcs. That's step five in solving mysteries, *eliminate the obvious*.

"Just a question that popped into my head. Who owns this land?"

"It's government land, just like the swamp. Nobody uses it," said Tommy.

"That's good. This is where you and Little Mouse take over. Can you walk the arcs a few times and see if you notice any difference in the ground? Is there a bump, a soft spot, or even a mound of rocks that might be out of place?"

"You mean like this spot right here?" said Sarah. She was standing on the closest arc almost parallel to the creek. "There's a little mound here, and the grass is much thinner. No deep roots."

Lenny was so excited he sprinted to her side. Sarah jumped out of the way just as he swung the pick he was carrying into the hard ground. "Careful Lenny," she said. "I'm still here."

"Oh my. I didn't hurt you did I. I'm just so excited."

"We are too Lenny," said Cinnamon. "Let's take it a little slower and use a shovel."

"Good plan," said Lenny. I'll dig." We all sat back and watched as Lenny through sand, dirt, and grass into the air. Some of it landed back in the hole, some ended up on his hat, and a little on us. Lenny didn't seem to notice. He was on a mission. If there was something here, he'd find it.

"I just heard a clunk," he said as he threw down the shovel. He reached into the hole, dug around with his hands, and pulled up a leather strap. "This isn't gold," he said as he threw the strap over his shoulder

"Wait Lenny. Let me see that." I examined the strap carefully. It was definitely old leather. The dry sandy soil had preserved it, but you could still see holes for a buckle. "Guys, I don't believe it, but Sarah, you found the spot, and Lenny, I think you found your uncle's saddlebags. Dig a little slower and a little deeper. See if the whole bag is down there."

Lenny decided to use his hands and not the shovel. He loved treasures and if he could uncover his uncle's saddlebags, he'd have a big piece of family history. In just a few short minutes the bags came loose, complete with straps and a U.S. monogram on the side.

Lenny brushed off the bag, carefully unbuckled the straps and reached inside. When he pulled his hand back, it was filled with several gold nuggets the size of marbles.

"Lenny, I believe you're rich," I yelled over everybody's screams of joy.

"I believe we all are," Lenny responded.

The walk back to the schoolhouse was slow and exhausting, but we didn't care. We had just discovered gold. The saddlebags were

heavy, but Lenny wouldn't part with them. He emptied most of the gold into bags we brought, but the saddlebags were his treasure. The gold was no big deal.

We arrived back at the schoolhouse with a pretty good plan. Lenny would keep his new treasure, but we'd lock the gold up in Mr. Winter's safe at the pool hall. We'd ask Uncle Bud McCabe what to do with it. We were all pretty sure that it belonged to the Odetts, but we needed to know if the government had a claim on it. We vowed not to let the Slim Stanley come anywhere near it. He could rot in Alcatraz as far as I was concerned.

Old Man Winter was shocked when we burst through the door of the pool hall. We were still excited and all tried to tell him about how we solved the mystery of Beauregard Puce's gold. He finally got us calmed down with some cold root beers and asked Cinnamon to give him the details. I had to drink mine pretty fast because I was due at the school in twenty minutes. I made them all promise to fill me in later as I strolled out the pool hall door, mounted *Phantom*, and rode off into the sunset. That's the image I hope I left with them; *When in doubt call Rocky Malone. He'll solve your mysteries.*

I stopped by the hotel just long enough to change into some jeans and a clean white T-shirt. I didn't have time to wash up but I thought that would be okay. Football players are all smelly. I was sure I'd fit right in. I grabbed my hat, told Ned to stay, and headed out the door. I wanted Ned to go along, but I didn't think dogs were allowed on the field during games. I was really tired and my legs felt like lead, but I had a job to do. I wouldn't let the team down.

I made it to the school just as Coach Nelson was unlocking the door to the equipment room. "Hello Rocky. Right on time. Why don't you sit back and relax a little while I draw up our game plan on the chalkboard. I'll fill you in as we go. By the way, here's a jersey for you. It's the smallest I have. You have to look official out on the field." He tossed me jersey number 3.

"Thanks Coach, That's a good number." Then I thought about

Seven Friends. Seven was a great number. I almost asked Coach for a jersey with number 7, but thought I might be pushing my luck just a little. Number 3 would work just fine. Maybe next year I could be number 7. I sat down on the team bench and tried to catch my breath. I was still pumped up about our discovery. I hoped my friends got some good advice from Uncle Bud. I was sure they would share all the details after the game.

The team arrived a little later and joined me on the bench. Coach brought in some sandwiches and everyone ate as he talked. This was game day and Coach didn't want us to eat too much, but we couldn't miss a meal. I found out that it was important to eat some food for energy, but you shouldn't stuff yourself on game day. "Lean and mean," Coach announced. I only ate four sandwiches.

Coach had drawn out several plays on the board and talked about pass patterns, blocking assignments, and running plays. I didn't understand any of it, but shook my head a few times and grunted "Yeah Coach. I got it" a few times just like the players. I think I fit right in. Eddie smiled and gave me a thumbs up. It felt pretty good.

Once Coach was finished, the team got dressed and took the field. I filled a few water buckets, organized towels, and picked out some of the best balls for the ball bag. Eddie showed me his favorite and asked me to give it to the officials when they arrived.

"Why do they need the ball? They're not playing."

"That's our game ball. They'll want to check it out to make sure it's okay to use. It's the one you'll bring out when we're on offense."

"Got it," I grunted. Eddie laughed.

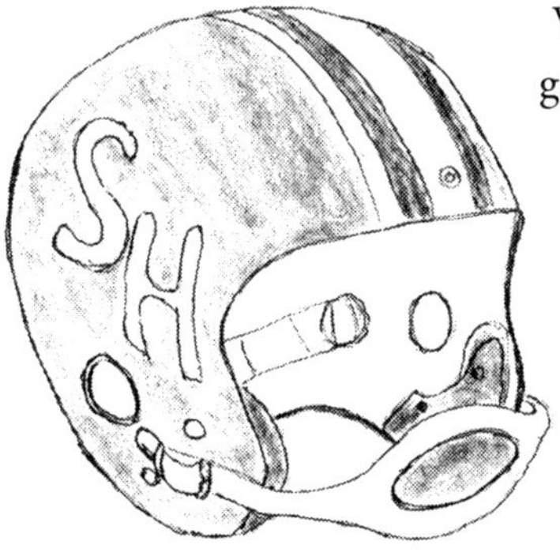

Warm-ups were a whole hour before game time. The other team had arrived and all the players were busy running, passing, kicking, and blocking each other. I thought they'd all be tired by the time the actual game started.

Ten minutes before the game Coach brought us back into the

locker room. "Helmets off and take a knee boys," he said. I was waiting for him to ask us to think of three people to pray for and three thankfuls.

Instead Coach talked about how proud he was of them, how hard they had worked to get ready for the season, and if we came together as a team, good things would happen. I thought about the Seven Friends and what we had done in the last few weeks. Coach was right on with what he said. I'd tell him just that after the game.

As the team captain, Eddie had a few words to say as well. I was hoping Coach wouldn't ask me to say anything. I was the ball boy though. I should have written out a short speech in my notebook.

All of a sudden Coach yells out "Let's do it." Everybody jumped up and start bouncing and chanting "Go, Go, Go, Go" faster and faster. Someone decided that it was game time and we all sprinted back onto the field. I was glad I was in the back because I would have been trampled. Those guys are huge.

The game started and the crowd cheered. I looked to see where my friends were sitting but it took a while to spot them. There had to be over two hundred people there. Where did they all come from? Skunk Hollow wasn't that big.

The other team was good but we were better. Eddie ran and passed for lots of touchdowns. I ran for lots of balls and water. The Skunk Hollow Raiders was a well-oiled machine. I only fell once carrying the water bucket, but only Little Mouse noticed. She cheered for me every time I came off the field. On that trip, I could hear her yell "That's okay Rocky. You'll do better next time."

And then the game was over. We had won 34 to 21 and everybody was happy. Coach congratulated everybody including me. I was exhausted, but proud to be a Raider. We were number one, at least for today.

I wasn't sure how I got home, but when my head hit the pillow it was lights out. Boy, did I need some sleep.

Chapter Twenty-three

"Rise and shine Rocky. Today's our big day. We can't be late for our own grand opening." I could tell Dad was super excited. It was still dark out, and I mean super vampire dark.

You've got to be kidding. It's morning already? "Just a few more minutes Dad. I promise I'll be down for breakfast in a little bit."

"Come on Rocky. We're burning daylight."

Is this what it's like in the army? If it is, I think I'll pass on army life. A kid my age needs his sleep. I'm still recovering from yesterday.

"I'd hate to have to drag you downstairs in your PJs. I wonder what Cinnamon would say about long underwear?"

That did it for me. I couldn't tell my dad that Cinnamon had already seen me in my PJs, and I really wasn't up for a second viewing. I rolled out of bed, put on some jeans, my new T-shirt, shoes and socks, and I was almost ready for the day. Just needed my baseball cap to cover my hair.

I followed Dad down the stairs groping my way through the dark. "Dad, nobody's up. I'll go back to my room and wait for breakfast."

"Nonsense Rocky. I can make us breakfast. It'll be ready in a flash. Now where's that coffee maker."

Memories of last Saturday and Thursday exploded in my head. Bran flakes, Spam, beans, and coffee. I can't eat that junk again and survive. "Hold on Dad. There's a note on the table."

I read it out loud. "Hello Buzz and Rocky. I knew you wanted an early start. Help yourself to cinnamon rolls, hard-boiled eggs, and orange juice in the fridge. We'll be along later. Mrs. Brickle."

"Remind me to give Mrs. Brickle a big hug. She saved my life today." I opened the fridge and dug into another amazing breakfast. Dad could have all the bran flakes he wanted. This was real food.

"Saved your life? Bran flakes would have been just fine for us Rocky. They keep you regular. I swear they spoil you around here."

"I'm okay with that," I said as I stuffed another egg into my mouth. If I worked at it, I could get a whole egg into my mouth all at once. Now there's a hidden talent. I bet Tommy couldn't do that. Charlie maybe. Sam wouldn't try.

Ned, Dad, and I got in our pickup and headed up to the garage. I knew I was going to be there all day long, so riding with Dad was a good plan. I could maybe take a short nap in the front seat before Dad needed me.

"Son, as soon as we get to the garage I'll need you to make up a few signs. I have some pieces of cardboard and finger paint for you. You can use all that creative talent you have."

"Dad, have you ever seen my pictures? I don't think this is a good idea. Maybe Cinnamon can make some signs. She's really good."

"Sorry Son. We need them right away. Yours will be just fine."

So much for the nap, and who thought up signs made with finger paint? I tried that stuff in first grade. My picture of an elephant looked like a duck, and my duck looked like a rock with wings. This was not a project I wanted to work on.

We pulled into the driveway and there were a bunch of men in overalls already waiting at the door. "Wow! People sure get up early around here."

"I'll bet they're farmers," said Dad. "They always start their day when the sun comes up."

"That's for sure. Change of plans Rocky. I'll open up and greet people. You make up a quick batch of lemonade and put out some cookies."

"Roger on that Dad." I was an old pro at making lemonade and throwing a few cookies on a table would be easy-peasy. I'd have to sample a few of the chocolate chip ones.

Dad was excited. Most of the men were holding on to lawn mowers, chain saws, or small engines. I bet all of them needed repairs. I could already see that Buzz' Small Engine Repair was just what Skunk Hollow needed. Way to go Dad! You called that one right.

More and more people were arriving by the minute. I was making and pouring lemonade by the buckets. Finally, right before eight o'clock, Mom, Mrs. B, and Cinnamon arrived. Miss Odetts had seen the people coming and came right over as well. "Nice job getting things started Rocky," said Mom. "We'll take over from here. Why don't you take a quick break and have some cookies and lemonade."

I could do that, even though that would be my sixth cookie. They were so good. I'd tell Miss Odetts that later. Mom probably wouldn't be pleased that I had eaten that many so early in the morning.

"Cinnamon, my dad asked me to make up some signs with finger paint. Do you think you could help me? I'll just make a mess."

"Piece of cake Rocky. Let's go see what your dad wants on them."

"You're a lifesaver, Cinnamon. Want a cookie?"

"No thanks. I just had breakfast." So did I. That didn't stop me.

We made three big signs for Dad. One was a WELCOME sign, one said REPAIRS THIS WAY, and the last said THANKS FOR STOPPING IN. YOUR BUSINESS IS APPRECIATED. Cinnamon made them look almost professional. I held the cardboard so it wouldn't wiggle.

It was an amazing open house. I bet every person in Old Town and New Town showed up some time during the day. Tons of people brought in tools to be repaired. Dad tagged them all and placed them on shelves he had built in the garage. He was going to be busy for a long time.

Old Man Winter and Uncle Bud McCabe stopped by around noon. I took a break and sat with them at a table out back. "You and your friends have been pretty busy this week," said Uncle Bud. I heard how you found old Beauregard's gold. You have the makings of a pretty good detective or lawyer some day."

"Thanks," I said. "I had lots of help. My friends deserve most of the credit. I could feel my face changing color.

"Rocky, we told Lenny and your friends what we could do about the gold, but we though you'd like to hear it from us directly," said Mr. Winter.

"It was smart to have it locked up in Thaddeus' safe. Bringing it to the bank would be asking for trouble. Slim Stanley owns that. I'll need to check on a few things, but I'm pretty positive the Odetts have claim to it all. That could take a few months, but I assured them it would be safe. Once I've covered all the bases, they can find out what it's worth and set up a deposit. I know several banks that would be happy to work with them."

"Can Lenny keep the saddlebags? They belonged to his uncle."

"That's not a problem at all. By the way, the Odetts have already told us what they would do with most of the money if it really does belong to them."

"How would they spend it? Lenny didn't seem to care about the gold at all. He just wanted the bags."

"That gold is worth a lot of money in today's market. They'd like to use it to give Old Town a big facelift. New store fronts, sidewalks, and a safe bridge."

"What a great idea. I especially like the idea of a new bridge. That old one is big time scary."

"Your mom and Miss Odetts have been talking and I think we can get started on their ideas right away. They'd like to turn this so-called house into a store. They'd keep the tables and chairs, put in a counter and sell cookies and coffee to people. Your mom would like to run a seamstress business in the back. Lenny wants to run a malt shop and sell root beer floats. It could become Old Town's first mini-mall. Three businesses under one roof."

"A malt shop would be awesome, but where would we live? I like the hotel, but we can't stay there forever."

"That's where I come in," said Old Man Winter. I just happen to have a house that I own that needs a good family. I built it many years ago, but don't live there any more. The house is just too big for me to take care of."

"The store idea sounds great and so does the house, but my parents can't take out another loan right now."

"I'm not asking for money Rocky. I don't need it. We could work out a deal like I have with Mr. Jingles. He takes care of my property on the North side of the lake. Your family could help out over there. It won't be rent-free. You'd be paying with some good, hard work. If you're interested, here are the keys. You and your friends can all go take a look later today."

"A real house with a yard and trees. I'm there. I hope my parents think it's a good plan. Maybe I can get some goats to help out with the yard work."

"You need to take a look first. It might not be a move you or your parents want to make."

"Thank you Mr. Winter. Thank you Mr. McCabe." I grabbed the keys and headed off to find Cinnamon and my parents.

Cinnamon was busy handing out cookies, but I managed to tell her about my conversation with Uncle Bud and Mr. Winter. I still couldn't bring myself to calling Mr. Winter Old Man, and I sure wasn't going to call him Thaddeus. He'd probably cancel the deal on the house.

Cinnamon was excited for me, but kinda sad at the same time. "That's great news Rocky. Of course I'll go with you to see it. I've been there many times. I'll miss your red jammies though."

"I'll leave them with you. I want new ones anyway."

"No Rocky, I really mean I'll miss you."

"I'll always be around,Cinnamon. You and I are best friends forever." I came around the table and gave her a huge hug. I think that was the first time I started a hug with a girl. It felt pretty good. When I let go, Cinnamon had a tear in her eye. She was okay though. She was smiling.

By four o'clock most of the people who had come to the open house were gone. I got a chance to talk to my parents about my meeting with Uncle Bud and Mr. Winter. They were actually more excited than me. Mom said we'd talk things over after church tomorrow. I planned on doing some serious praying and I had lots of thankfuls.

Dad said we were off the hook for the day, but I was to show up at New Town Park for a potluck party at 7:00. I guess this was an annual back-to-school get together to meet parents, teachers, and coaches. I promised I'd be there. I couldn't miss eating my way through tons of desserts before even thinking about the main dishes. That potluck was a no-brainer.

Cinnamon and I rounded up our friends and headed over to Mr. Winter's old house. Ned and I were the only one who had never seen it. With five tour guides, I got to see every piece of that house and the yard. The house had a big living room, dining room and kitchen. There was one bedroom on the first floor and three more upstairs. I knew my parents would want the downstairs bedroom. The whole upstairs could be mine. The only scary part was the attic. I thought maybe I could nail that door shut with some silver spikes. The house had been empty for a few years. I couldn't take a chance on a couple of vampire bats hanging out up there. Barring the attic, this house was perfect. This could be Rocky's castle. There was plenty of room for me and my friends when they stayed over. I hoped my parents thought it was cool.

We all got to the park just as people were setting out dishes. I was so busy at the open house I had forgotten all about lunch. I decided to start my meal off with a couple of pieces of pie. I'd save a little room for the main dishes. I love my system and whoever thought of potlucks was a genius.

Music started at about 9 o'clock and everybody celebrated on into the night. Someone even brought fireworks, and I even managed to dance a slow dance with Cinnamon. It was an Elvis tune, so I had to give it a shot. I only stepped on her toes twice. The lessons must have worked.

Chapter Twenty-four

Wake up Sweetie. You have to get ready for your first day of school."

I can't seem to get a break on this early morning routine. "Can't I sleep a little longer Mom? I'm so tired and I really don't want to go." I tried to use my best "I'm sooooo tired" whine, but Mom somehow saw through my performance and got me moving. I do wish she wouldn't call me Sweetie. Cinnamon or Eddie might hear. That's not a good way to start the morning.

"Cinnamon's waiting for you and Mrs. Brickle has bacon, blueberry pancakes, and scrambled eggs on the table."

That's all it took. Food always got me rolling. I could smell the bacon way up here on the third floor. I pulled on my best jeans with matching knee patches, a clean white T-shirt, pretty clean socks, and my high-top tennis shoes. You have to work with what you have. Another bad hair day, but a couple of dabs of Brylcreem, a quick comb and I was set. I used the comb Sam gave me, but still hadn't used the brush. Maybe I could use the brush on Ned. Dogs liked to be brushed. I just can't let Sam know. I don't think she'd be too pleased.

Lucky thing I took a bath last night. The thought of being called "Stinky" on the first day wouldn't be a good start either. I was sure I'd have enough problems adjusting to a new school. Adding B.O. would not improve my standing in the classroom. I knew first impressions were important, even though my first encounters with Cinnamon, Sam, and Tommy hadn't gone as well as I had hoped. I practically ran Cinnamon over, thought Sam was a boy, and fell down a hill meeting Tommy. I vowed meeting my new teacher and class would be better.

I had planned everything out and I was ready to make my mark at Skunk Hollow School.

I ran down the hallway, took the stairs two at a time, and practically flew into a chair at the dining room table. Mrs. Brickle must have anticipated my entrance. A big stack of pancakes hit the table just as my backside landed on the chair next to Cinnamon.

"Nice entrance Sweetie," Cinnamon teased as I tucked a napkin under my chin, reached for the syrup, and grabbed my fork.

I should have thrown out a comeback, but I was way too tired, too hungry, and too embarrassed. I had to have a mother-son talk soon. I was way too old and too cool to be called Sweetie by my mother. "Thanks," I mumbled as the first bite hit my mouth.

"Rocky, where are your manners this morning."

"Sorry Mom. Mrs. Brickle's food is always so good. I was just showing her a compliment."

"It might be better if you thank her rather than show her by stuffing your mouth. "

"You're right Mom," I said as I swallowed and put down my fork. "Mrs. Brickle, you are an amazing cook. Thanks for the great breakfast."

"You are so welcome Rocky. Dig in, you need to meet the bus in twenty minutes." I now had permission to feed the hungry giant. Six pancakes, five strips of bacon, and a plate of scrambled eggs! Wash it down with a big glass of OJ and I was set until lunchtime.

"Where's Eddie this morning? Doesn't he start school today? Do seniors get the first day off?" I had heard about Senior Skip Day in Chicago. Maybe it came early in Skunk Hollow.

"Eddie's already at school working out," replied Cinnamon. "He runs a captain's practice with the football team. Says it gives him an edge. He never takes the bus."

I pretended to know all about giving somebody an edge. If Eddie got one, I was all for it. Eddie deserved an edge. After all, Eddie was cool.

"Are you ready to go Rocky? Mom packed us both some lunches."

"I just need to run back upstairs. Back in a flash." I excused myself from the table, raced up the steps, gave Gerty some water, put my sling in my back pocket, grabbed my good-luck stone, and closed the door to my room. I was pretty sure making my bed was optional today, so I let it go. No one would care. Maybe a quick "Do Not Enter" sign on my door would help. Oh, forget it. That was way too much trouble. I'm outta here.

"Okay Cinnamon, I'm ready," I barked as I slid down the last banister.

"Aren't you forgetting a few things Rocky?" Mom asked as I moved toward the hotel door.

"Oh yeah. Ned you have to stay here. Bye Mom. I love you."

"Thank you Rocky, but you have syrup on your T-shirt, sticky hands, and a napkin under your chin. Maybe one more trip upstairs would be in order."

I was happy Mom saved me again, but I was getting tired of all those steps. Maybe I should keep a list of things to do before school in my notebook. I could put that in my other back pocket.

"Ned, Gerty, clean T-shirt, bye Mom, thank you Mrs. Brickle. Okay, Cinnamon, now I'm ready." I said tripping down the last flight of stairs I hoped to cross for the last time this morning.

"It'll be a great day Rocky. Just stick with me."

"That's a ten-four good buddy."

"What on earth do you mean Rocky?"

"Oh never mind Cinnamon. That's just detective talk."

"I think you'd better work on talking normal today. Miss Larson will appreciate that."

"Okay. Got it. Over and out."

"Rocky, knock it off and take your lunch," Cinnamon said in her always-calm voice. I thought it best not to respond. Where did my mother find that Hopalong Cassidy lunch box? I'm too old for cowboy lunch boxes. I'll ask for a brown paper bag tomorrow.

We walked to the Old Town side of the bridge. Cinnamon said it was safer to walk across the bridge together rather than one at a time.

I wasn't so sure. Counting us, there were eight kids waiting to cross the bridge, Tommy and Sarah Two Feathers, Charlie Potts, Samantha Torgeson, and two kids even smaller than Little Mouse.

"Hi Tommy, Sarah, Sam, and Charlie. Who are these two?"

"*Hau le mita kola*," greeted Tommy in perfect Lakota.

"These are the Anderson sisters, Nellie and Ada," said Little Mouse. Their family owns a farm west of the railroad tracks. We've known them for years."

"Hello," I said as the two girls ducked behind Tommy.

"They're pretty shy around lots of people." This from Mr. Quiet?

"Here comes the bus," said Cryin' Charlie. "Let's get everyone across the bridge. "

As I started out a little hand reached up and grabbed mine. For a quick moment, I thought it was Little Mouse guiding me again, but it wasn't. It was little Nellie Anderson. She smiled up at me as if I was her security blanket. Not to be outdone, Ada quickly grabbed my other hand.

"I think they like you Rocky," said Sam in a very sincere voice.

"Stick with me girls," I said. "I'll keep you safe." Tommy gave me a big smile.

"At school too?" peeped Nellie. "It's awfully big."

"Of course. Whenever you need me, I'll be right down the hall." Now all I needed was a friend or two to keep me safe. I was sure George and the Slimeballs would be gunning for me on day one. Maybe Ned could stay in my new classroom. He'd keep those toughs away.

The bus wasn't much to look at, but I recognized the driver right away. "Hey Charlie, it's your dad."

"Yup! He's our driver. He gets us to school and delivers mail at the same time."

"Hello Mr. Potts," we greeted as we climbed into the bus one by one.

Nellie and Ada had to sit next to me on the bus. On the short ride to school they filled me in as best they could on what it was like living on a farm. I told them I'd like to visit their farm some time this week since I'd never seen chickens in the wild. Both girls laughed as if I had said something real funny. We never had chickens running around in Chicago, so I didn't quite get it. They were both very excited that I wanted to visit their farm.

And then we arrived at my new school. My elementary school in Chicago was as big as Skunk Hollow's K-12 school, but it was still big when you don't know your way around. Nellie and Ada asked if I would bring them to their classrooms. I said sure and then quickly asked Cinnamon to come with us. Four of us, Charlie, Sam, Cinnamon, and I would be in the same classroom. Tommy was a grade older and Little Mouse was in fourth grade. Their classrooms were right down the hall.

We found Nellie's and Ada's rooms at the far end of the school near the playground and bathrooms. That made sense with little kids. They each gave me a hug and then off they went to start their day. Cinnamon and I turned down the hall again and immediately ran into the prides of Skunk Hollow: George Stanley, Clyde, and Freddie.

"Well lookie here. If it isn't my dear friend coming to school to get some smarts. You and your friends are going to pay for what you did to my dad." I'd have to say, George had one goal in mind. Make my life miserable. He was off to a good start today.

"Leave him alone George. You are so rude." Cinnamon barked.

"Hiding behind a girl, little city boy," George grunted as his two greasy friends snorted.

"I'd have a battle of wits with you, but I see you're unarmed. Maybe another day." I'd been working on that line for two weeks.

"What's he mean by that?" snorted Clyde.

"I don't know, but I think he's asking for trouble, and you found it here, buddy boy."

"Weenie, turnip, worm, stink weed, and now buddy boy. You still don't remember my name, George. I'll say it slower this time. It's Rocky, R-O-C-K-Y. Even better, I'll write it down for you. You can read, right?" I think my sharp tongue was getting me into more trouble. George's face had turned almost the color of Cinnamon's hair. I had to think of another approach. Maybe I should run.

Just then Eddie and his football buddies came around the corner from the gym. "Hey Rocky. Good to see you. Can you make it to practice after school today? Coach Nelson wants to talk to you more about our away game on Friday. He'll get you out of school early if you want to ride the team bus. Hi Cinnamon. Get lost George." George and company quickly disappeared down the hall.

"Hi Eddie. You bet. I'm hoping Coach still wants me to be the ball boy at all the games." Pay dirt on two counts! I couldn't believe I'd be riding with the team and I didn't get my nose smashed in.

"That's the plan," said Eddie. " Let us know if George or his buddies give you any grief. Our team sticks together." The whole football team was looking out for me? Suddenly, Skunk Hollow School felt a little safer. This might turn out to be a pretty good year.

We all waited in the hallway until our teacher, Miss Larson, called us in to the classroom. She didn't look like any of the teachers I had back in Chicago. Gray hair stacked in what they called a beehive, wire-rimmed glasses that hung on the end of her nose, crystal blue eyes, a faded blue dress that hung loosely over a slightly plump body. She had to be somebody's grandma. And then she spoke . . .

"Come in my children and locate your desk. You will be sitting alphabetically by first name. Quickly now, find your name tag so we can get started." Her voice was like a cold, hissing wind blowing across an icy lake. The kind that can freeze you in your tracks before you had a chance to say "Yes Miss Larson."

I hustled to the back of the room just as I heard her say "As in the back, Zs in the front," even though I was pretty sure we'd have no Zs. Her voice trailed off and a cold shiver ran down my spine. I did an about-face and moved toward the front. I hated sitting in the front of the classroom. Hiding in the back was more my style. Each desk held two students. What's with that? Oh well. I wonder who I'll be sitting next to?

"Hey Rocky. You're my partner."

I was Sam's partner? Really? No other S's? I could think of at least five S's in my Chicago class and we didn't even sit alphabetically. I liked Sam but had my doubts about sitting next to her for a whole year. We got along most of the time, but sometimes, not so much. Maybe Miss Larson made a mistake.

"Mr. Malone, would you kindly take your seat? We're all waiting."

"Uh, yes ma'am." I slid into my seat and bumped elbows with Sam.

"Not so close Gumball. I'm left-handed."

Great! Unless I could get Miss Larson to let us switch sides or change seats, we'd be bumping elbows every time we wrote something. I also need to tell her to drop Gumball and just call me Rocky. I raised my hand.

"Yes Mr. Malone."

"Miss. Larson, Sam's left-handed."

"That's nice Mr. Malone. Thank you for sharing."

The entire class started laughing. I was going to raise my hand again to explain, but didn't get the chance. A strong, icy north wind blew in with just one word. "Class!" And the laughter stopped. There was no doubt who was in charge in this classroom.

"Class, our first order of business is to meet our new students. We have three new boys that moved into our fair city, two that live in New Town and one in Old Town. Boys would you come up to the front and introduce yourselves?" We all lined up in front of the class. The two boys from New Town went first. They had to be brothers, but they didn't look alike. They kinda reminded me of Stan and Ollie. Maybe they had different dads or they were adopted. I hoped for a few jokes.

"Hi, I'm Billy Benson," said the first boy as he wiped his nose on his sleeve. That was funny, but nobody laughed.

"And I'm Bobby Benson. We're twins and we moved here from Butte, Montana."

"Our parents are taking over the cafe down on Central Avenue."

"Our specialty is hamburgers."

Bobby would say something, then Billy, then back to Bobby, and so on. This ping-pong game went on for about ten minutes, although it seemed like hours. My legs were falling asleep, I had to go to the bathroom, and I wanted a drink of water. The class needed to hear some good stuff about Chicago and the Old Town mysteries, not about the Benson Burger Boys from Butte. What happened to the jokes? I planned on springing a few on the class with my speech. Mom always said laughter was the best medicine.

Finally, it was my turn. I'd put them on the edge of their seats. "Hello, I'm Rocky Malone and yes, that's my real name. We just moved here from Chicago and my father is starting up a new small engine repair shop in Old Town. Our open house was Saturday and we had a great turn out. Anyway, this sure isn't like Chicago. I've only been here a little over a week and I've made lots of friends. Hi Cinnamon, Charlie, and Sam. My friends Tommy and Sarah are in other classes. I'm helping the football team Friday night. Eddie Brickle is the team captain and he and I are best buddies."

"Rocky, sorry to interrupt, but what is that in you back pocket?"

"Oh this? It's a sling Miss Larson." I can show everybody how it works." I pulled it out and gave it a couple of swings. "We do have 'Show and Tell' here. Right?" I was sure I had the whole class on the edge of their seats, just waiting for my big finish.

"I think not Mr. Malone." The class started giggling. "Please bring that to my desk. Sit right here please. Class, we'll hear more from Rocky a little later today. Now I'd like everyone to take out some paper and write three paragraphs on what you did this summer. Spelling and penmanship count. This will be your first grade."

Everyone quickly took out paper and pencils except me. I occupied the chair next to Miss Larson's desk. I couldn't believe I was in trouble already. This was not looking good for the Rock.

"May I have the sling please Mr. Malone. We'll just put it in this drawer for safekeeping. I've heard quite a bit about you in the two weeks you've been here. I'd like you to stay in a recess and tell me about some of the things that you have accomplished since you arrived in Old Town."

"Yes ma'am, and I am so sorry for whatever I did," as I passed the sling to her.

Suddenly the cold, icy voice had melted away. "Oh Rocky. Don't be sorry for anything. I grew up in Old Town and still live there. Katherine Odetts and I are very good friends and I taught her brother Lenny years ago. I'm thrilled that you're in my class and helping out our friends in Old Town. Moving is always tough, but this is going to be an exciting year for you, and just maybe you and I will both learn a few things from each other along the way. That's a beautiful sling by the way. It looks like Tommy Two Feathers' work."

I nodded and I swear she winked at me. No really! Well, maybe it was just a twitch in her eye, but I was beginning to think she would be okay as my teacher. Tomorrow I'd bring my snake Gerty to class. I know she'll be a hit with Miss. Larson. "Okay Miss Larson. See you at recess." Maybe she wanted to learn how to use a sling. I'd just follow Tommy's steps. She couldn't be any worse than me.

"Now Mr. Malone, get back to work." The icy voice was back but I noticed a smile on her face as I sat down at my desk. I pulled out some paper, bumped elbows with Sam, and composed the best three paragraphs ever written about a summer vacation, at least by my standards. I decided to draw a badge on the last page. It might be worth a few bonus points. I think I'll break out one of my crimefighter magazines for a few quotes. Detective Bill Perkins would be proud.

To be continued....

Acknowledgements

So many people helped make this book a reality. My lovely bride Bette gave me so much support as she edited each page and chapter, and made sure everything connected. Thanks to my brothers Mike, Bruce, and Duane for tagging along with me on my "research outings". A big thank you goes out to all the fantastic people at the Grant County Historical Museum, the Codington County Heritage Museum, the Lake Norden Historical Museum, and the South Dakota State Archives for allowing me the opportunity to dig through archived documents, pictures, and bygone memories. Special thanks also to the residents and towns throughout Western Minnesota and Eastern South Dakota for letting me photograph and then draw their homes, stores, and buildings. I do apologize for not being a better illustrator. Although some readers may recognize events and locations, the story, characters, and the town of Skunk Hollow are complete fiction. Hope you enjoy the ride down memory lane.

CPSIA information can be obtained at www.ICGtesting.com
Printed in the USA
LVOW11s0328240616

493926LV00002B/7/P

9 781614 934257